CAPTAIN RAVENSHAW

"THERE WAS EXCHANGE OF THRUST AND PARRY."

(See page 333).

CAPTAIN RAVENSHAW

OR,

THE MAID OF CHEAPSIDE

A Romance of Elizabethan London

By

Robert Neilson Stephens

Author of "Philip Winwood," "A Gentleman
Player," "An Enemy to the King," etc., etc.

Illustrated by
HOWARD PYLE
and others

*"Hang him, swaggering rascal! . . . He a captain! . . . He
lives upon mouldy stewed prunes and dried cakes."*
— King Henry IV., Part II.

Boston: L. C. PAGE &
COMPANY Publishers. *Mdcccci*

Colonial Press

Electrotyped and Printed by C. H. Simonds & Co.

Boston, Mass., U. S. A.

PREFACE.

HERE is offered mere story, the sort of thing Mr. Howells cannot tolerate. He will have none of us and our works, poor "neo-romanticists" that we are. Curiously enough, we neo-romanticists, or most of us, will always gratefully have him; of his works we cannot have too many; one of us, I know, has walked miles to get the magazine containing the latest instal-ment of his latest serial. This looks as if we were more liberal than he. He would, for the most part, prohibit fiction from being else than the record of the passing moment; it should reflect only ourselves and our own little tediousnesses; he would hang the chamber with mirrors, and taboo all pictures; or if he admitted pictures they should depict this hour's actualities alone, there should be no figures in cos-tume.

But who shall decide in these matters what is to be and what is not to be? Who shall deny that all kinds of fiction have equal right to exist? Who shall dictate our choice of theme, or place, or time? Who shall forbid us in our faltering way to imagine forth the past if we like? The dead past, say you?

As dead as yesterday afternoon, no more. " Where's he that died o' Wednesday ? " As dead as the Queen of Sheba. But on the pages of Sienkiewicz, for example, certain little matters of Nero's time seem no more dead than last week's divorce trial in the columns of those realists, the newspaper report-ers. All that is not immediately before our eyes, whether dead or distant, can be visualised only by imagination informed by description, and a small transaction in the reign of Elizabeth can be made as sensible to the mind's eye as a domestic scene between Mr. and Mrs. Jones in the administration of McKinley. But how can one describe authentically what one can never have seen ? You may propound that question to the realists ; they are often doing it, or else they see extraordinary things now and then

But, now that I remember it, Mr. Howells is not really illiberal. He has, upon occasion, admitted a tolerance — nay, an admiration — for " genuine ro-mance." But what is genuine romance ? Is psycho-logical romance, for instance, more " genuine " than melodramatic romance ? Are we not all — we " neo-romanticists " — aiming at genuine romance in some kind ? Shall there not be many misses to a hit ? many inconsiderable achievements to a masterpiece ? And we suffer under limitations which the great romancers had not to observe. We must be watchful against anachronisms, against many liberties in style and matter which the esteemed Sir Walter, for instance, might take — and did take — without stint. One's fancy was less restrained, in his day. One cannot, as he did, bring Shakespeare to Greenwich palace before the festivities at Kenilworth occurred; or let a shopman recommend a pair of spectacles to a doctor of divinity with the information that the king, having tried them on, had pronounced them fit for a bishop; or make the divine buy them with the cheerful remark that a certain reverend brother's advancing age gives hopes of an early promotion. Fancy such an exchange of jocularity between a shop "assistant" in Piccadilly and Doctor Ingram, while the late Doctor Creighton was Bishop of London! Flow of fancy is easier upon such terms; or, when one may even, as the great Dumas did, be so free of care for details as to have the same character in two places at the same time.

It is not meant to be implied that Mr. Howells is thought to consider the work of Scott or Dumas genuine romance. If he has anywhere mentioned an example of what he takes to be true romance, I have missed that mention. I should like to read his definition (perhaps he has published one which I have not seen) of genuine romance. But I would rather he taught us by example than by precept. What a fine romance he could write if he chose!

But as for us less-gifted ones, the "neo-romanticists," shackled as Scott and Dumas were not, we
must work a while under the new conditions, the
new checks upon our imagination, ere we shall get
a masterpiece. Meanwhile none of us yields to Mr.
Howells in admiration of a true romance, and none
of us would be sorry to lay down the pen, or shut
up the typewriter, some fine afternoon and find it
achieved. But until then may we not have indifferent romances, just as we have indifferent realistic
novels ? Why not, pray ? Again, shall one man,
one group, one school, decide what shall be and what
shall not ? "Dost thou think, because thou art
virtuous, there shall be no more cakes and ale ?"

Now, of merits which mere story may possess, and
usually does possess in measure greater than the
other sort of thing does, one is — construction.
Wherefore, the opponents of this sort of thing
belittle that merit. But it is a prime merit, nevertheless. Is not the first thing for praise, in a
picture, its composition ? in a building, its main
design ? in a group of statuary, its general effect ?
So, too, in a work of fiction. "Real life does not
contrive so curiously," says Professor Saintsbury.
Precisely ; if it did, what would be the good of
fiction ? Neither does nature contrive well-ordered
squares of turf, with walks, flower-beds, hedge-rows,
shrubbery, trees set with premeditation ; shall we, on

that account, make no gardens for ourselves? Who shall ordain that there be no well-constructed plots in fiction because life, seen in sections as small as a novel usually represents, is not well constructed? It is time somebody put in a word for plot. When all is said and done, the main thing in a story *is* the story.

Mr. Howells said, long ago, that the stories were all told. It is doubtful. But even if it were certain, what of it? Because there was an old tale of a king's wife whose lover lost the ring she gave him, whereupon the king, finding out, bade her wear it on a certain soon-coming occasion, and she was put to much concern to get it in time, was the world to go without the pleasure of D'Artagnan's mission for Anne of Austria? And what though Dumas himself had used the old situation of a real king imprisoned, and his "double" filling the throne in his place, were we to have no "Prisoner of Zenda?" Or even if the story of the man apparently wooing the handsome sister, while really loving the plain sister, had already been told, as it had, was Mr. Howells prohibited from making it twice told, in "Silas Lapham?"

Now, as to this little attempt at romance in a certain kind, I wish merely to say, for the benefit of those who turn over the first leaves of a novel in a bookstore or library before deciding whether to take or leave it, that it differs from the usual adventure-story in being concerned merely with private life and unimportant people. Though it has incidents enough, and perils enough, it deals neither with war nor with state affairs. It contains no royal person; not even a lord — nor a baronet, indeed, for baronets had not yet been invented at the period of the tale. The characters are every-day people of the London of the time, and the scenes in which they move are the street, the tavern, the citizen's house and garden, the shop, the river, the public resort, — such places as the ordinary reader would see if a miracle turned back time and transported him to London in the closing part of Elizabeth's reign. The atmosphere of that place and time, as one may find it best in the less known and more realistic comedies of Shakespeare's contemporaries, in prose narratives and anecdotes, and in the records left of actual transactions, strikes us of the twentieth century as a little strange, somewhat of a world which we can hardly take to be real. If I have succeeded in putting a breath of this strangeness, this (to us) seeming unreality, into this busy tale, and yet have kept the tale vital with a human nature the same then as now, I have done something not altogether bad. Bad or good, I have been a long time about it, for I have grown to believe that, though novel-reading properly comes under the head of play, novel-writing properly

comes under the head of work. My work herein
has not gone to attain the preciosity of style which
distracts attention from the story, or the brilliancy
of dialogue which — as the author of "John Ingle-
sant " says — "declares the glory of the author more
frequently than it increases reality of effect." My
work has gone, very much, to the avoidance of
anachronisms. This is a virtue really possessed by
few novels which deal with the past, as only the
writers of such novels know. It may be a virtue
not worth achieving, but it was a whim of mine to
achieve it. Ill health forbade fast writing, the success of my last previous book permitted slow writing,
and I resolved to utilise the occasion by achieving
one rare merit which, as it required neither genius
nor talent, but merely care, was within my powers.
The result of my care must appear as much in what
the story omits as in what it contains. The reader
may be assured at the outset, if it matters a straw to
him, that the author of this romance of Elizabethan
London (and its neighbourhood) is himself at home
in Elizabethan London ; if he fails to make the
reader also a little at home there in the course of
the story, it is only because he lacks the gift, or
skill, of imparting.

ROBERT NEILSON STEPHENS.

LONDON, June 1, 1901.

CONTENTS.

LIST OF ILLUSTRATIONS.

CAPTAIN RAVENSHAW.

CHAPTER I.

MEN OF DESPERATE FORTUNES.

"Though my hard fate has thrust me out to servitude,
I tumbled into th' world a gentleman." — The Changeling.

IT was long past curfew, yet Captain Ravenshaw
still tarried in the front room of the Windmill tavern, in the Old Jewry. With him were some young
gentlemen, at whose cost he had been drinking
throughout the afternoon. For their bounty, he
had paid with the satirical conversation for which
he was famed, as well as with richly embellished
anecdotes of his campaigns. Late in the evening,
the company had been joined by a young gallant
who had previously sent them, from another chamber, a quantity of Rhenish wine. This newcomer
now ordered supper for the party, a proceeding at
which the captain dissembled his long-deferred pleasure — for he had not eaten since the day before.
Moreover, besides the prospect of supper, there was
this to hold him at the tavern : he knew not where

he should look for a bed, or shelter, upon leaving it. The uncertainty was a grave consideration upon so black and windy a night.

Master Vallance, the gentleman who had ordered supper, had listened to the last of Ravenshaw's brag with a rather scornful silence. But the other young men had been appreciative; it was their pose, or affectation, to be as wicked as any man might; hence they looked up to this celebrated bully as to a person from whom there was much to be learned, and in whom there was much to be imitated.

The group had been sitting before the wide fire-place. But as soon as the roast fowls were brought in, there was a movement to the long table in the middle of the room. The captain was gifted with active, striding legs and long, slashing arms. So he was first to be seated, and, as he leaned forward upon his elbows, he seemed to cover more than his share of the table. He had a broad, solid forehead, an assertive nose, a narrow but forward chin, gray eyes accustomed to flash with a devil-may-care defiance, a firm mouth inured to a curve of sardonic derision. His rebellious hair, down-turning moustaches, and pointed beard were of a dark brown hue. He was a man of good height; below the sword-belt, he was lank to the ground; above, he broadened out well for chest and shoulders. His voice was quick, vigorous, and not unpleasantly metallic. He was under thirty, but rough experience had hardened his visage to an older look. His jerkin, shirt, hose, shoes, and ruff also betokened much and severe usage.

Master Vallance, in spotless velvet doublet and breeches, and perfectly clean silk stockings, looked at him with contemptuous dislike.

"Take heed you scorch not the capon with your nose, roaring Ravenshaw," said the youth, quietly.

It was not Ravenshaw's habit to resent allusions to his character as a "roaring boy;" indeed he encouraged the popular idea which saddled him with that title, at that time applied to bullies of the taverns. But some circumstance of the moment, perhaps something in the young coxcomb's air of aristocratic ridicule, guided the epithet to a sensitive spot.

"*Captain* Ravenshaw, by your leave," he said, instantly, in a loud tone, with an ironical show of a petitioner's deference.

"Forsooth, yes; a captain of the suburbs," replied the young gentleman, with a more pronounced sneer.

Now at this time—toward the end of the reign of Queen Elizabeth—and for a long time after, certain of the suburbs of London were inhabited numerously by people of ill repute. There were, especially, women whom the law sometimes took in hand and sent to the Bridewell to break chalk, or treated to a public ride in a cart, as targets for rotten vegetables, addled eggs, and such projectiles. Many an unemployed soldier, or bully who called himself soldier, would bestow, or impose, his protection upon some one of these frail creatures in the time of her prosperity, exacting from her the means of livelihood. Hence did Ravenshaw see in the title of "captain of the suburbs" an insult little less than lay in that of "Apple-John," or "Apple-squire," itself.

When a gentleman calls another by the name of a bad thing, it is not necessarily implied that he thinks the other is that thing; but it is certain that he means to be defiantly offensive. Therefore, in this case, the captain's part was not to deny, but to resent. Not only must he keep up his reputation with the other gentlemen as a man not to be affronted, but he really was in a towering rage at being bearded with easy temerity by such a youngling.

"What!" quoth he. "Thou sprig! Thy wits are strayed away, methinks. Or has thy nurse been teaching thee to use a pert tongue?"

"Nay, save your own tongue for the tasting of yon capon. I speak only truth. Your reputation is well known."

"Why, thou saucy boy, I may not spit butterflies on my sword, nor provoke striplings by giving them the lie; else —"

The captain finished with a shrug of vexation.

"Look ye, gentlemen, he lays it to my youth," continued the persecutor, "but there's yet a horse of another colour. This captain is free enough with his bluster and his sword; he has drawn quarts of blood for a single word that misliked him, upon occasion; but he will bear a thousand scurvy affronts from any man for the sake of a supper. You shall see — "

"Supper!" echoed the captain, springing up. "Do you cast your filthy supper in my teeth? Nay, then, I'll cast it in thine own."

With this, thoroughly enraged, Captain Ravenshaw seized the particular capon to which the gallant had alluded, and flung it across the table into the gallant's face. It struck with a thud, and, rebounding, left the young man a countenance both startled and greasy. Not content, the offended captain thereupon reached forth to the fowl which had been served as companion to the capon, and this he hurled in the same direction. But he aimed a little too high, moreover the fop ducked his head, and so the juicy missile sped across the room, to lodge plump against the stomach of a person who had just then come into view in the open doorway.

This person showed lean in body and shabby in raiment. He made a swift, instinctive grasp at the thing with which he had come so unexpectedly in contact, and happened to catch it before it could fall to the floor. He held it up with both hands to his gaze a moment, and then, having ascertained beyond doubt its nature, he suddenly turned and vanished with it.   Let us follow him, leaving behind us the scene in the tavern room, which scene, upon the landlady's rushing in to preserve order for the good name of the house, was very soon after restored to a condition of peace by the wrathful departure of Ravenshaw from the company of an offender too young for him to chastise with the sword.

The ill-clad person who clutched the cooked fowl, which accident had thus summarily bestowed upon him, made short work of fleeing down the stairs and out into the black, chill February night.   Once outside, though he could not see his hand before his face, he turned toward Cheapside and stumbled forward along the miry way, his desire evidently being to put himself so far from the Windmill tavern that he might not be overtaken by any one who could lay claim to the fowl.

The air was damp as well as cold.   The fugitive, keeping his ungloved hands warm by spreading them around the fowl, which was fresh from the spit, had to grope his way through an inky wind.   He listened for possible footfalls behind him, but he heard none, and so he chuckled inwardly and held his prize close to his breast with a sense of security.   Now and then he raised it to his nostrils, in anticipation of

the feast he should enjoy upon arriving at the rest-
ing-place he had in mind. He would have made a
strange spectacle to anybody who might have been
able to see him from one of the rattling casements
as he passed ; but so dark it was that downlookers
could no more have seen him than he could see
the painted plaster, carved cross-timbers, projecting windows, and gabled roof-peaks of the tall
houses that lined the narrow street through which
he fled.

At one place a lantern hanging over a door threw
a faint light upon him for a moment, and showed a
young man's face, with sharp features and a soft
expression ; but the face was instantly gone in the
darkness, and there was no other night-walker abroad
in the street to have seen it while it was visible.

"Surely," he meditated, as he went, "the time of
miracles has returned. And even a starved scholar
is found worthy of Heaven's interposition. With the
temerity of the famished, I enter a tavern, ascend
the stairs, and steal into a room which I take to be
empty because no sound comes from it, my only
hope being to pilfer a little warmth nobody will
miss, perchance to fall heir to a drop of wine at
the bottom of a glass, or a bone upon an uncleared
table. And lo, I find myself in the presence of a
gentleman asleep before a pot of mulled canary,
which he has scarce wet his throat withal. In three

swallows I make the canary my own, just in time to set down the pot before in comes a tapster. I feign I am in search of friends, who must be in t'other chamber. To make good the deceit, I must needs look in at t'other chamber door; when, behold, some follower of Mars, who looks as hungry as myself, pelts me with poultry. It is plainly a gift of the gods, and I am no such ill-mannered clown as to stay and inquire into the matter. Well, *gaudeamus igitur*, my sweet bird; here we are at St. Mary Cole Church, on the steps of which we shall make each other's better acquaintance. Jove!—or rather Bacchus!—what tumult a pint or so of mulled wine makes in the head of a poor master of arts, when too suddenly imbibed!"

He went half-way up the steps and sat down, crouching into the smallest figure possible, as if he might thus offer the least surface to the cold. Sinking his teeth into the succulent breast of the roast fowl, he forgot the weather in the joy of eating. But he had scarce taken two bites when he was fain to suspend his pleasure, for the sound of rapid footfalls came along the way he had just traversed. He took alarm.

"Sit quiet now, in God's name, Master Holyday!" he mentally adjured himself. "'Tis mayhap one in search of the fowl. Night, I am beholden to thee for thy mantle."

The person strode past and into Cheapside without apprehension of the scholar's presence upon the steps. The scholar could not make out the man's looks, but could divine from sundry muttered oaths he gave vent to, and from his incautious haste of movement, that he was angry.

"God 'a' mercy! how he takes to heart the loss of a paltry fowl!" mused Master Holyday, resuming the consumption of his supper on the church steps. "For, certes, 'twas from the Windmill he came; from his voice, and the copiousness of his swearing, I should take him to be that very soldier whom the gods impelled to provide me with supper. Well, he is now out of hearing; and a good thing, too, for there comes the moon at last from the ragged edge of yon black cloud. Blow, wind, and clear the sky for her. Pish! what is this? Can I not find my mouth? Ha, ha! 'tis the mulled wine."

The scholar had indeed struck his nose with the fowl, when he had meant to bring it again between his teeth. He was conscious of the increased effect of the wine in other ways, too, and chiefly in a pleasanter perception of everything, a sense of agreeable comicality in all his surroundings, a warmed regard for all objects within view or thought. This enhanced the enjoyment of his meal. The moonlight, though frequently dimmed by rushing scraps of cloud, made visible the streets near whose junction he sat, so that the house fronts stood strangely forth in weird shine and shadow. The scholar, shivering upon the steps, was the only living creature in the scene. Yet there seemed to be a queer half-life come into inanimate things. The wind could be heard moaning sometimes in unseen passages. The hanging signs creaked as if they now and then conversed one with another in brief, monosyllabic language.

"In the daylight," thought the scholar, "men and women possess the streets, their customs prevail, and their opinions rule. But now, forsooth, the house fronts and the signs, the casements and the weathercocks, have their conference. Are they considering solely of their own matters, or do they tell one another tales of the foolish beings that move about on legs, hurrying and chattering, by day? Faith, is it of me they are talking? See with what a blank look those houses gaze down at me, like a bench of magistrates at a rogue. But the house at the end, the tall one with the straight front, — I swear it is frowning upon me. And the one beside it, with the fat oriel windows, and whose upper stories belly so far out over the street, — as I'm a gentleman and a scholar, 'tis laughing at me. Has it come to this? — to be a thing of mirth to a monster of wood and plaster, a huge face with eyes of glass? For this did Ralph Holyday take his degrees at

Cambridge University, and was esteemed as able a disputant as ever came forth of Benet College? Go thy ways, Ralph; better wert thou some fat citizen snoring behind yon same walls, than Master Holyday, *magister artium*, lodging houseless on the church steps with all thy scholarship. Not so, neither; thou wouldst be damned rather! Hark, who is it walks in Cheapside, and coming this way, too?"

He might have recognised the tread as the same which had some minutes before moved in the opposite direction; though it was now less rapid, as if the owner of the feet had walked off some of his wrath. Coming into view at the end of the Old Jewry, that owner proved to be in truth the very soldier of whom Holyday had caught a glimpse at the tavern. The soldier, turning by some impulse, saw the scholar on the steps; but his warlike gaze had now no terror for Master Holyday, who had put at least half of the fowl beyond possible recovery, and whose appetite was no longer keen.

"God save you, sir!" said the scholar, courteously. "Were you seeking a certain roast fowl?"

"Not I, sirrah," replied Captain Ravenshaw, approaching Holyday. "You are he that stood in the doorway, perchance? Rest easy; the fowl was none of mine. I should scorn to swallow a morsel of it."

And yet he eyed it in such a manner that Master Holyday, who was a good judge of a hungry glance, said, placidly:

"You are welcome to what is left of it here." Which offer the scholar enforced with a satisfied sigh, indicating fulness of stomach.

The captain made a very brief pretence of silent hesitation, then accepted the remainder of the feast from the scholar's hands, saying:

"Worshipful sir, it should go hard with me ere I would refuse true hospitality. Have I not seen you about the town before this night?" He sat down beside Holyday, and began to devour the already much-diminished fowl.

"I know not," replied the scholar, who had a mild, untroubled way of speaking. "'Twas last Michaelmas I came to London. I have kept some riotous company, but, if I have met you, I remember not."

"'Slight! you know then who I be?"

"Not I, truly."

"Yet you call me riotous."

"That argues no previous knowledge. Though I be a Cambridge man, it takes none of my scholarship to know a gentleman of brawls at sight, a roaring boy, a swaggerer of the taverns — "

"Why, boy, why! Do you mean offence in these names?"

"No offence in the world. You see I bear no sword, being but a poor master of arts. None so bold of speech as the helpless, among honourable men of the sword."

"Some truth in that. Look ye, young sir, hast ever heard of one Ravenshaw, a captain, about the town here?"

"Ay, he is the loudest roarer of them all, I have heard; one whose bite is as bad as his bark, too, which is not the case with all of these braggadocios; but he is a scurvy rascal, is he not? a ragged hector of the ale-houses. Is it he you mean?"

"Ha! that is his reputation? Well, to say truth, he may comfort himself by knowing he deserves it. But the world used him scurvily first — nay, a plague on them that whine for themselves! I am that Ravenshaw."

"Then I must deal softly; else I am a hare as good as torn to pieces by the dogs."

"Why, no, scholar, thou needst not be afeard. I like thee, young night-walker. Thou wert most civil concerning this fowl. 'Od's light! but for thee, my sudden pride had played my belly a sad trick this night. Thou art one to be trusted, I see, and when I have finished with this bird, I will tell thee something curious of my rascal reputation. But while I eat, prithee, who art thou? and what is it hath sent thee to be a lodger on the steps of St. Mary Cole

Church?   Come, scholar; thou might do worse than
make a friend of roaring Ravenshaw."

"Nay, I have no enemies I would wish killed.
But I am any man's gossip, if he have inclination for
my discourse, and be not without lining to his head-
piece.   My name is Ralph Holyday; I am only son
to Mr. Francis Holyday, a Kentish gentleman of
good estate.   He is as different a manner of man
from me as this night is from a summer day.   He
is stubborn and tempestuous; he will have his way,
though the house fall for it.   He has no love of
books and learning, neither; but my mother, seeing
that I was of a bookish mind, worked upon him un-
ceasingly to send me to the university, till at last,
for peace' sake, he packed me off to Cambridge.
While I was there, my mother died — rest her soul,
poor lady!   After I took my degrees, my father
would have it that I come home, and fit myself to
succeed him.   Home I went, perforce, but I had no
stomach for the life he would lead me.   I rather preferred to sit among my books, and to royster at the
ale-house in company with a parson, who had as great
love for learned disputation as for beer and venison.
Many a pleasant day and night have I sat with good
Sir Nicholas, drinking, and arguing upon the soul's
immortality.   This parson had sundry friends, too,
good knaves, though less given to learning than to
tossing the pot; they were poachers all, to say truth,

and none better with the crossbow at a likely deer
than the vicar. Thus, when I ought to have been
busy in the matter of preserving my father's deer,
I would be abroad in forbidden quest of other men's ;
'twas, I know not how, the more sportive and curious
occupation. Well, my father stormed at these ways
of mine, but there was no method of curing them.
But one day he became fearful his blood should die
out. He must have descendants, he swore, and to
that end I must find a wife straightway. Here is
where we crossed weapons. I am not blind to the
charms of women, but I am cursed with such timidity
of them, such bashfulness when I am near them, that
if I tried to court one, or if one were put upon me
as wife, I should fall to pieces for shaking. I would
sooner attempt anew the labours of Hercules than go
a-wooing for a wife."

"'Tis a curious affliction," remarked the captain,
pausing in his feast. "But many men have it ; fighting men, too. There was Dick Rokeby, that was
my comrade in France ; he that fought with Harry
Spence and me, each one 'gainst t'other two, upon
the question of the properest oath for a soldier to
swear by. Harry was one of your Latin fellows,
and held for 'the buckler of Mars.' Dick Rokeby
said an Englishman could do no better than swear
by the lance of St. George. And I vowed by the
spurs of Harry Fift' I would put down any man

that thought better of any other oath. We fought it out, three-cornered, in Grey's Inn Fields; and the spurs of Harry Fift' won the day. As for women, I am their enemy on other grounds. There was one I trusted, and when I was at the wars she wronged me with my friend. I have sworn revenge upon the sex, curse 'em! So you would not marry?"

"That I would not. The only women I can approach without trembling at the knees, and my face burning, and my tongue sticking fast, are serving-maids and common drabs, and such as I would not raise to a place of quality. So the end was that, after he had raged and threatened for six months, my father cast me forth, swearing I should never cross his doorsill, or have a penny of him, till I should come back with a wife on my arm. And so I came last Michaelmas to London."

"And how hast made shift to live since then?"

"Why, first upon some money my friend Sir Nick thrust upon me; then by the barter of my clothes in Cornhill; and meanwhile I had writ a play, a tragedy, that Master Henslowe gave me five pounds for."

"I would fain see thy tragedy. How is it named?"

"God knows when it may be played; it has not yet been. It is 'The Lamentable Tragedy of Queen Nitocris.' The story is in a Greek history."

"What, you dare not even discourse with a mere gentlewoman, yet write the intimate histories of queens?"

"Yes, friend; there are many of us poor poets do so. We herd with trulls, and dream of empresses. (A passable decasyllabic line, that!) But I have not been able to sell another tragedy, nor yet to have my sonnets printed, whereby I might get ten pounds for a dedication. And so you see me as I am."

"Well," said the captain, having by this time pretty well stuffed himself, "I like thee the better for being a poet. Such as you know me to be, you will scarce believe it; but I am one — or was once — fitted by nature to take joy in naught so much as in poetry, and the sweet pastoral life that poets praise so. But never whisper this; I were a dead man if the town knew the softness underneath my leathern outside. But in very truth, as for books, I would give all the Plutarchs in the world for one canto of 'The Faerie Queene' or ten pages of the gentler part of Sidney's 'Arcadia.' Had I won my choice, I had passed my days, not in camps and battles, taverns and brawls, but in green meadows, sitting and strolling among flowers, reading some book of faery or shepherds — for I never could make up poetry of my own."

"That picture belies the common report of Captain Ravenshaw."

"Ay, Master Holyday; swaggering Ravenshaw is no shepherd of poesy. But hearken to what I promised thee: I, too, am a gentleman's son; the family is an old one in Worcestershire, — observe I call it not *my* family. I was early a cast-off scion, and for no fault of mine, I swear. 'Twas the work of a woman, a she-devil, that bewitched my father. But God forbid I should afflict any man, or rouse mine own dead feelings, with the tale of my wrongs! I was no roaring boy then; I was a tame youth, and a modest. But when I found myself out in the world, I soon learned that with a mild mien, unless a man have a craftiness I lacked, he is ever thrust backward, and crushed against the wall, or trodden upon in the ditch. And so for policy I took the time and pains to make myself a master of the sword, not that I might brawl, but that I might go my ways in peace. In good time, I killed two men or so that were thought invincible; and I supposed the noise of this would save me from affronts after that."

"And was it not so?"

"Perchance it had been, if my manner had comported with the deed. But I still went modest in my bearing, and so my prowess was soon forgot; some may have thought my victories an accident of fortune; besides, strangers knew not what I had done, and saw no daring in me; and so I found myself as unconsidered as ever. And at last, when the woman

I loved turned treacherous and robbed me of the
friend at court on whom my fortune hung, and
malice was hatched in me, I bethought me of a
new trick. I took on a bold front, an insolent
outside ; I became a swearer, a swaggerer, a roaring
boy, a braggart ; and lo ! people soon stepped aside
to let me pass. I found this blustering masquerade
a thousand times more potent to secure immunity
than my real swordsmanship had been. The transformation was but skin-deep at first ; but the wars,
and my hard life and my poverty, helped its increase,
so that now it has worked in to the heart of me.
There was a time it made me ill to sink my rapier
into a man's soft flesh, but I grew to be of stronger
stomach. And when I first put on the mask of
brazen effrontery, I was often faint within when I
seemed most insolent. But now I am indeed roaring
Ravenshaw, all but a little of me, and that little often
sleeps."

"But this insolence of thine, real or false, seems
not to have made thy fortune."

"Nay, but it has made my poverty the less con-
temptible. Lay not my undoing to it. When the
war lasted, I fared well enough, as long as I kept
the captainship my friend had got me ere the woman
played me false. A score of things have happened
to bring me to this pass. My braggadocio, ofttimes
enforced with deeds, hath neither helped nor hin-

dered my downfall; it hath stood me in good stead in fair times and foul.   Pish, man, but for my reputation, and the fear of my enmity or violence, could I have run up such scores at taverns as I have done, being penniless?   How often have I roared dicing fools, and card-playing asses, out of the stakes when they had fairly won 'em?   Could any but a man who has made himself feared do such things, and keep out of Newgate or at least the Counter i' the Poultry here?"

" Why, is not that rank robbery, sir?"

"Yes, sir, and rank filling of my empty stomach. Tut, scholar, you have been hungry yourself; roofless, too.   Be so as oft as I have been, and with as small chance of mending matters, and I'll give a cracked three farthings for what virtue is left in you. Boy, boy, hast thou yet to learn what a troublesome comrade thy belly is, in time of poverty?   What a leader into temptation?   Am I, who was once a gentleman, a rascal as well as a brawler?   Yes, I am a rascal.   So be it; and the more beholden I to my rascality when it find me a dinner, or a warm place to sleep o' nights.   Would it might serve us now. Who are these a-coming?"

Some dark figures were approaching from up the Old Jewry, attended by two fellows bearing links, for the moonlight was not to be relied upon. The figures came arm in arm, at a blithe but unsteady gait, sway-

ing and plunging. Presently the captain recognised
the gentlemen who had been his afternoon companions at the sign of the Windmill. But Master Vallance was not with them, having doubtless taken
lodging at one of the inns near the tavern. The
sparks, jubilant with their wine, no sooner made out
the captain's form than they hailed him heartily.

"What, old war boy!" cried Master Maylands, a
spruce and bold young exquisite. "Well met, well
met! Hey, gentles, we'll make a night on't. Captain, you shall captain us, captain!"

"Ay, you shall captain us about the town," put in
Master Hawes, who spoke shrilly, and with a lisp,
for which he would have been admired had it been
affected, but for which he was often ridiculed because
it was natural. "You shall teach us to roar as loud
as you do. What say you, gallants? Shall we go to
school to him to learn roaring? He is the master
swaggerer of all that ever swaggered."

The proposal was received with noisy approval, the
roysterers gathering around the captain where he
sat, and grasping him by the sleeves to draw him
along with them.

"Softly, gentlemen, softly," said the captain. "Ye
seem of a mind here. But do you consider? There
is much I might impart, in the practice of swaggering. Would you in good sooth have me for a
tutor?"

There was a chorus of affirmative protestation.

The captain thought it politic to urge a scruple.

"But bethink ye," quoth he, "to be a true swag-gerer is no child's play. And you are of delicate rearing, all; meant to play lutes in ladies' cham-bers; court buds, gallants."

"Why, then," said Maylands, "we shall be gallants and swaggerers, too; an you make swaggerers of us, we will make a gallant of you, will we not, boys?"

"Nay," replied Ravenshaw, "I have been a gallant in my time, and need but the clothes to be one again; and so does my friend here, who is a gentleman and a scholar, though out of favour with fortune. Now there be many tricks in the swaggering trade; the choice of oaths is alone a subtle study, and that is but one branch of many. I'll not be any man's schoolmaster for nothing."

"Faith, man, who asks it?" cried Master May-lands. "We'll pay you. For an earnest, take my cloak; my doublet is thick." He flung the rich broadcloth garment over the captain's uncloaked shoulders. "You need but the clothes to be a gal-lant again? 'Fore God, I believe it! Tom Hawes, I've cloaked him; you doublet him. Barter your doublet for his jerkin; your cloak will hide it for the night; you've a score of doublets at home."

Master Maylands, in his zeal, fell upon the unob-jecting Hawes, and in a trice had helped to effect the transfer, the captain feigning a helpless compliance in the hands of his insistent benefactors. It occurred to another of the youths, Master Clarington, to exchange his jewelled German cap of velvet for Ravenshaw's ragged felt hat; whereupon Master Dauncey, not to be outdone, would have had his breeches untrussed by his link-boy, to bestow upon the captain, but that the captain himself interposed on the score of the cold weather.

"But I'll take it as kindly of you," said Ravenshaw, "if you should have a cloak for my scholar friend. How say you, Master Holyday? Thou'lt be one of us? Thou'lt be a swaggering gallant, too?"

Master Holyday, inwardly thanking his stars for the benevolent impulse which had made him share the fowl, and so elicit this gratitude, would have agreed to anything under the moon (except to woo a woman) for the sake of warmer clothes.

"Yes, sir," said he, with his wonted studious gravity of manner; "if these gentlemen will be so gracious."

The gentlemen were readily so gracious. After a few rapid exchanges, which they treated as a great piece of mirth, they beheld the scholar also cloaked and richly doubleted and hatted. He wore his fine garments with a greater sense of their comfort than of his improved appearance, yet with a somewhat pleasant scholastic grace.

The captain strutted a little way down the street, to enjoy the effect of his new cloak; but, as he stepped into Cheapside, the moon was clouded, and he could no longer see the garment tailing out finely over his sword behind. A distant sound of plodding feet made him look westward in Cheapside, and he saw a few dim lanterns approaching from afar.

"Lads, the watch is coming," said he. "Shall we tarry here, and be challenged for night-walkers?"

"Marry," quoth Master Maylands, leaping forward to the captain's side, "we shall take our first lesson in swaggering now; we shall beat the watch."

"As good a piece of swaggering gallantry as any," said the captain. "Come, my hearts!"

And he led the way along Cheapside toward the approaching watchmen.

CHAPTER II.

DISTURBERS OF THE NIGHT.

" I will have the wench."
" If you can get her." — *The Coxcomb.*

THE captain gave instructions, as he and his pupils
strode forward. The two boys with the lights were
left behind to take shelter in a porch, so that the
peace-breakers might advance in the greater darkness. It was enough for their purpose that they
had the lanterns of the watch to guide them.

The watchmen came trudging on in ranks of two.
Presently there could be heard, from somewhere
among them, a voice of lamentation, protest, and
pleading, with a sound of one stumbling against
sundry ill-set paving-stones of the street.

" They have a prisoner," said the captain to his
followers. " We'll make a rescue of this. Remember, lads, no swords to be used on these dotards;
but do as I've told ye."

In another moment, and just when the watchmen
seemed about to halt for consideration, but before
their leader had made up his mind to cry, " Stand ! "
the captain shouted, " Now, boys, now; a rescue !

a rescue!" and the roysterers rushed forward with a chorus of whoops.

The watch, composed for the most part of old men, had scarce time to huddle into a compact form when the gallants were upon them. The assailants, keeping up their shouting, made to seize the watchmen's bills, with which to belabour them about their heads and shoulders. One or two were successful in this; but others found their intended victims too quick, and were themselves the recipients of blows. These unfortunate ones, bearing in mind the captain's directions, essayed to snatch away lanterns, and to retaliate upon the watchmen's skulls; and whoever failed in this, rushed to close quarters, grasped an opponent's beard, and hung on with all weight and strength.

The captain's operations were directed against the pair who had immediate charge of the prisoner. Possessing himself of the bill of one, whom, by the same act, he caused to lose balance and topple over, he obtained the other's voluntary retreat by a gentle poke in the paunch. The prisoner himself proved to be a man of years, and of port; he had a fat, innocent face, and he showed, by his dress and every other sign that became visible when the captain held up a lantern before him, to be a gentleman. What such a guileless, well-fed old person could have done to fall afoul of the night-watch, Captain Ravenshaw could not imagine. For the time, the old person's astonishment and relief at being set free were too great to permit his speaking.

Meanwhile, Master Holyday, having been the last to come up, found the melée so suddenly precipitated, and so complete without his intrusion, that he stood back looking for a convenient place and time for him to plunge into it. But it seemed impossible for him to penetrate the edge of the scuffle, or to connect himself with it in any effective way. So he hung upon the skirts; until at last two of the watchmen, being simultaneously minded for flight, bore down upon him from out of the hurly-burly. He instinctively threw out his arms to stay their going; whereupon he found himself grappled with on either side, and from that instant he had so much to do himself that he lost all observation of the main conflict. Nor had the other fighters any knowledge of this side matter. But their own sport was over ere their wind was out; the watchmen, being mainly of shorter breath and greater prudence than their antagonists, soon followed the example of flight; and the gallants, soberer by sundry aches, smarts, and bruises, were left masters of the field. None of the watch was too much battered to be able to scamper off toward the Poultry.

"A piece of good luck, sir," began Captain Ravenshaw, to the released prisoner, around whom the gallants assembled while they compared knocks and trophies. "You had been scurvily lodged this night, else."

"Sirs, I thank ye," replied the old gentleman, finding at last his voice, though it was the mildest of voices at best. He was still shaky from having been so recently in great fright; but he gathered force as his gratitude grew with his clearer sense of escape. "God wot, I am much beholden to ye. You know not what you have saved me from."

"To say truth, a lousy hole behind an iron grating were no pleasant place for one of your quality," said Ravenshaw.

"Oh, 'tis not that so much, though 'twere bad enough," said the gentleman, with a shudder. "'Tis the lifetime of blame that would have followed when my wife had heard of it. You must know, sirs, I am a country gentleman, and I am not known to be in London; my detention would be noised about, and when it reached my wife's ears —'sfoot, sirs, I am for ever your debtor in thankfulness!" And he looked his meaning most fervently.

"Why did the watch take you up?" inquired the captain.

"Why, for nothing but being abroad in the streets. The plaguey rascals said I was a night-walker, and that I behaved suspiciously. I did nothing but stand and wait at the Standard yonder, for one I had agreed to meet; but when I saw the watch coming I stepped back, to be out of their lantern-light. This stepping back, they said, proved I was a rogue; and so they clapped hands on me, and fetched me along. But now I bethink me, sirs: the person I was to meet — what will she do an she find me not at the place?" The old gentleman showed a reawakened distress, and, turning toward the direction whence the watch had brought him, looked wistfully and yet reluctantly into the darkness.

"Oho! She!" quoth the captain. "No wonder your wife — "

"Nay, think no harm, I beg. Nay, nay, good sirs! Sure, 'tis an evil-thinking world. Well, I must e'en bid ye good night, and leave ye my best thanks. Would I might some day repay you this courtesy. My name, sirs — but no, an ye'll pardon me, I durst not; the very stones might hear it, and report I was in London. But if I might know — "

"Surely. We have no wives in the country, that we must keep our doings from, have we, boys? And we are free of the streets of London, aren't we, boys? My name, sir, is Ravenshaw — Captain Ravenshaw; and this gentleman — "

He was about to introduce his companions by the names of great persons of the court, when, casting his eyes over the group for the first time since the link-boys had come up with their torches, he was suddenly otherwise concerned.

"Why, where's Master Holyday? Where the devil's our scholar?"

The gallants looked from one to another, and then peered into the surrounding darkness, but saw no one; nor came any answer to the captain's shout, "What ho, Holyday! Hollo, hollo!"

"An't please you," spoke up one of the link-boys, "while we waited yonder, the watchmen ran past us; and methought two of them dragged a man along between them; but 'twas so dark, and they went so fast—"

"Marry, that's how the wind lies," cried the captain. "Gallants, here's more business of a roaring nature. A rescue! Come, the hunt is up! To the cage, boys! We may catch 'em on the way."

Without more ado, Ravenshaw led his followers, link-boys and all, on a run toward the Poultry, leaving the grateful old gentleman in the darkness and to his own devices.

They hastened to the night-watch prison, but overtook no one on the way; it was clear that the watchmen had made themselves and their prisoner safe behind doors. An attack on the prison would have been a more serious business than the captain could see any profit in. So, abandoning the luckless scholar to the course of the law, the night-disturbers made their way back to Cheapside, wondering what riotous business they might be about next.

"What asses are these!" thought the captain. "They have warm beds to go to, yet they rather wear out their soles upon the streets in search of trouble. Well, it helps me pass the night, and I am every way the gainer by it; so if puppies must needs learn to play the lion, may they have no worse teacher."

When they came to the Standard, that ancient stone structure rising in the middle of the street, they walked around it to see if the old gentleman was there; but the place was deserted.

"Here were a matter to wager upon, now," observed the captain: "Whether he met his mistress after all and bore her away, or whether he found her not and went wisely to bed."

A few steps farther brought the strollers opposite the mouth of Bread Street. The sound of men's voices came from within this narrow thoroughfare.

"Marry, here be other fellows abroad," quoth the captain. "How if we should 'light upon occasion for a brawl? Then we should see if we could put them down with big words. Come, lads."

They turned into the narrow street and proceeded toward a group whose four or five dark figures were indistinctly marked in the flickering glare of a single torch. This group appeared to be circled about a closed doorway opposite All-hallows Church, at the farther corner of Watling Street, in which doorway stood the object of its attention.

"Some drunken drab o' the streets, belike," said the captain, in a low voice, to his followers. "We'll feign to know her, and we'll call ourselves her friends; that will put us on brawling terms with those gentlemen. They are gallants, sure, by their cloaks and feathers."

The gentlemen were, it seemed, too disdainful of harm to interrupt their mirth by looking to see who came toward them. The heartless amusement on their faces, the tormenting tone of the jesting words they spoke, gave an impression somewhat like that of a pack of dogs surrounding a helpless animal which they dare not attack, but which they entertain themselves by teasing.

The captain stepped unchallenged into the little circle, and looked at the person shrinking in the doorway, who was quite visible in the torchlight.

"'Slight!" quoth the captain. "This is no trull; 'tis a young gentlewoman."

His surprise was so great as to make him for the moment forget the plan he had formed of precipitating a quarrel. The young gentlewoman looked very young indeed, and very gentle, being of a slight figure, and having a delicate face. She leaned close against the door, at which she had, as it seemed, put herself at bay. Her face, still wet with tears, retained something of the distortion of weeping, but was nevertheless charming. Her eyes, yet moist,

were like violets on which rain had fallen. Her lips
had not ceased to quiver with the emotion which had
started her tears. Her hair, which was of a light
brown, was in some disorder, partly from the wind;
for the hood of the brown cloak she wore had been
pulled back. It might easily be guessed who had
pulled it, for the gentleman who stood nearest her,
clad in velvet, and by whose behaviour the others
seemed to be guided, held in his hand a little black
mask, which he must have plucked from the girl's
face.

This gentleman was tall, nobly formed, and of a
magnificent appearance. His features were ruddy,
bold, and cut in straight lines. He wore silken black
moustaches, and a small black beard trimmed to two
points.

At the captain's words, this gentleman looked
around, took full note of the speaker in a brief
glance, and scarce dropping his smile, — a smile careless and serene, of heartless humour, — said, calmly :

" Stand back, knave ; she is not for your eyes."

The captain had already thought of the inequality
between this fragile damsel and her persecutors ;
despite his account against womankind, her looks
and attitude had struck within him a note of com-
passion ; and now her chief tormentor had called
him a knave. He remembered the purpose with
which he had arrived upon the scene.

"Knave in your teeth, thou villain, thou grinning Lucifer, thou — thou—!" The captain was at a loss for some word of revilement that might be used against so fine a gentleman without seeming ridiculously misapplied. "Thou beater of the streets for stray fawns, thou frighter of delicate wenches!"

"Why, what motley is this?" replied the velvet gallant. "What mummer that is whole-clad above the girdle, and rags below? what mongrel, what patch, what filthy beggar in a stolen cloak? Avaunt, thing!"

The gentleman grasped the gilded hilt of his rapier, as if to enforce his command if need be.

"Ay, draw, and come on!" roared the captain. "You'll find me your teacher in that."

At the same moment a restraining clutch was put upon the gentleman's sleeve by one of his companions, who now muttered some quick words of prudence in his ear. Whether it was due to this, or to the captain's excellent flourish in unsheathing, he of the double-pointed beard paused in the very movement of drawing his weapon, and a moment later slid the steel back into its velvet scabbard. In his desistance from a violent course, there was evidently some consideration private to himself and his friend, some secret motive for the avoidance of a brawl.

"Say you so?" quoth the gentleman, blandly, as if no untoward words had passed. "Well, if you can be my teacher, you must be as good a rapier-and-dagger man as any in the kingdom, and there's an end on't. Are you that?"

"Sir, you might have tried me, and **found out**," said the captain, considerably mollified at the other's unexpected politeness, and putting up his sword.

"Why, marry, another time I may have occasion to see your skill — nay, I mean not a challenge; I should enjoy to see you fight any man."

"But what of this gentlewoman, sir?" said the captain, interrogatively.

"Why, you will not dispute, it is my prize, by right of discovery. You a swordman, and not know the laws of war? Faith, we men of the sea are better learned."

"Nay, but is she of the breed to make a prize of? Methinks she looks it not."

"Pish, man, a pretty thing or so; a citizen's filly, mayhap, that hath early slipped the halter; she will not tell her name; but what we find loose in the streets after curfew, we know what it is, whatsoever it may look."

The girl now spoke for the first time since the captain had seen her. Her voice, though disturbed by her feelings, was not shrill like a child's, but had the fulness of blossoming womanhood, and went with the smoothness common to well-bred voices.

"I was never in the streets at night before," she said, sobbingly. "There was one I was to meet, who was waiting for me at the Standard in Cheapside."

"Eh!" quoth the captain, with a suddenly increased interest.

"Some gallant 'prentice, belike," said the gentleman in velvet, with his singular smile of gaiety and cruelty. "Some brave cavalier of the flat cap, whom we frighted off."

"'Twas not so!" cried the girl. "He was not frighted off. I was going to him, and was near the place, but I could not see him yet, 'twas so dark. And then the watch came, with their lanterns, and I stood still, so they might not observe me. But I saw them go to the Standard, and take my — my friend that waited for me. I knew not what to do, and so I stayed where I was, all dismayed. And then, but not till the watch had gone away with him, came you cruel gentlemen and found me. So he was not frighted by you. Alas, if he had but seen me, and come to meet me!"

"But he was soon free of the watch," said the captain, wondering what such a damsel should have to do in surreptitiously meeting such a worshipful old married gentleman. "Came he not back to the place? 'Tis a good while since."

"How know you about him?" queried the girl, with wonder.

" 'Tis no matter," said the captain, forgetting for the nonce to brag of an exploit. " He ought to have come back to the place to seek you ; he was no true man, else."

" Belike he did, then," said the girl, quickly, with hope suddenly revived.

" Nay, 'tis certain he waits not at the Standard; we came from there but now. Doubtless his taking up by the watch gave him his fill of waiting there. He seemed a man with no stomach for night risks."

" Then," said the girl, mournfully, " he must have come back after I had run from these gentlemen. Then he would think I could not meet him ; 'twas past the time we had set. Oh, villains, that I should run from you, and miss my friend, and yet be caught at last ! He would give all up, and go to his inn, and back to the country at daybreak. All's over with me ! Oh, ye have much to answer for ! "

" How prettily it cries ! " quoth the handsome gentleman.

" Faith, sir," said the captain, good-humouredly, " let's see an 'twill laugh as prettily. How if we led this dainty weeper to her friend's inn, and roused him out ? Perchance then we shall have smiles for these showers. Where does he lie, little mistress ? "

" Alas, I know not. 'Twould be near the river, I think."

"Oho, that he might take boat quicker," said the gentleman. "And now will he fly without thee at daybreak, say'st thou? Never sorrow, sweetheart; I'll boat thee to Brentford myself to-morrow."

"There be scores of inns near the river," said the captain to the girl. "But we might make trial at some of them, an we knew by what name to call for your friend."

"Nay, that I'll never tell! I know not if he would give his true name at the inn. Alas, what shall I do?"

"Why, come to the tavern and make merry," said Velvet Suit, "as we have been inviting you this half-hour."

"I'll freeze in the streets sooner!"

"Is there need of that, then?" asked the captain. "Hast no place in London to go to? Came you not from some place to meet your friend?"

"From my father's house, of course."

"Then why not go back to it? What's to fear? 'Twas late when you came forth, was it not? I'll wager thy people were abed. Did they know you meant to play the runaway?"

"'Tis not like they know it yet," she replied, a little relieved from complete dismay, but still down-hearted.

"And sure the way you came by must be open still," went on the captain.

"I locked the door behind me; but I left the key where I can find it, if you gentlemen will let me go. You will, sirs; I'll thank ye so much! I am undone every way, else."

"Of course we'll let you go," said the captain, decisively, with an oblique eye upon the velvet gallant. "We'll be thy body-guard, forsooth; we'll attend thee to thy door."

"Nay, let me go alone, I beg!"

"Why, would you risk more dangers?"

"I have not far to go. Pray, pray, follow me not! Pray, let me be unknown to ye, good sirs! Think, if my mishap this night were noised about, and my name known — think, if my father were to hear it!"

"Ay, true," said the captain. "Go alone, but on condition, if you see harm ahead, you turn back to us; you must cry for help, too. And so we give our words of honour not to — "

"Softly, softly, Master Meddler," broke in the handsome gentleman. "Be not so free with your betters' words of honour. I know not what hath allowed you to live so long after thrusting in upon this company — "

But again he was checked by the man at his elbow. This was a broad-breasted man of medium height, who seemed, as well as his plain dark cloak would show, to be of solid, heavy build; as for his face, its

lower part was so covered by a thick, spade-shaped
beard, and the upper part so concealed by the brim
of a great Spanish hat, purposely pulled down over
the eyes, that one could not have obtained a sufficient
glimpse for future recognition. He spoke to his gay
companion in a brief whisper, but his words had
instant weight.

"Tush! 'tis not worth bloodshed," said the gay
gentleman, having heard him. "Let the wench go;
what is one fawn among so many? But on condition. I crave more of your acquaintance, Sir Swordman; we may come to a fight yet, with better
reason; so my friends and I will let the girl go hang,
an you and your party come drink with us."

"We are your men there," replied the captain,
warming up within, at such a happy issue; "but the
taverns are barricaded at this hour."

"I know where the proper knock will open doors
to us. 'Tis agreed, then. Wench, go your ways;
good night!"

He moved aside to let her pass, and the girl,
stepping from the doorway, with a single look of
thanks to the captain, ran swiftly toward Cheapside.
She was out of the range of the torchlight in a
moment. As soon as her figure was invisible in the
night, the gentleman in velvet left his companion,
and, taking the captain fraternally by the arm, started
toward Knightrider Street.

Ravenshaw, yielding in spite of an inclination to
stay and listen for any distant sign of alarm from
the girl, strode mechanically along; he heard his
own followers and the gentleman's friends coming
close behind, and starting up conversations. Lighted
by the two link-boys and the other torch-bearer, the
party at length stopped before a tavern door in
Thames Street.

The handsome gallant knocked a certain number
of times, and, while he waited for answer, the party
huddled into a close group before the door. Every
face was now in the torchlight, and the captain cast
a glance over the little company. Suddenly a strange
look came into his face.

"What's this?" he said to the gentleman, quickly.
"Where's your other friend — he with the hat pulled
over his eyes?"

For answer, the gentleman gave a curious smile,
showing white teeth; and his eyes sparkled mock-
ingly.

"Death and hell! Gods and devils!" cried the
captain, roaring in earnest, and whipping out his
sword. "He slunk back and followed the maid,
did he? Ye'd trick me, would ye? Now, by the belly
of St. George —" At this point, though the velvet
gallant had swiftly drawn in turn, the group having
opened a clear space at the captain's first excla-
mation, Ravenshaw broke off to another thought.

"Nay, we'll go after that hound first; the scent's warm yet; and then we'll look to you. Come, lads of mine!"

He dashed through the group, and headed for Cheapside; his four pupils and the two link-boys tarried not from following him. The other gentlemen looked to their leader for direction; whereupon he, as the tavern door opened, put up his sword and, laughing quietly, led them into the house.

"They'll be rare dogs an they catch Jerningham," quoth he. "The fools! their noise would warn him even if they should chance upon his track."

The captain and his companions found Bread Street and Cheapside black, silent of human sounds, and, wherever they carried their lights, empty of human forms. They traversed two or three of the side streets, and listened at the corners of others, but without result. Where, in this night-wrapped London, did the two objects of their search now draw breath?

If the girl had indeed not had far to go, she was probably safe; and if she were safe the man's doings mattered little. So, and as the gallants were beginning to show signs of weariness, the inspiriting effect of their last wine having died out, the captain piloted them back to the tavern at whose door he had left his quarrel scarce begun.

He found the tavern door barred; and no amount

of knocking and shouting sufficed to open it. The tired gallants were yawning, leaning against one another (they dared not lean against the tavern, lest something might be dropped upon them from an upper window), and talking of bed. Therefore the captain drew off to a safe distance from the tavern, and thus addressed his following :

"Ye have had but a poor lesson in swaggering to-night, masters. To be true roaring boys, we should have forced a brawl on those gallants — rather for the brawl's sake than for the girl's. To help the helpless hath nought to do with true swaggering, save where it may be a pretext. But this lambkin looked so tender, I forgot myself, and behaved discreetly, seeing her cause was best served that way. The essence of roaring is not in concern for the cause, but in putting down the enemy. If you be in the wrong, so much the greater your credit as a bully. And now, if we wait for those cozeners to come forth — "

"Oh, let 'em come forth and be damned," said Master Clarington, sleepily. "I'm for bed. Light me to my lodging, boy. Who'll keep me company to Coleman Street ? "

As the three other young gentlemen had, at the time, their city lodgings in that direction, they were quite ready to avail themselves of Master Clarington's initiative in yielding to the claims of fatigue.

The captain was not such a fool as to risk their favour by opposing their decision, seeing how their zest for adventure had oozed out of them. He therefore accompanied them northward through Bow Lane with outward cheerfulness. On the way, he considered within himself whether or not to fish for an invitation to a night's lodging, or for the loan of money to pay for a bed himself. He bethought him that man was fickle, particularly in the case of would-be daredevils who soon grew sleepy on their wine; if he would retain the patronage of these four, he must not go too far upon it at first. He had too much experience to sacrifice to-morrow's pound for to-night's shilling. So, when he came to Cheapside, where his companions should turn eastward, he stopped, and said:

"I must wish ye good night here, gentlemen. You will be at the Windmill again to-morrow, mayhap?"

"What?" said Master Maylands, carelessly. "Go you no farther our way? Where lodge you, then?"

"Oh, I lodge out Newgate way," replied the captain, vaguely. "A good night to ye all! Ye'll find me at the Windmill after dinner. Merry dreams, lads! Faith, I shall be glad to get under cover; the wind is higher, methinks."

A chorus of good nights answered him drowsily, and he was left in darkness, the link-boys going with

the four gentlemen, who hung upon one another's
arms as they plodded unsteadily along.

The captain trudged westward in Cheapside, in
mechanical obedience to the suggestion pertaining
to his lie.

"I should better have got myself taken up of the
watch," he mused, as he gathered his new cloak
about him, and made himself small against the wind.
"Then I should have lain warm in the Counter.
That scholar is a lucky fellow. But that would
have lost me the opinion of my four sparks. Well,
it shall go hard but they continue bountiful. Cloak,
doublet, and bonnet already — a good night's booty.
'Tis well I found 'em in the right degree of drink.
As for that wench — I was an ass, I should have
let those roysterers have their way of her; 'twould
have served my grudge against the sex. But such a
child — ! Hey! What fellow comes here with the
lantern and the wide breeches? An it be a constable, I'll vilify him, and be lodged in the Counter
yet. How now, rascal! — what, Moll, is it thou, up
to thy vixen tricks again?"

The newcomer, who now faced Ravenshaw and
held up a lantern to see him the better, wore a
man's doublet and hose, and a sword; but a careful
scrutiny of the bold features would have revealed to
any one that they were those of a sturdy young
woman, of the lower class. The daughter of Frith,

the shoemaker of Aldersgate, had yet to immortalise herself as Moll Cutpurse, but she had some time since run away from domestic service and taken to wearing men's clothes.

"Good even, Bully Ravenshaw," quoth she, in a hoarse, vigorous voice. "Why do you walk the night, old roaring boy?"

"For want of a lodging, young roaring girl."

"Is it so? Look ye, then; I'm abroad for the night, on matters of mine own. Here's my key; 'tis to the back yard gate of the empty house in Foster Lane, where the spirit walks. Dost fear ghosts?"

"Fear ghosts? Girl, I make 'em!"

"Then you'll find in that yard a penthouse, wherein is a feather-bed upon boards. 'Tis a good bed — I stole it from a brewer's widow."

And so the captain lodged that night in a coalhouse, thankfully.

CHAPTER III.

"I must and will obtain her; I am ashes else." — *The Humourous Lieutenant.*

Now it happened that while Captain Ravenshaw and his companions were speeding up Bread Street toward Cheapside, the Spanish-hatted gentleman of whom they were in quest was plodding down Friday Street toward the tavern at whose door they had left his friends. When he arrived there, he gave a knock similar to that which had served to open the house to the handsome gallant of the double-pointed beard; and presently, after being inspected through a small grating in the door, he was admitted.

"Is Sir Clement Ermsby above?" he asked the sleepy menial who had let him in.

"Yes, your worship. An't please you, he and his friends came in but a little while ago. They're in the Neptune room. A cold night, your worship."

"How many of his friends?"

"Three, sir. There were e'en five or six more with him outside, at first; but they went their ways. Methinks there was some quarrel, but I know not."

57

The gentleman pushed his hat back from his brow, and looked a trifle relieved. He stood for a moment with his eye on the servant, as if to see that the man barred the door properly, and then he went up-stairs to a room at the rear of the tavern. The tapestry of this chamber represented the sea, with the ocean god and a multitude of other marine figures. Around the fire sat the newcomer's friends, smoking pipes; they greeted him with laughter.

"Ho, ho!" cried the handsome gallant. "She 'scaped you, after all! The pinnace was too fleet!"

"I gained all I wished," said the broad-breasted gentleman, coolly, speaking in curt syllables. "I had no mind to close in combat. I did not even let her know I was giving chase. But I saw what port she made into; I know where to seek her when the time is propitious."

With a faint smile of triumph over his comrades, the gentleman, who had thrown off his plain cloak while speaking, stepped close to the fire, removed his gloves, and began to warm his fingers. He was of middle stature, thick-bodied, heavily bearded, of a brown complexion; his expression of face was melancholy, moody, dreamy; as he gazed into the fire he seemed lost in his own thoughts. His momentary smile had brought a singularly sweet and noble light into his face; but that light had vanished with the smile.

"I must thank you, Ermsby, and all of ye," he said, after a short silence. "You drew the fellow away like the best of cozeners. How got you rid of him so soon?"

"Faith, by his taking note of your absence, and guessing what was afoot," replied the handsome gallant. "He's e'en looking for you now. A murrain on him! his ribs should have felt steel, but for thy fear of a brawl, Jerningham."

"Thou'rt a fool, Ermsby," answered Jerningham, continuing to gaze with saturnine countenance into the fire; "and my daring to call thee so tells how much I fear a fight for its own sake. How often must I put it to you in plain terms? If I be found concerned in roystering or rioting, I forfeit the countenance of my pious kinsman, the bishop. With that I forfeit the further use of his money in our enterprise. Without his money, how are we to complete the fitting of our ship? No ship, no voyage. No voyage, no possessing the fertile islands; and so no fortune, and there's an end. Pish, man, shall we lose all for a sight of some unknown rascal's filthy blood? Not I. You shall see me play the very Puritan till the day my ship lifts anchor for the Western seas."

"You have played the Puritan to-night, sooth," said Ermsby. "To steal after a wench under cover of night, and find out her house for your hidden purposes in future, — there's the soul of Puritanism. Where does she live ? "

" I'll still be puritanical, and keep that knowledge to myself," said Jerningham, with the least touch of a smile.

" Nay, man, the secret is ours, too ! " protested Ermsby. "We helped you to it. Come, you had best tell ; that will put us on our honour to leave her all to you. If you don't, by my conscience, I'll hunt high and low till I find out for myself, and then I won't acknowledge any right of yours to her. Tell us, and make us your abettors ; or tell us not, and make us your rivals."

Jerningham was silent for a moment, while he motioned the attending servant to pour him out some wine ; then, evidently knowing his men, he replied :

" She led me but a short chase ; which was well, as I had to go upon my toes — the sound of her steps was all I had to guide me. When the sound stopped, in Friday Street, I heard the creaking of a gate ; it meant she had gone into a back yard. I went on softly, feeling the walls with my hands, till I came to the gate ; and there I heard a key turning in a door. I had naught to do but find out what house the gate belonged to. 'Twas the house at the corner of Cheapside."

" And Friday Street ? Which side of Friday Street ? "

"' SHE LED ME BUT A SHORT CHASE.' "

"The east side. 'Tis a goldsmith's shop. Does any one know what goldsmith dwells there?"

No one remembered. These were all gentlemen who, when they were not at sea, divided most of their time between the country and the court; at present they lodged toward the Charing Cross end of the Strand, in a row of houses opposite the river-side palaces of the great. But Jerningham himself lived with his kinsman, the bishop, in Winchester House, across the Thames.

"Time enough to learn that, and win a score of goldsmith's daughters, and tire of 'em too, ere the ship is fitted," said Ermsby, losing interest in the subject; whereupon the conversation shifted to the matter of the ship, then being repaired at Deptford.

From this they fell to dicing, — all but Jerning-ham, who sat looking steadily before him, as if he saw visions through the clouds of tobacco smoke he sent forth. Presently was heard the noise of pounding at the street door below.

"'Tis that rascal come back, ten to one; he has given over hunting you," said Ermsby to Jerningham.

"Then be sure you open not, Timothy," said Jerningham, addressing the tavern drawer who was staying up to wait upon those privileged to use the house after closing hours.

"No fear," replied Timothy. "They may ham-mer till they be dead, an they give not the right knock. I'll e'en go look down from the front window, and see who 'tis."

Ermsby went with him; and presently returned with him, saying:

"'Tis our man; and Timothy here knows him. It seems he is one Ravenshaw, a roaring captain. I've heard of the fellow; he talks loud in taverns, and will fight any man for sixpence; a kind of ranger of Turnbull Street — "

"Nay," corrected Timothy; "he is no counterfeit, as most of those rangers be. He roars, and brags, and looks fierce, as they do; but he was with Sir John Norris in Portugal and France, and he can use the rapier, or rapier and dagger, with any man that ever came out of Saviolo's school. I have seen him with the foils, in this very room, when he made all the company wonder. And 'tis well known what duels he has fought. One time, in Hogsdon fields — "

"Oh, that is the man, is it?" said Jerningham, cutting off the drawer's threatened torrent of reminiscence. "Then so much the better he has grown tired of beating at the door. He has gone away, I trust. As ye love me, gentlemen, no scandals till the ship is armed, provisioned, manned, and ready every way for the tide that shall bear us down the Thames."

"And look that you bring no scandal in your siege of this goldsmith's daughter," said Ermsby, jocularly.

"Trust me for that," replied Jerningham.

It was several weeks after this night, and the chilling frown of winter had given place to the smile of May, when, upon a sunny morning, Sir Clement Ermsby, followed by a young page, stepped from a Thames wherry at Winchester stairs to confer with Master Jerningham upon the last preparations for their voyage. They were to sail in three days.

Jerningham was pacing the terrace, frowning upon the ground at his feet, his look more moody than ever, and with something distraught in it; now and then he drew in his breath audibly between his lips, or allowed some restless movement of the hands to belie his customary self-control.

"What a devil is it afflicts you, man?" was Ermsby's greeting, while his page stood at a respectful distance, and began playing with two greyhounds that came bounding up. "This manner is something new. I've seen it for a week in you. Beshrew me if I don't think an evil spirit has crept into you. What's the matter?"

"Nothing's the matter," said Jerningham, in a growling tone. "'Tis my humour."

"'Tis a humour there's no excuse for, then, on a day like this, and with such a prospect before one's eyes." As Sir Clement spoke, he looked over the balustrade to the Thames and the countless-gabled front of the spire-studded city.

The Thames and London were fair to see then. The river was wider than it is now, and was comparatively clean. Swans floated upon its surface, and it was lively with passenger craft, — sailboats, rowboats, tilt-boats, and boats with wooden cabins, gaily decorated barges belonging to royalty and nobility. The Thames, with its numerous landing-stairs, was the principal highway of London. When the queen went from Whitehall to Greenwich, it was, of course, by this water thoroughfare. It was the more convenient way of transit between the city and Westminster, where the courts were held. It had but one bridge at London then, — the old London Bridge of the children's song, "London Bridge is falling down;" the bridge that was a veritable street of houses, and which stood some distance east of where the present London Bridge stands. To many people the better way of crossing to Southwark, when they went to the playhouses or the bear-gardens, was by boat. Water-men were at every landing-place, soliciting custom. When at work, they often sang as they plied the oars. The rich, when they would amuse themselves upon the river in their handsome tilt-boats, took musicians with them. On a fine May day, in the reign of Elizabeth, when the little green waves sparkled in the sunshine, the Thames alone was a sight worth looking at from the terrace of Winchester House, which, as everybody knows, was on the Southwark side, west of the beautiful Church of St. Mary Overie (now St. Saviour's), and which thus commanded a fine view of river and city-front.

Beginning at the far west, where the river came into sight after passing Westminster and Whitehall, its northern bank presented first the long row of great houses that came as far as to the Temple, — houses that were really town castles, with spacious gardens, whose river walls were broken by gates, whence were steps descending to the water. Nearer, grew the stately trees of the Temple garden ; nearer yet, rose from the river's edge the frowning walls of the Bridewell, once a palace, and of Baynard's Castle. And here the eye was drawn up and back from the water-front, which henceforth abounded with wharves, by the huge bulk of St. Paul's, which stood amidst a multitude of ordinary buildings like a giant among pigmies, — the old St. Paul's, Gothic, with its square tower in the centre, its crosses crowning the ends and corners, its delicate pinnacles rising from its flying buttresses, its beautiful doorways and rose windows. Coming still eastward, the eye swept a great mass of gabled houses ascending in irregular tiers from the river, the sky-line broken by church towers and steeples innumerable. Directly opposite Winchester House, the river stairs that fell from the tall, narrow buildings were mainly for commercial uses. A little further east, the view was shut in by the close-packed houses on the bridge, so that one could not see the Tower, or the larger shipping off the wharves in the lower river.

But this morning the sight was nothing to Master Jerningham, whose only answer to his friend was to look the more harassed and woebegone. Ermsby suddenly took alarm.

"How now? Has anything ill befallen at Deptford?" he asked.

"No. All goes forward fast — too fast." And Jerningham sighed.

"How too fast? How can that be? Good God, man, have you lost heart for the voyage?"

"Never that. You know me better. But we shall soon be sailing, and the hours go, and yet I am no further with — oh, a plague on secrecy, 'tis that wench. There is no way under heaven I can even get speech of her."

"What wench?" inquired Ermsby, in whose thoughts there had been more than one wench since the reader first made his acquaintance.

"What wench! Gods above, is there more than one? — worth a man's lying awake at night to sigh for, I mean."

"And is there one such, then? Faith, an there be, I have not seen her of late."

"Yes, you have. Scarce three months ago."

"That's three ages, where women are concerned. Who is this incomparable she?"

"That goldsmith's daughter — you remember the night we chased her from Cheapside down Bread Street, and came near a quarrel with Ravenshaw the bully, and I followed to see where she lived?"

"Faith, I remember. A pretty little thing. And she has held you off all this time? Man, man, you must have blundered terribly! What plan of campaign have you employed against her?"

"I have not been able to pass words with her, I tell you. She rarely goes forth from home at all, and when she does 'tis with both parents, and a woman, and a stout 'prentice or two. I have stood in wait night after night, thinking she might try to run away again; but she has not."

"Why, you know not your first letter in the study of how to woo citizens' womankind. Go to her father's shop while she is there, and contrive to have her wait upon you. Flattery, vows, and promises sound all the softer for being whispered over a counter."

"I have watched, and when I have been busy at the ship, my man Gregory has watched. But she never comes into the shop. She has a devil of shrewdness for a father; a rock-faced man, of few words, with eyes on everything. He already suspects me; for now whenever I go near his shop he comes from his business and stares at me as if he offered defiance."

"A plague on these citizens. They dare outface gentlemen nowadays. They are so rich, and the law is on their side, curse 'em! A goldsmith thinks himself as good as a lord."

"This one has taught his very 'prentices to look big at me as I pass. And Gregory — he is a sly hound, as you know, and when I put him on his mettle for the conveyance of a letter to the girl's waiting-woman, he was ready to sell himself to the devil for the wit to accomplish it. But he could not; and they have smelt a purpose in his doings, too. The last time he went near the shop, and stood trying to get the eye of some serving-maid at a window, two of the goldsmith's 'prentices came out and, pretending not to see him, ran hard against him and laid him sprawling in the street."

"And he let them go with whole skins? Had he no dagger?"

"Of what use? They are very stout fellows, all in that shop. And they would have had only to cry 'Clubs,' and every 'prentice in Cheapside would have come to cudgel Gregory to death. They have too many privileges in the city, pox on 'em!"

"You should have begun by making friends with the goldsmith openly, and so got access to his house.

Then you could have cozened him when the time
came."

"But 'tis too late for that now.   Besides, these
citizens distrust a man the first moment, when they
have wives and daughters.   Oh, we have tried every
way, both myself and Gregory.   Gregory found a
pot-boy, at the White Horse tavern, that knew one
of the maids in the house, and we tried to pass a
letter by means of those two.   But the letter got
into the father's hands, and the maid was cast off,
and I'm glad I signed a false name.   I know not
if Mistress Millicent ever saw the letter."

"Is Millicent her name?"

"Ay.   She is the only child.   Her father is
Thomas Etheridge, the goldsmith, at the sign of the
Golden Acorn, in Cheapside at the corner of Friday
Street.   And nothing more do I know of her, but
that I am going mad for her.   And now that I have
opened all to you, in God's name tell me what I
shall do.   Though we sail in three days, I must have
her in my arms for one sweet hour, at least, ere
I go.   Laugh if you will!   Call it madness.   'Tis
the worse, then, and the more needs quenching.
What shall I do?"

"Use a better messenger; one that can get the
ear of the maid and yet 'scape the eye of the father;
one that can win her to a meeting with you.   Such
things are managed daily.   Howsoever hedged by

husbands, or fenced by fathers, the fair ones of the city are still to be come at.   Employ a go-between."

"Have I not tried Gregory? Where he has failed, how shall any other servant fare? Not one of those at my command has a tithe of his wit. Nor has any of our sea-rogues."

"Why, the look of being a gentleman's serving-man will damn any knave in the eye of a wary citizen, nowadays. And Gregory hath the face of a rascal besides. Employ none of that degree. As for our sea-rogues, we chose 'em witless, for our own advantage."

"Troth, you might serve me in this matter, Ermsby. You have the wit; and you should find good pastime in it."

"Faith, not I. I know the taste of 'prentice's cudgel. I'll tell you a tale; 'twill warn you that, when love's path leads into the city, you'd best see it made sure and smooth ere you tread it yourself. One day as I was going to the play in Blackfriars, my glance fell upon as handsome a piece of female citizenship as you'll meet any day 'twixt Fleet Street and the Tower. She saw me looking, and looked in turn; and I resolved to let the play go hang, and follow her. She had with her an old woman and a 'prentice boy, and her look seemed to advise me not to accost her in their presence. So I walked behind her, smiling my sweetest each time she turned her head around. She led me into a grocer's shop in Bucklersbury. I could see by her manner there that she was at home; there was no husband in sight, the shop being kept by two 'prentices. Here she forthwith sent the woman up-stairs, and turned as if she would attend upon me herself. Now, thought I, my happiness is soon to be assured; and I was rejoicing within, for each time I had seen her face she had looked more lovely. Sooth, the ripe-ness of those lips — !"

"Well, well, what happened?"

"I went but to open the matter with a courteous kiss on the cheek; but the more luscious fruit hung too near, so I stopped me at the lips instead, and stopped overlong there. She made pretence — I swear 'twas pretence — to push me away, and to be much angry and abused. But the zany 'prentices knew not this virtuous resistance was make-believe, and they ran at me as if I were some thief caught in the act. I met the first with a clout in the face, but they were stout knaves and made nothing of laying hands upon me. I shook them off, and then, being at the back of the shop, drew my sword to ensure my passage to the street. But that instant they raised the cry, 'Clubs!' and ran and got their own cudgels, and came menacing me again. While I was making play with my rapier, thinking to fright them off, all the 'prentices in Bucklersbury began to pour into the shop, shouting clubs and brandishing 'em at the same time. I saw there was naught to do but cut my way through by letting out the blood of any grocer's knave or 'pothecary's boy that should stand before me. But ere I had made two thrusts in earnest, my rapier was knocked from my hand by a club. A cloud of other clubs rained on my head, shoulders, and body. And so I cowered helpless, seeing nothing before me but the chance of being pounded to a jelly by the crowd."

"And what miracle occurred?"

"The wit of woman intervened. She that I had followed laid hold of some box or bag, and thrust her fingers in, and began flinging the contents by handfuls into the air. It was ground pepper. In a moment every man Jack in the shop was sneezing as if there were a prize for it. Such a shaking, and bending forward of bodies, and holding of noses, was never seen elsewhere. Every fellow was taken with a sneezing fit that lasted minutes, for the woman still threw the pepper about, regardless of the work it had done. Limp and half-blind as every rascal was, and busied with each new spasm coming on, they paid no more heed to me; and so, sneezing like the rest, I pushed through unregarded to the street. I fled down Walbrook, and came not to an end of sneezing till I had taken boat at Dowgate wharf. I went home, then, and put my bruises to bed; and

I know not how many days it was till I had done aching. Be thankful thou hast not fared in the goldsmith's shop e'en worse than I fared in the grocer's; for there is no pepper kept in goldsmith's shops."

" I know not then what kind of emissary to send. As you say, a serving-man is too easily seen through. A gentleman will not risk the cudgel. I know a lawyer, a beggarly knave eager for any sort of questionable transaction."

" Nay, he'll make a botch of it, as lawyers do of everything they set their hands to."

" How if I tried a woman? 'Tis often done, I believe. As thieves are set to catch thieves, so set a woman —"

" Ay, women have zest for the business; especially the tainted ones — they joy to infect their sisters whose purity they secretly envy. They that have spots take comfort in company, as misery doth. Yet they will serve you ill; for they ever bring entanglement on those they weave their plots for, as well as on those they weave against. City husbands and fathers have grown wiser, too; they've learned to look for love-plots in their women's fellowship with other women. Unless you'd risk some chance of failure with this maid —"

" By God, that I will not! I must have a sure messenger."

"I would mine own page yonder had the wit, that I might lend him. But when I choose a servant, 'tis rather for lack of wit in him; else he might take it into his head to outwit his master. My boy there serves well enough to carry sonnets to court ladies; but he would never do for your business. You say this goldsmith is watchful. Therefore, you want a man the most unlike the common go-betweens in such affairs; a man that looks the last in the world to be chosen as love's ambassador."

"Some venerable Puritan, perchance," said Jerningham, with the slight irony of one not quite convinced.

"Ay, if one could be found needy enough to want your money; but that's hopeless. We must seek a poor devil that hath a good wit and can act a part. If we had one such in our ship's company — What, Gregory! Have you been listening, knave?"

Sir Clement's break was caused by his perceiving, upon suddenly turning around, that Jerningham's man stood near, with a suspicious cock of the head. This Gregory was just the fellow to steal up without noise; he had long cultivated the silent footfall. He was a lean man of about thirty-five years; a little bent, and with a long neck, so that his head always seemed hastening before his body, which could never catch up. He had a small, sharp face, of an ashen complexion, and with fishy, greenish eyes; his expression was that of cunning cloaked in calm impudence.

"No offence, sirs," said he, glibly, stepping forward with bowed head. "I couldn't help hearing a little. If I may say so, sirs, my master needn't yet look abroad for one to do his business. I think I have a shift or two still, if I may be so bold."

"You may not be so bold, Gregory," said Jerningham. "Disguises are well enough in Spanish tales and stage plays; but you'd be caught, and all brought home to me and the bishop's ears. He could stay our ship at the last hour, an he had a mind to. Go to; and do and speak when you are bid, not else."

The serving-man stepped back, looking humiliated.

"He's already green with jealousy of the man you shall employ," said Ermsby, with unkind amusement at the knave's discomfiture.

"Ay, he's touchy that way. A faithful dog — and bound to be so, for I know a thing or two that would hang him. But to reach this maid, I must have another Mercury. Where shall I find this witty poor rascal that is to cozen old Argus, her father, and get me access to her?"

"Why, but for going to Deptford, we might seek

him forthwith. The hour before dinner is the right time. But —"

"Then let us seek. There's no need we go to Deptford to-day. We cannot haste matters at the ship; all's in good hands there. In God's name, come find me this fellow."

"Bid Gregory hail a boat, then," said Ermsby; and, after the servant had been sent ahead to the stairs on that errand, and Ermsby had motioned his own page to go thither, he continued: "We shall go to Paul's first, where we got so many of our shipmates; there we shall have choice of half the penniless companions, starved wits, masterless men, cast soldiers, skulking debtors, and serviceable rascals in London. Of a surety, you can buy any service there; there's truth in what the plays say."

The two gentlemen, attended by Gregory and the page, were soon embarked in a wherry whose prow the watermen headed against the current, the destination being some distance up-stream on the opposite bank.

"What of Meg Falkner?" Ermsby said, suddenly, in a tone too low for the servants to hear. "Are you rid of her yet?"

Jerningham's brow turned darker by a shade.

"That were as great a puzzle as to reach this goldsmith's wench," he replied. "I would have

married her to Gregory; it seemed no mean fate for
a yeoman's daughter that had buried a brat; but
she'd have none of that. I durs'n't turn her out lest
she make a noise that might come to the bishop.
I'm lucky she hath kept quiet, as it is."

"She lives still at your country-house?"

"Ay; where else to lodge her? Rotten as it is, it
does for that; and that is the only use it hath done
me this many a year. There's a cow or two for her
maintaining, and some hens. And for company,
there's old Jeremy that's half-blind. He can quiet
her fears o' nights, when the timbers creak and she
thinks it is a ghost walking."

"And what of the house when you are away on
the voyage?"

"Troth, all may out then, I care not! Let 'em
sell the estate for the debts on it; they'll find themselves losers, I trow. And Mistress Meg will be left
in the lurch, poor white-face! As for me, when the
ship sails, I shall be quit of that plague."

"Ay, but you'll be quit of this goldsmith's wench,
too. Will your 'one sweet hour' or so suffice, think
you?"

The faintest smile came into Jerningham's face.

"I will not prophesy," said he, softly. "But, as
you well know, when we come to that island, if all
goes well, I shall be in some sort a king there."

"Certainly; but what of that, touching this wench?"

" Why, will not the island have room for a queen as well ? "

" Oho ! " quoth Ermsby, after a short silence. " So the wind blows that way in thy dreams ! "

Presently they landed at Paul's Wharf, climbed to Thames Street, which was noisy with carts and drays, and went on up a narrow thoroughfare toward the great church.

CHAPTER IV.

THE ART OF ROARING.

"Damn me, I will be a roarer, or't shall cost me a fall." — *Amends for Ladies.*

ON the February morning when he rose from bed in the coal-house attached to the haunted dwelling in Foster Lane, Captain Ravenshaw waited about the yard for Moll Frith to return from her excursion of the night. When she appeared, he gave her back the key to the gate, and borrowed two angels from her. Armed with these, he bade her repent of her sins, and hastened to Cheapside, turning eastward with the purpose of finding out how and where his new friend, the scholar, fared in the hands of the law.

Cheapside, which was in a double sense the Broadway of Elizabethan London, was already thronged with people going about their business, the shops and booths of the merchants being open, and the shopmen and 'prentices crying out their wares with the customary "What d'ye lack?" At the great conduit, the captain pushed his way through the crowd of jesting and quarrelling water-carriers who were filling their vessels, and washed his hands and face. Looking about for a means of drying himself, while the water dripped from his features, he espied a woman with a pitcher, to whom the uncouth water-carriers would not give place. The captain knocked several of them aside, gallantly took the woman by the hand, led her to the fountain, and enabled her to fill her pitcher. While she was doing this, he, with courteous gestures, took her kerchief from her head and dried himself therewith; after which he returned it with a bow so polite that, between her amazement and her sense of flattery, she could not find it in her to say a word against the proceeding.

Going on his way refreshed, the captain suddenly met Master Holyday, who looked as unconcerned as if he had never been near a prison in his life.

"What, lad, did not the watch take thee, then?"

"Yes, faith, and kept me all night in a cage, where I think I have turned foul inside with the smell of stale tobacco smoke. I am come but now from the justice's hall."

"Man, you've had a quick journey of it. By this light, you must have found money in those new clothes, and tickled the palm of a constable."

"No; the justice might have sent me back to the stinking hole, for all the money I had to give anybody. When he asked me my name, I bethought me to reply, 'Sir Ralph Holyday;' which was no more than my right at Cambridge, when I became

a graduate there. But, seeing me in these clothes
instead of in black, the justice thought the ' Sir' was
of knighthood, not of scholarship. And so he said
he could make nothing out of the watchmen's stories,
which agreed not. I then addressed him respect-
fully in Latin; and, lest it might be seen that he
did not understand me, he got rid of me forthwith."

" We'll drink his health — but not yet. While I
have money to show, we'll bespeak lodgings, and so
make sure of sleeping in-doors, for a week o' nights,
come what may. These clothes will get us curtseys
and smiles from any hostess — except them that
have already lodged me."

" Ay, we are fine enough above the waist, but our
poor legs and feet are sorry company for our upper
halves."

" Why, we must see to that when we meet our
four asses again. Meanwhile our cloaks will cover
us to the knees, and if we carry our heads high
enough, nobody will dare look scornful at our feet.
Remember, we are gallants while these clothes last ;
swaggering gallants, that give the wall to no man.
And while we go seek lodgings, I'll tell thee how
thou shalt earn thy share of these coxcombs' wast-
ings. Hast ever travelled abroad ? "

" No," said the scholar, falling into the captain's
stride as the pair went westward.

" No matter. Thou hast read books of other

countries, and heard travellers tell of foreign cities ? "

" Yes ; I've read and heard much ; and remembered some of it."

" Then bear in mind, you are a great traveller. Your gentleman that hath not been abroad is counted a poor thing among gallants. Now these four silken gulls have never been out of England, and they look sheepish whene'er a travelled man talks of France or Italy in their company. They would give much to pass for travelled gallants ; to talk of French fashions and Italian vices without exposing their inexperience. You shall instruct 'em, so they may fool others as you fool them. I'll broach the matter softly, and in such a way that they shall see the value of it. Thus, while you fill 'em up with tales of the foreign cities you have seen, we shall eat and drink at their cost. And so we shall hold 'em when they be tired of the swaggering lessons I mean to give 'em."

" Well, I will do my best. What I don't know, I will e'en supply by invention. My stomach will inspire me, I trust."

They took lodgings at the top of a house in St. Lawrence Lane, not far from its Cheapside end ; and passed the time in walking about the streets till near noon, when they went to dinner at an ordinary where long tables were crowded with men of different de-

grees, who dined abundantly and cheaply. The two
companions finally repaired to the Windmill tavern,
where they had to wait an hour before their young
gentlemen appeared.

The four were now sober, and showed hardly as
much relish in meeting the captain as he might have
wished. They cast somewhat rueful glances at the
clothes they had given away in their vinous generosity, and which they had now replaced with other
articles suitable to their quality. They manifested
no eagerness for lessons in swaggering, and seemed
at first to have forgotten any understanding they
may have formed with the captain in regard thereto.

But Ravenshaw was prepared for this apathy.
He took the risk of inviting the gentlemen to drink,
and with the air of an accustomed host he bowed
them into the room to which a tapster directed him.
He trusted they would be of different mood when
the time to pay the score should come.

A little drinking, and a few of the captain's tales,
warmed them up to some enthusiasm for his society ;
and in an hour he had them urging him to proceed
straightway to their further education in the art of
roaring. After some reluctance and some unwilling-
ness to believe that their proposal of the previous
night had been serious, he was persuaded to consent.
With the faintest grimace of triumph, for the eyes of
Master Holyday alone, who smoked a pipe temper-

ately by the fire, he rose and began by illustrating
how your true bully should "take the wall" of any
man about to pass him in the street.

The arras-hung partition of the room served as a
street wall. The captain started at one end, Master
Dauncey at the other. When the two met at the
middle, the instructor enacted an elaborate scene of
disputing the right to pass next the wall and so avoid
the mud of the mid-street. He showed how to plant
the feet, how to look fierce, how to finger the sword-
hilt, what gestures to make; then what speeches to
use, first of ironical courtesy, then of picturesque
abuse, finally of daunting threat. Master Holyday, looking on from the fireplace, was amazed to
see how much art could be displayed in what had
ever seemed to him quite a simple matter. The
captain went through every possible stage short of
sword-thrusts; but there he stopped, saying that
roaring ended where real fighting began.

"If your man has not given way by this time," said
he, "and you think he may be your better with the
weapons, the next thing is to come gracefully out
of the quarrel, by some jest or other shift. This
is what many swaggering boys do, out of fear. When
I do it myself, 'tis because I would avoid bloodshed,
or out of mercy to my antagonist. But 'tis, in any
case, a most important thing in the art of swaggering;
I shall give examples of it in my next lesson."

He then caused the gallants, in pairs, to go through such a scene as he had enacted. They made a foolish, perfunctory business of it at first, though he schooled them at every moment in attitude, gesture, or look, and supplied them with terms of revilement that made the scholar stare in admiration, and sanguinary threats before which a timid man might well tremble in his shoes.

It would not do to carry his pupils too far forward at a step ; he must keep them dependent upon him as long as possible. Nor was it safe to tire them with repetitions. So he put an end to the lesson in good time ; and then, to hold them for the rest of the day, he set forth the possibility of their learning to pass as men that had travelled abroad. Master Holyday, while modestly admitting the extent of his wanderings in foreign countries, showed some disinclination to the task of imparting the observations he had made.

"For, look ye," quoth he, "I once had a gossip whom I was wont to tell of things I had seen abroad. Like yourselves, he had never crossed the narrow seas ; but by noting carefully my talk, he was able to make other people think he had travelled as far as I. There was one thing I had told him, which I had chanced to forget afterward. A dispute arose betwixt us one day, before company that knew not either of us well, touching certain customs in Venice.

By my not mentioning the thing I had forgot, and by his parading it as a matter well known, which others in the company knew to be the case, I was made a laughing-stock, and he got reputation as a great traveller. And to this day he keeps that reputation, all at my expense."

This ingenious speech brought the desired insistence; and that very afternoon was begun, at Antwerp, an imaginary journey through the chief cities of Europe, in which were seen many things more astonishing than any foreign traveller had ever observed before.

It took several evenings to go through Flanders and France, and would have taken more, but that, after the gallants had satisfied their curiosity regarding Paris, they were in haste to arrive in Italy as soon as might be. Italy was then the great playground of English travellers; the fashions came from there, so did the inspiration to art and literature; the French got their cookery and their vices from Italy; the English imported some of the vices, but not the cookery.

While the scholar led his four charges from city to city by routes often unusual and sometimes impossible, Captain Ravenshaw conducted them stage by stage toward proficiency in swaggering. He showed them how differently to bully their betters, their equals, their inferiors; how to bully before company,

how without witnesses, how in the presence of ladies ;
how to overbear in every situation, from a simple
jostle in the street to a dispute about a woman ; how
to meet a contradiction in argument, how to give and
receive every degree of the lie, how to intimidate a
winner out of the stakes at a gaming-table ; and
finally how, when the opponent was not to be talked
down, either to slip out of a fight or to carry one
through.

The progress of the four would-be bullies in
their fireside travels, and their swaggering education,
was accompanied by further improvement in the
dress of their instructors.   At last the soldier and
his friend were able to go clad in breeches, stockings,
shoes, shirts, ruffs, and gloves, quite worthy of the
cloaks, doublets, and hats they had previously received.   The four young gentlemen were now eager
to try their new accomplishments about the town.
The captain postponed the test as long as he could ;
but finally their impatience was so peremptory that
he had to consent.

Now the captain knew that if his four apes should
make a failure of their first attempt at swaggering,
his favour with them were swiftly ruined ; conversely,
a success would warrant his demanding a substantial
reward in money.   Thus far his only payment, and
Master Holyday's likewise, had been in the shape of
dinners, suppers, tobacco, and clothes.   The two had

been compelled, from time to time, to put off payment for their lodgings, and to temporise with their
laundress ; and now their hostess's face wore a more
and more inquiring look each morning as they went
out.   Ravenshaw had, it was true, obtained a little
coin in the card-playing and dicing, by means of
which he had illustrated to his pupils the uses of
roaring in those pastimes.   But this amount, small
enough, he decided to lay out in ensuring the desired success of his coxcombs in their first bullying
exhibition.

He therefore made a sudden and secret excursion
to the suburbs beyond Newgate.   After searching
the lower taverns and ale-houses about Holborn and
Smithfield, he found, in a cookshop in Pye Corner,
a man with whom he forthwith entered into negotia-
tion.   This man was a burly, middle-aged fellow,
with a broken nose, a scarred cheek, a sullen attitude,
and a husky voice.   While he talked, he frequently
spat in the rushes that covered the floor ; and now
and again he would finish a remark with the words,
added without the least sense, " And that's the hell
of it."   He wore a dirty leather jerkin over other
clothes, and his attire was little better than Ravenshaw's had been before his change of fortune.

After some talk, Captain Ravenshaw handed over
some money to this man, promised a further sum
upon the issue of the business, received the bravo's

assurance that all should go well, and hastened
back alone to meet his companions at the sign of
the Windmill.

It was evening when the party sallied forth, the
four coxcombs as keen for riot as ever was a colt for
kicking up heels in a field. They would have barred
the street against the first comers, or sought a brawl
in the first tavern, but that Ravenshaw bade them
save their mettle for adversaries worthy of their
schooling.

"I mean to pit ye 'gainst the first roarers of the
suburbs," said he. "Nothing short of the kings of
Turnbull Street shall suffice ye, lads. What think
ye of Cutting Tom himself? I know where he and
his comrades take their supper nowadays. Save
your breath for such; an ye roar them down in
their own haunts, it shall be heard of. Waste no
wind upon citizens or spruce gallants. Strike high,
win supremacy at the first trial, and you are made
men."

With such counsel he restrained them until he had
led them through Smithfield to Cow Cross, near the
town's edge.

Like a bent arm, lying northwestward along the
fields toward Clerkenwell, was the narrow lane of
ramshackle houses called Turnbull Street. Leaving
his followers, the captain went into one of these
houses. He soon came back.

"'Tis excellent," said he. "Cutting Tom and his friends are in the front room at the top o' the stairs. They are feasting it with the hostess and some of her gossips. You four shall go up and claim the room by right of superior quality. Master Holyday and I will stay below in talk with the bar-boy so they sha'n't know I'm with you; but if need be, call me."

"Nay, we shall want no help," said Master Maylands; but the quaver of his voice belied his show of confidence.

"'Tis well," replied Ravenshaw. "A rare thing to roar these braggarts from their own table, before the womankind of their own acquaintance! Come."

A minute later the four sparks, huddled close together, and with white faces, thrust themselves into an ill-plastered room where four villainous-looking fellows and as many painted women sat at table. These people suddenly ceased their loud talk and coarse laughter, and one of them, — the broken-nosed rascal with whom Ravenshaw had that day conversed in the cook-shop — demanded thunderously:

"Death and furies! Who the devil be these?"

"Your betters, bottle-ale rogue!" cried Maylands, somewhat shrilly, and like an actor in a play.

"Betters!" bellowed the broken-nosed man, rising to his feet. "Plagues, curses, and damnations! Does the dog live that says 'betters' to me? I am called Cutting Tom, thou bubble!—Cutting Tom, and that's the hell of it!"

"An you be called Cutting Tom," replied May-lands, taking a little courage from the sound of his own voice, "'tis plain you are called so for the cuts you have received, not given. The wounds in your dirty face come not from war, but from bottles thrown by hostesses you've cheated. Out of this room, dog-face!—you and your scurvy crew. 'Twould take a forest of juniper to sweeten the place while you're in it. You are not fit for the presence of such handsome ladies."

"A gentleman of spirit," whispered one of the ladies, audibly.

"What, thou froth, thou vapour, thou fume!" roared Cutting Tom. "Avaunt! ere I stick you with my dagger and hang you up by the love-lock at a butcher's stall for veal."

"Hence, thou slave," retorted Maylands, "thou pick-purse, thou horse-stealer, thou contamination, thou conglomeration of all plagues—!"

"Thou bundle of refuse!" put in Master Hawes.

"Thou heap of mud!" added Master Dauncey.

"Thou filth out of the street-ditch!" cried Master Clarington.

Meanwhile the women had scampered to the fire-place for safety. Cutting Tom's three comrades had found their feet, and they now joined their voices to his in a chorus of abuse, defiance, and threat; they beat the table fearsomely with their sheathed swords. In turn, the young gentlemen half-drew their blades and then pushed them violently back again, and trod angrily upon the rushes. Cutting Tom's party had all got to that side of the table farther from the door. The four intruders therefore advanced to the table, and with terrible words belaboured their adversaries across it.

"A step more," cried Cutting Tom, banging his sword handle upon the table, "and I'll spit ye!"

"And roast ye after at the fire!" said one of his men.

The gallants showed that they could rattle their hilts upon the innocent board as fiercely.

"Out of the room," shouted Maylands, "ere we pin ye to the wall and set dogs on ye!"

This was but the beginning of the contest, which soon attained a scurrility too shocking, not for Elizabethan ears, but for these pages. Meanwhile, Ravenshaw and Holyday waited below. At last a noise was heard in the passage above, and the four ill-favoured fellows came bounding down the stairs. Three of them left the house at once, but Cutting Tom, seeing that the gallants did not follow, stopped to whisper with the captain.

"'Twas good as a play," quoth he. "We held our own awhile, as you bade. Then we let 'em overbear

us, and at last we feigned such fear they said they'd
e'en make us tie their shoes. 'They're tied already,'
quoth I. 'Then untie 'em,' said they. We untied
'em; and then they'd have us depart a-crawling on
our hands and knees; and so we left 'em, on all
fours; and that's the hell of it! I thought the
women would have burst a-laughing."

"Here's the rest of the money," said Ravenshaw,
parting with his last coin. "Now vanish, and come
not here again this night, or you'll have me to
answer!"

Cutting Tom examined the money by the candle-
light, and went his way with a grunt.

"So far, good," said Ravenshaw, chuckling. "Our
young cocks will think themselves the prime swaggerers of Christendom."

"Until they come upon the truth," said Holyday.
"The next men they meet, they'll be for bullying;
and then they're not like to come off as well."

"But they shall meet no men this night. The
ladies above will keep 'em here till they be too sleepy
with wine for any desire of roaring. We'll see 'em
safe home, and to-morrow at dinner I'll ply 'em for a
fat remuneration. When that's in our pockets, they
may learn the truth and go hang. We'll hire a page
to attend us, and we'll live like gentlemen. We're
lucky to have found 'em constant so long. Come;
we'll up to them, as if we happened in."

" Nay, not I, where there be women."

" Oh, plague, man, you'll not be long bashful afore these trollops ! " And he pulled the unwilling scholar after him by the arm.

CHAPTER V.

PENNILESS COMPANIONS.

" I walk in great danger of small debts. I owe money to several hostesses." —
The Puritan.

THE next day, after dinner, finding the four dupes as much puffed up with imagined valour as he had hoped, Ravenshaw put forward the matter of a fit reward. That they might more freely consider, he left them for half an hour, taking Holyday with him.

" Troth," began Master Hawes, when the four were alone, " I think we have bestowed somewhat already upon these two. If they are pressed for money, why don't they pawn some of the clothes we've given 'em ? "

" They consider they must be well clad to go in our company," said Clarington.

" If it comes to that," said Maylands, " we can dispense with 'em. We roared down this Cutting Tom and his Turnbull rangers, why should we be still beholden to this captain ? "

" And we've learned as much of t'other one's travels as we're like to remember," added Dauncey.

"Let them go hang for any more gifts!" said Maylands.

"Will you tell them so?" queried Hawes.

"Faith, yes! An we can roar down four Turnbull rangers, can we not roar down this one captain? He has taught us all he knows himself."

"Yet I would not have him think us stingy," said Hawes, who, as he was stingy, was sensitive as to being thought so.

"Why, look you," replied Maylands. "When they come back, I'll say we'll satisfy 'em, touching a gift of money, ere the day be done. Then, presently, we'll find some occasion in their talk for a quarrel. Thereupon, we'll roar 'em down, and so break with 'em."

The occasion arrived when Master Holyday was in the midst of a wonderfully imagined tale of travel. He told how he had escaped from Barbary pirates in the Mediterranean, and swum ashore to the harbour of — Fez!

"What, man?" broke in Master Clarington. "Fez is not on the seacoast."

"Most certainly it is," said the scholar, imperturbably.

"'Tis not. I had an uncle, a merchant adventurer, was there once. He had to journey far inland."

"Oh, ay," said Holyday, a little staggered; "the

city of Fez is inland, but the country borders on the sea. 'Twas that I meant."

"Nay, you spoke of the harbour; you must have meant the city."

"Tush, tush!" put in Ravenshaw, anxious to keep up the scholar's credit. "He meant the country; a fool could see that."

"Ay, truly," said Master Maylands, "a fool; but none else."

"I'll thank you for better manners," said Ravenshaw, sharply.

"Manners, thou braggart!" cried Maylands, seizing his opportunity. "Thou sponge, thou receptacle of cast clothing! Talk you of manners?"

"What! — what! — what! — what!" was all the answer the amazed captain could make for the moment.

"Ay, manners, thou base, scurvy knave; thou houseless parasite, thou resuscitated starveling! — thou and thy hungry scholar!" put in Master Hawes.

"Oho! 'Tis thus? Ye think to try my swaggering lessons against me?" said the captain, springing to his feet.

"Pish! You are no better than Cutting Tom," retorted Maylands.

Ravenshaw's wrath knew no bounds. The four rebellious pupils and providers were on their feet, defiant and impudent.

"You'd raise your weak breath against me, would ye? And you'd finger your sword-hilts, would ye?" he roared. "By this hand, ye shall draw them, too! Draw, and fend your numbskulls 'gainst the whacks I'll give 'em! Draw, and save your puny shoulders! I scorn to use good steel against ye, dunces, lispers, puppies! I'll rout ye with a spit!"

They had drawn swords at his word, thinking he would wield his rapier against them. But, as it was, they had an ill time enough to defend themselves against the spit he had seized from the fireplace. Nimbly he knocked aside their blades, violently he charged among them, swiftly he laid about him on pates and bodies; so that in small time they fled, appalled and panic-stricken, not only from the room, but down the stairs. The captain did not take the trouble to follow them beyond the doorsill of the room.

"Hang them, bubbles!" quoth he. "They shall come on their knees and lick my shoes, ere I'll take 'em back to favour again."

But the scholar philosophically shrugged his shoulders.

To make matters worse, as the two were about to leave the tavern, they were called upon to pay the score. Ravenshaw said the young gentlemen would pay, as usual.

"Nay," said the hostess, "they went away cursing

my tavern, and saying they would never come near it again. 'Twas you ordered, and I look to you to pay. 'Tis bad enough an you drive good customers from my house, and give it a bad name with your swaggering."

"Peace, peace, sweetheart. We have no money to pay; there's not a groat between us."

"Then you have clothes to pawn. I'll have my money, or I'll enter an action. So look to't, or, by this light, ye'll find yourselves in prison, I swear to ye!"

The two unfortunates fled from her tongue, down the Old Jewry. It rains not but it pours; and when they reached their lodgings in St. Lawrence Lane they were confronted by the woman of the house, whose distrust had been brought to a head by their absence the previous night. She must have her money; let them go less bravely clad, and pay their honest debts, else they had best beware of sheriff's officers.

When they were alone in their room, Holyday was for selling their fine clothes.

"Never, never!" said Ravenshaw. "If we cannot make our fortunes in fine clothes, how shall we do it in rags? Though we go penniless, while we look gallant we shall be relied upon. Some enterprise will fall our way."

The next morning they rose before their hostess,

and took leave of her house without troubling her
with farewells. They found new quarters in a shoemaker's house in St. Martin's-le-Grand, and avoided
their old haunts for fear of arrest.

The question of meals now grew difficult. Ravenshaw had become so well known that possible
adversaries at the gaming-tables shunned him. What
little credit he could still compass at ordinaries and
taverns soon prepared the way for new threats
of arrest. Sometimes the two companions contrived
to eat once a day, sometimes once in two days.
After a time, the captain agreed that Holyday might
barter his clothes. The scholar speedily appeared
in a suit of modest black, as if he were his gallant
companion's secretary; and for awhile the two
feasted daily. But anon they were penniless again,
and went hungry. The captain swore he would not
part with his fine raiment; though he should starve,
it would be as a swaggering gallant still.

No Lent was ever better kept than was the latter
part of that year's Lent (though to no profit of the
fishmongers) by those two undone men. Their
cheeks became hollow, their bellies sank inward,
they could feel their ribs when they passed their
hands over their chests. They went feverish and
gaunt, with parched mouths and griped stomachs.
As hunger gnawed him, and the fear of sheriff's
officers beset him at every corner, and hope grew

feeble within him, the captain became subject to alternations of grim resignation and futile rage. The scholar starved with serenity, as became a master of the liberal arts, being visited in his sleep by dreams of glorious banquets, upon which in his waking hours he made sonnets.

In May the patience of the shoemaker in St. Martin's-le-Grand was exhausted, and the two penniless men had other lodgings to seek.

They spent much of their time now in St. Paul's Church. Here employment was like to offer, and here was comparative safety from arrest, certain parts of the church being held sanctuary for debtors. To St. Paul's, therefore, they went on the morning that found them again roofless; keeping a lookout on the way thither for any sheriff's men who might with warrant be in quest of them. It was fortunate that none waylaid them, for the captain was in such mood that he would have gone near slaying any that had. Neither he nor Holyday had eaten for two days.

They took their station against a pillar in the middle aisle of the great church, and watched with sharp eyes the many-coloured crowd of men, of every grade from silken gallants to burden-bearing porters, that passed up and down before them, making a ceaseless noise of footfalls and voices, and sometimes giving the pair scant room for their famished bodies.

The St. Paul's of that time was larger than the present cathedral. It covered three and a half acres, and was proportionately lofty. Thanks to its great doors and wide aisles, it afforded a short way through for those foot-goers in whose route it lay, — porters, labourers, and citizens going about their business. But its wide aisles served better still as a covered lounging-place for those on whose hands time hung heavy, — gentlemen of fashion, men who lived by their wits, fellows who sought service, and the like. These were the true " Paul's walkers." It was a meeting-place, too, for those who had miscellaneous business to transact ; a great resort for the exchange of news, in a day when newspapers did not exist. Certain of the huge pillars supporting the groined arches of the roof were used to post advertising bills upon. The services, in which a very fine organ and other instruments were employed, were usually held in the choir only, and the crowd in the nave and transepts did not much disturb itself on account of them. The time of most resort was the hour before the midday dinner ; and it was then that Ravenshaw and Holyday took their stand before the pillar on this May morning.

" There walks a poet that hath found a patron," said the scholar. " Yet 'tis ten to one the verses he is showing are no better than these sonnets in my breeches pocket here."

" If you had a capon's leg or two in your breeches pocket it were more to the purpose," replied the captain.

" 'Troth, my sonnets are full of capon's legs and all other things good to eat," sighed Holyday. " I've conceived rare dishes lately; I have writ of nothing else."

" If we could but eat the dishes out of thy sonnets!" muttered Ravenshaw. " How can you write sonnets while you are hungry?"

" Why, your born poet finds discomfort a spur. There was the prophet Jonas writ a sonnet in the whale's belly."

" Faith, I'd rather undertake to write one with a whale in my belly! I feel room for a whale there. Who the devil comes here?"

It was none other than Master Maylands, and following him were Clarington, Dauncey, and Hawes, the four being attended by a footman and a page. These gallants, in coming down the aisle, had espied the captain before he had seen them. They had stopped and held a brief colloquy.

" Pish! who's afeard?" Maylands had said. " He won't fight in the church."

" And if he will," said Clarington, " we can 'scape in the crowd."

" Hang him, hedgehog!" said Dauncey. " I think the spirit has gone out of him, by his looks."

"It makes me boil," said Hawes, "to see the dog dressed out like a gentleman in clothes of our giving."

The gallants advanced, therefore, looking as supercilious and impudent as they could.

"God save you, dog of war!" said Maylands.

"God lose you, pup of peace!" replied the captain.

"Faith, I had thought 'twas a warm day," said Maylands, "but for seeing you wear a heavy cloak. Or is it that you durs'n't leave it home, lest it be seized in pawn for debt?"

"You are merry," quoth the captain, briefly; for the gallant had mentioned the true reason.

"It shows your regard for us," put in Hawes, "that you always wear our clothes, to avoid their being seized."

"A finger-snap for your clothes!" said the captain, his ire engendered by their daring to make so free of speech with him.

"Nay, you value 'em more than that," said Clarington. "They're all you have."

"Is it so?" said the captain.

"Ay," said Maylands, "you must needs wear our livery still, whether you will or no."

"Your livery, curse ye!" cried Ravenshaw, observing that some in the crowd had halted to see what game of banter was going on. "Why, monkeys, I've worn these clothes about the town in hope

of meeting ye, that I might give 'em back. Since
I did ye the honour to take your gifts, I've heard
things of ye that make it a shame to have known ye.
I've sought ye everywhere; but the fear of a beating
has kept ye indoors. Now that I meet ye, for God's
sake take back your gifts, and clear me of all behold-
ing to such vermin! Your cloak, say you? Yes,
lap-dog, there's for you. I thank God I'm free of
it!" Acting on the impulse which had come with
the inspiration for his retort, and wrought up beyond
all thought of expediency, he had flung the cloak in
the astonished gallant's face. "This bonnet will better fit an empty head," and he tossed his cap to
Clarington. "Here's a doublet, too; I've long ached
to be rid of it," he cried, divesting himself of that
garment as fast as he could, to hurl it at the head
of Master Hawes. "This ruff has choked me of
late; I pray you, hang yourself with it; there'll be
an ass the less. The shoes are yours, coney; take
'em, and walk to hell in 'em!" He threw them one
after another at their former owner, and began drawing off his stockings. "I'll be more careful in accepting gifts hereafter; a gift is a tie, and a man should
make no tie with those he may come to hear foul re-
ports of. Your stockings, sir! The breeches, — nay,
I must take them off at home, and send 'em to you
later; them and the shirt, and sundry linen and such,
that are with the laundress. Take these gloves,

though, and this handkerchief; and you your hanger
and scabbard, and the rest.   Take 'em, I bid ye,
or — And now, whelps, you've got what's yours.
Thank God, the sword and dagger are my own!   My
weapons may go naked while my body does.   Vanish,
with your gifts!   I scorn ye!"

His voice and looks were such that the four gentlemen thought best to obey.   Hastily entrusting the
captain's cast raiment to the footman and page, who
closely followed them, they pushed through the grinning crowd that had witnessed the scene; and the
captain was left in his shirt and breeches, with his
sword and dagger in his hands, to the amused gaze
of the assembly, and the somewhat rueful contempla-
tion of Master Holyday.

CHAPTER VI.

REVENGE UPON WOMANKIND.

" Get me access to th' Lady Belvidere,
But for a minute." — Women Pleased.

AMONG newcomers who at that moment pressed
forward to see what was the matter, were Master
Jerningham and Sir Clement Ermsby. Followed by
Gregory and the page, they had but then entered
the church upon the quest we know of. By standing
upon their toes, they got a view of the half-naked
man. At the same time they heard the name,
" Roaring Ravenshaw," passed about.

" Ravenshaw ? " said Ermsby to his friend. " So
'tis. And your very man."

" What, for such an affair ? A swaggering cast
soldier ? "

" Ay, indeed. The last man in the world to be
suspected in your particular case."

" But can he compass it ? "

" Trust these brawlers, these livers by their wits,
for a thousand shifts. They get their bread by
tricks."

" But will he undertake it ? "

"For pay?   Look at him."

"But he was her champion that night."

"A mere show, to cross us.   Should they know each other again, 'twill gain him her confidence the sooner.   Go; make use of his present need."

"Shall you come with me?"

"He might remember me as his adversary that night.   He saw you not well enough to recognise you.   Better he shouldn't know you are my friend. I'll be gone, ere he see us together.   Meet me at Horn's ordinary when you have done with him.   To him straight."

Beckoning his page, Sir Clement hastened from the church, while Jerningham, with Gregory at his heels, elbowed imperiously forward till he was face to face with the captain.   Ravenshaw had, in the meantime, been bandying jests with the crowd, though inwardly wondering what he should do next.

"When a soldier of your ability comes to this plight," said Jerningham, in a courteous, kindly tone, "'tis plain the fault's not so much his own as it is the world's."

Ravenshaw gazed at the speaker; manifestly without recognition.

"Sir," said the captain, "whatever faults the world hath done me, I dare yet put my dagger to the world's throat, and cry 'Deliver!'"

"Still the swaggerer," quoth Jerningham, with his soft smile.

"Ever the swaggerer," replied Ravenshaw. "'Tis my policy. This craven world will give nothing out of love or pity; 'twill give only out of fear; and so I bully out of it a living."

Jerningham went close to him, and spoke in tones not to be heard by the crowd, which presently, seeing that no more amusement was to be afforded, began to melt into the usual stream of saunterers.

"I take it," said Jerningham, "you are as good at cozening as at bullying."

"I am not such a coward as to deny it. There be some so tame, the fiend couldn't find it in his heart to bully them; at the same time, their lack of wit must needs tempt me to cozen them."

"You have a persuasive speech at will, too, I see."

"Seest thou?"

"Look you: I could mend your fortunes if you could persuade, or cozen, or bully, to a certain end for me."

"Prove you'll mend my fortunes, and I'm your man," said the captain, jumping at the hope.

Jerningham regarded him for a moment thoughtfully, then said:

"Perhaps I'd best prove it first, ere I tell you what service I require."

" I care not what the service is. Anything that a man can do, I can do."

"And will do ? "

"And will do — if it be not too black. I'll not murder."

" Oh, the business has no murder in it. Here's proof I'll mend your fortune — all such proof that is in my purse, as you see. Meet me here after dinner, dressed so as not to draw everybody's eyes upon us as we talk. You shall hear then what the service is. And there shall be more pay when it is done."

The captain took the money with unconcealed avidity, betraying his feelings by the readiness with which he promised good faith and promptitude. Seizing Holyday's arm, he then hastened off to Smithfield, reckless alike of the appearance he made in the streets, and of the risk of meeting sergeants. In the second-hand shops of Long Lane he remedied his nakedness at a price which left sufficient for his dinner and the scholar's at Mother Walker's three-halfpenny ordinary. When he reappeared in St. Paul's, which was now comparatively empty between hours of resort, he wore a suit of faded maroon with orange-tawny stockings and a brown felt hat.

Meanwhile, Jerningham, glad to have committed the swaggerer to the business before the latter knew its nature, had told the news to Sir Clement at dinner, and was already back in the church. The faithful Gregory still attended him, more disgruntled than ever, for he considered that he might have had some of the money his master had bestowed, and would yet bestow, upon this swaggering captain. Gregory regarded the captain blackly; he viewed this new engagement as a thing most unnecessary, most injurious to himself; and he found his wrath increase each time he looked upon the interloper. Jerningham bade him wait out of hearing, and beckoned the captain into a darkish corner of the church, whither Master Holyday did not follow.

"Well," said Ravenshaw, with after-dinner joviality, "what's the business? What is it you would have me bully, or cozen, or persuade for you?"

"In plain words, a certain wench's consent to a meeting," was the reply.

"What the devil!" cried the captain, aflame. "Do you take me for a ring-carrier?"

Jerningham was silent a moment; then said:

"I take you for no better — and no worse — than any disbanded soldier that lives upon his wits about the town here."

"What others do, is not for me to be judged by. I am Ravenshaw."

"I never heard any reason why Ravenshaw should be thought more tender of women than his comrades are."

"Tender of women! A plague on 'em! I owe them nothing but injuries. 'Tis not that."

"What is it, then, offends you?"

"'Tis that you should think me a scurvy fellow that you dare affront with the offer of such an errand."

"Why, 'tis no scurvy errand. I only ask you to persuade her to meet me. I would approach her myself, but I am suspected and cannot come at her without her connivance. I need one whom her people have not marked, to speak to her for me. I take it you have the wit to reach her ear. I would have you carry her my praises, and vows, and solicitations for a meeting; and describe me to her as you see me, as a liberal, well-inclined gentleman."

"Ay, in short, you ask me to play the go-between."

"Oh, pshaw, man! stumble not at mere names."

"The names for such business are none too sweet, in troth!"

"They are but names. And sweet names may be coined for it. Love's ambassador, Cupid's orator, heart's emissary, — call yourself so, and the business becomes honourable."

"Faith, I have long known things are odious or honourable in accordance with the names they're called by. But I am not for your business."

"Why, you have no choice. You are bound to it by the clothes you wear, bought with my money —"

"I can e'en doff these clothes, as I have doffed others," said the captain, though somewhat disconsolately.

"By the very dinner you have eaten," went on Jerningham.

"I can scratch up the money to pay you for that."

"And by the further service I intend for you. Beshrew me, man, you may find yourself nested for life if you keep my favour. No more nakedness and starvation." Jerningham, on the eve of his long voyage, could afford any promise; besides, 'twas not impossible this redoubtable fellow might really be useful to him indefinitely, one way or another.

Ravenshaw glared at him with the tortured look of a man sorely tempted.

"Moreover," added Jerningham, "what profit can you have in any kind of virtue, when your reputation is so villainous?"

"Hang my reputation! I'll not be taken for a love-messenger. I'll help no man to any woman."

"You are an ass, then. For aught you know, my love may be honest enough."

"If it were, you would go about it otherwise."

"You know not the world, to say so. Does honest love always work openly? Hath not every case its peculiar circumstances? Because you fear, without known grounds, that you may be a means of harm to a wench, will you go hungry to-morrow?

You are fed now, but will you be fed then? Troth, I ne'er knew a craving stomach to have nice scruples."

"Oh, faith, I know that want is an evil counsellor."

"Evil or not, it speaks so loud as to silence all others. Is it not so? Come, captain, be not a fool. If I mean no harm to the girl, 'tis no harm in your bringing us together."

"But if you do mean harm?"

"Can I do her harm against her will? She shall name the place and time of meeting. Is it for grown men to be qualmish merely because a petticoat is concerned?"

"Petticoats to the devil! I owe no kindness to women, I say. 'Twas a woman's wiles upon my father robbed me of my patrimony. 'Twas a woman's treason to my love poisoned my heart, deprived me of my friend, changed the course of my fortunes, and made me what I am. Calamities fall upon the whole she-tribe, say I!"

"Why, then, if at the worst chance I should be the cause of harm to this one, 'twould be so much amends to you on the part of the sex."

A sudden baleful light gleamed in Ravenshaw's eyes.

"By God, that were some revenge!" he muttered. "Who is the woman?"

"A goldsmith's daughter, in Cheapside."

"A goldsmith's daughter — some vain minx, no
doubt ; deserving no better fate, and desiring no
better. As for the goldsmith — they are cheaters
all, these citizens that keep shops ; overchargers,
falsifiers of accounts ; they rob by ways that are
most despicable because least dangerous. And they
call *me* knave ! And their women, that flaunt in
silks and jewels bought with their cheatings — 'twas
such a woman cozened me ! 'Twas such that made
a rogue of me ; if I were e'en to pay back my
roguery upon such ! — I'll do it ! By my faith, I'll
do it ! I'll be your knave in this, your rascal ; I
take it, a knave is better than a starveling, a rascal
is choicer company than a famished man. And 'tis
time I settled scores with the race of wenches !
Let's hear the full business."

Jerningham set forth exactly the situation. He
laid stress on his requirement that the meeting
should occur within the next two days. But he
said nothing of the projected voyage ; nor did he
mention the circumstances in which he had first seen
the girl. When he told her name and abode, he
looked for any possible sign of recognition on the
captain's part. But none came ; Ravenshaw had
never learned who was the heroine of that February
night's incident.

When Jerningham took his departure, the captain
strode over to where Holyday awaited him.

"Rogue's work," said Ravenshaw ; "but a rogue am I, and there's an end. I must get access to a rich man's house, and to the private ear of a wench ; and move her to meet secretly a gentleman she knows not ; and all within two days. How is it to be done ? "

" Is the rich man a gentleman — of the true gentry, I mean — or is he a citizen here, a man of trade ? " queried Holyday. "If a man of trade, the way to his house, or his anything, is to make him think there's money to be got out of you."

" He is a goldsmith in Cheapside."

" Why, then, let me see. There is a goldsmith lives there, somewhere, knows my father. They were friends together in their youth, in Kent. I haven't met him since I was a small lad ; but I might go to him as straight from my father ; and then introduce you as a country gentleman ; and so he might be got to commend you to the goldsmith you seek."

" There's no time for roundabout ways. Yet your father's friend may serve us one way or another. What's his name ? "

" Thomas Etheridge. As I remember, my father — "

" What ? Why, death of my life ! 'tis my very goldsmith ; the one whose daughter I must have speech with. Faith, here's a miracle to help us —

of the devil's working, no doubt. This Etheridge knows not you are at odds with your father ?"

"'Tis hardly possible he should. I have never sought him since I came to town. He never would go back to Kent, and so he could not see my father. He has an elder brother lives near my father ; but 'twixt that brother and the goldsmith there was an old quarrel, which kept the goldsmith from coming to visit our part of the country ; 'twould keep the brothers from communicating, as well."

"Have you means of assuring him you are your father's son ? Can he doubt ?"

"He would believe me for my likeness to my mother. He knew her."

"Then you shall carry him your father's good words this hour ; and you shall commend me to him as — but I must change my looks first. I'll to the barber's, and cast my beard, all but a small wit-tuft under the lip ; and have my moustaches pointed toward the sky. This goldsmith may have seen Roaring Ravenshaw in his time ; I'll be another man then."

"But the daughter — it must be managed so I shall not have to meet her — or any women o' the family."

"Oh, the devil, man ! if you be not introduced to the ladies, how shall your mere friend be ? But stay ; at best, will the friend be ? These citizens are wary with their hospitality. The son of your father might be invited to the table, the son's friend bowed out with a cool 'God be wi' ye, sir!' 'Tis all too round-about still. Body o' Jupiter, I have it! He hath not seen you since you were a lad, say you?"

"Not since a day my water-spaniel bit him in the calf o' the leg, the last time he came to see my father. I was twelve years old or so."

"Good. I shall remember the water-spaniel; and as we go to the barber's, you shall tell me other things I may recall to his mind; things none but you and your father could have known."

"Certainly; but how shall these serve you?"

"Why, I have neither letters nor likeness, to bear out my word. But the barber shall make me look the right age; and these old remembrances, with some further knowledge of matters at your home, and my assurance, — all these shall make me pass with Master Etheridge as Ralph Holyday, son of his old friend; and you need take no hand in the business — that is, if you'll allow this."

"With all my heart," said Holyday, glad to escape the risk of meeting women.

CHAPTER VII.

MISTRESS MILLICENT.

" 'Tis a pretty wench, a very pretty wench, — nay, a very, very, very pretty wench."
— *The Wise-woman of Hogsdon.*

THE house of Thomas Etheridge, goldsmith, was near facing the great gilt cross in Cheapside, the images around whose base — especially that of the Virgin — were chronically in a state of more or less defacement. A few doors east of Master Etheridge's, and directly opposite the cross, was the western end of Goldsmith's Row, described by Stow as "the most beautiful frame of fair houses and shops that be within the walls of London, or elsewhere in England." It consisted of "ten fair dwelling-houses and fourteen shops, all in one frame, uniformly built four stories high, beautified toward the street with the Goldsmiths' arms and the likeness of woodmen, . . . riding on monstrous beasts, all . . . cast in lead, richly painted over and gilt."

Master Etheridge's house, thrusting out an iron arm from which hung a blue-painted square board with a great gilt acorn, was quite as tall and "fair"

as any of the ten in the neighbouring "frame."
It supper stories were bright with the many small
panes of wide projecting windows. The shop, whose
front was usually open to the street by day, occupied
the full width, and a good part of the depth, of the
ground floor. Behind the shop was a "gallery" or
passage, with a private entrance from the side street,
and with a stairway; beyond this passage was the
kitchen; and over that, the dining-room, which
looked down upon a back yard that was really a
small garden.

Upon the low plastered ceiling of the dining-room
was moulded a curious design of golden acorns. The
walls were hung with tapestry representing a chase
of deer. The floor was covered with rushes, which
crackled under the feet of the boys that waited upon
the family at supper.

Captain Ravenshaw, with face clean-shaven all but
for the skilfully up-turned moustaches and the tiny
lip-tuft, leaned back in his carven chair after a com-
forting draught of his host's canary, drew his foot
away from the dog that was pretending to mistake
it for a bone under the table, and thought how lucky
were those who supped every day at the board of
Thomas Etheridge.

"Yes," said Master Etheridge, who was a man
square-faced, square-bodied, hard-eyed, hard-voiced,
looking and sounding as if he should deal rather in

iron than in the softer, sunnier metal, a man with a shrewd mouth and a keen glance; but just now, for once, a little mellowed by the recollections of youth which his visitor had stirred; "your father was ever a man to have his will or raise a storm else. He led your poor mother many a mad dance. Be thankful all husbands are not as obstinate as Frank Holyday, Jane."

Jane, the goldsmith's wife, looked as if she could tell a tale or two of husband's obstinacy, that would match any to be told of the elder Holyday; but she sweetly refrained. She was a plump, handsome woman, who filled her velvet bodice and white stomacher to the utmost on the safe side of bursting; she was the complete housewife, precise about the proper starching of the ruffs and collars, nice in her dress, of an even temper, choosing serenity rather than supremacy. So she merely beamed the more placidly upon the visitor, and said :

"I warrant this young gentleman will not copy his father in that. His looks show the making of a kind husband. I wish you joy, Master Holyday."

For the pretended Holyday had told the goldsmith in the shop that he was about to marry a young lady of Kent, wherefore he wished presently to buy plate and jewelry. This news had turned the cool reception of an uninvited caller into the cordial welcome of a possible customer. And, as it

was a guarantee against his wooing the daughter of
the house, for whom a man of the Holydays' moder-
ate estate was no acceptable suitor, it had removed
the paternal objection to his presence in the family
circle.   Hence the goldsmith had honoured the
claims of hospitality, and invited his old friend's supposed son to supper.

On being introduced to the ladies, Ravenshaw
had promptly recognised the maid of that February
night.   On her part, his voice had seemed to touch
her memory distinctly, but the transformation wrought
by the razor had puzzled her as to his face.   At supper, sitting opposite him in silence, she had listened
alertly while he had continued deluding her father
with anecdotes of the elder Holyday ; and she had
shyly scrutinised his face.   He had covertly noticed
this.   No doubt she was racking her brain in efforts
to identify him.   Why not enlighten her ?   The
knowledge that he was in the secret of her attempted
flight would give him a power over her.   So he had
said, to her father :

" Oh, pardon my forgetting, sir.   I was wrong
when I told you I had not been in London except in
passing to Cambridge and back.   I was here over
night last February."   At this he had brought his
eyes to bear full on Mistress Millicent.   " I was in
this neighbourhood, too.   But the hour was so late,
I durs'n't intrude on you.   Indeed, no one was abroad

in the streets but roysterers, and brawlers, and runaways, and such."

The girl's face had turned of a colour with her
lips, her eyes had flashed complete recognition, had
met his for an instant in a startled plea for silence,
then had hid themselves under their long lashes.
Ravenshaw, feeling as if he had struck a blow at
something helpless, had glanced quickly at her
parents. They had been busy with their knives and
spoons, fingers and napkins, and had observed nothing.

Curiosity and fear, the captain had thought, would
now make her grant, if not seek, a word with him
alone. After that, he had not rested his look upon
her again during the supper. He had met her father's
eyes readily enough, and her mother's, and those of
the ladies' woman, the head shopman, and the other
dependents at the lower part of the table, but not
hers.

For, of a truth, she was not the vain and affected
hussy, or the stiff and supercilious minx, or the bold
and impudent hoyden, he had expected to find as the
only daughter of a purse-proud citizen. Every movement of her slim young figure, encased in a close
blue taffeta gown, seemed to express innocence and
gentleness; her oval face, rich in the colour of
blushes, lips, and blue eyes, had a most ineffable
softness; even her hair, brown and fine, parting

across her brow without too many waves, gave an impression of grace and tenderness; and over her countenance, whose natural habit was one of kindly cheerfulness, there now lay something plaintive. Ravenshaw found it not easy to face her, knowing for what purpose he had lied himself into her presence.

And now, the trenchers being nearly bare, and mouths having more leisure to talk than the voracious custom of that day allowed them during meals, Master Etheridge was minded for further reminiscence of his old friend.

"Ay, ay, many's the quart of wine we've drunk together after supper, in my rash days. Your father would have all drink that were about him. Even his dogs he would make drunk. A great man for dogs. I mind me of a prick-eared cur he had, would drink sack with the best of us, and sit on a stool at table with us, and howl with us when we sang our ballads. And there was a terrier, too; I have my reason not to forget him."

"Yes," quoth Ravenshaw; "he bit you in the calf o' the leg the last time you were at our house."

"Nay, that was a water-spaniel did that," said the goldsmith.

Ravenshaw remembered now that Holyday had said a water-spaniel; but he thought it would appear the more natural if he should seem to be in this point tricked by memory, as, in some detail or other, people often are.

"Nay," said he, "I am sure it was the terrier; I remember it as well —"

"Oh, no, never, never the terrier; 'twas the water-spaniel, on my word. Why, I never see the spaniels diving for ducks in the ponds at Islington but I think of it."

But Ravenshaw feigned to be unconvinced, and when, after some further talk, he yielded the point, it was as if merely out of courtesy. When the supper party rose from the table, the captain was for a pipe of tobacco, which he forthwith produced. But Master Etheridge said he was no tobacconist, and that the smoke made his lady ill. Ravenshaw replied that, by their leave, he would then take a turn or two, and a whiff or two, in the garden, whose beauty, observed by him from the window, invited closer acquaintance. Etheridge liked to hear his garden commended before his wife, as its implied sufficiency saved him the expense of a garden with a summer-house in the suburbs, which many a citizeness compelled her husband to possess. So he went cheerfully ahead to show the way.

"When you return, you shall find us in the withdrawing room, across the passage," said Mistress Etheridge.

Ravenshaw bowed to the ladies; in doing which,

he met Mistress Millicent's eyes with a look that said as plainly as spoken words: "I have something for your ears." This intimation, in view of the circumstances of their former meeting, could not fail to engage her interest.

The goldsmith led him down-stairs to the ground floor passage, whence a door opened to a narrow way running past the rear of the house to the little garden. This comprised a square of green turf, in the centre of which was an apple-tree, now in blossom; a walk led to and around this tree, and another walk enclosed the whole square. This latter walk was flanked on the outer side by rosemary and various shrubbery, banks of pinks and other flowers; which screened the garden walls except where a gate gave entrance from Friday Street. The farther side of the garden was sheltered by a small arbour of vines; beneath this was a bench, and another bench stood out upon the turf, so that one might sit either in sun or in shade.

It was still daylight; the regular household supper was taken early in those times, and English days are long in May. Yet an early star or two showed themselves in the clear sky. The scent of the pinks and apple-blossoms was in the air.

"A sweet night toward," said the goldsmith, manifesting an inclination to remain with his guest in the garden. But this was what Ravenshaw did

not desire. The captain, therefore, as soon as he
had lighted his pipe, took Master Etheridge's arm
so as to have the greater pretext for walking close to
him, and blew such volumes of smoke in the poor
man's direction that, for the sake of his eyes and
nostrils, being no "tobacconist," he was soon glad
to make excuse for returning into the house, and to
hasten back, coughing and blinking.

"If she is a woman," mused the captain, left alone,
"she will come to hear what I may tell her. She
has been on pins and needles. By this light, what
a piece of chance! — that this maid should be that
one! What shall I say to her? I must open upon
the matter of that night. Tut, has she not yet
observed I am alone here now? Or has she not the
freedom of the house? or the wit to devise means of
coming hither? Well, I will give her the time of
this pipeful. What a sweet evening!"

But the sweetness of the evening made him only
sigh uneasily, and feel more out of sorts with himself. Several minutes passed, and he was thinking
he might have to resort to some keen stroke of
wit to get private speech with her, after all; when
suddenly she appeared, with ghostlike swiftness, at
the corner where the passage along the kitchen
wing gave into the garden. He was, at the moment,
scarce ten feet from that spot.

She was blushing and perturbed. She cast a

look up at the dining-room window, then glanced at him, and, instantly dropping her eyes, sped over the turf to the farther side of the apple-tree. He quickly followed her; and when, thereupon, they stood together, the tree screened them from the house.

Without looking at him, and tremblingly plucking the apple-blossoms to hide her confusion, she said, quickly:

"Sir, I thank you for what you did that night. You will not tell them, will you?"

He thought that, by promising unconditionally, he should lose a possible means of controlling her actions; so he must, for the moment, evade.

"Then they know not?" he queried.

"Nay; I got in, and to my chamber, without waking any one."

"And had you no further molestation in the streets? One of those men tricked me, and followed you. I learned it after."

She looked at him with a little surprise. "Nay, I saw him not, nor heard him. I had no trouble. But you will not tell?"

Her wide-open eyes, round and large and of the deepest blue, were turned straight upon his face, as if they meant to leave him not till they should have a direct answer.

"Why — mistress," he blundered, and then

"'SIR, I THANK YOU FOR WHAT YOU DID THAT NIGHT.'"

dropped his own gaze to where he was beginning to scrape the gravel awkwardly with his shoe, "why need you ask? Did I not protect your secret that night?"

"Then why do you hesitate now?" she demanded, with a sudden unconcealed mistrust. "Oh, Master Holyday, what is in your mind? Why have you drawn me hither to speak with you alone? Why do you make a doubt of promising not to betray me? Come, sir, I have little time; they will soon be wondering where I am; either promise me, or I myself will tell them, and then, by St. Anne, I care not —"

There was a threat of weeping in her voice and face, and Ravenshaw impulsively threw up his hand, and said:

"Nay, fear not. I will not tell. I give my word."

Trouble fled from her face, and a smile of gratitude made her appear doubly charming.

Ravenshaw cleared his throat, without reason, and tried to meet her glance without seeing her, if that had been possible.

"You are a happy maid," quoth he, settling down to a disagreeable business. "'Tis proven that you may play the runaway for an hour or two, when you wish, and none be the wiser. There's many a maid would give her best gown thrice over, for that assurance."

"Troth, it serves me nothing," she said, with a forlornness he could not understand. "An I were to play the runaway again, whither should I run?"

He thought for an instant of going into the mystery of her former desire to run away; but he decided that, as time pressed, it were better to hold to the present design.

"Whither, indeed?" quoth he. "Faith, London has no lack of pleasant bowers, where beauty may hear itself praised by the lips of love. Sure, you look as if I talked Greek to you. Certainly you are wont to hear yourself admired?"

"Oh!" she murmured, at a loss, with a smile, and a blush of confusion.

"Troth, now," said he; "confess you enjoy to be admired."

"Oh, pray," she faltered, "talk not of such things. I know not how to answer."

"Yet you take pleasure in hearing them? Come, the truth, mistress. Faith, 'tis but a simple question."

"Oh — why — I do — and I do not."

"I warrant," quoth he, softly, "there would be no 'I do not,' if the right gentleman spoke them." The captain's tone seemed lightly gay and bantering; but, though she knew it not, his throat was dry, and he was trembling from head to foot like a shivering terrier.

"I am sure I know not," she answered, embarrassedly, but still smiling.

"Put it to the test," he whispered, huskily. "Give him the occasion to speak — one that adores you — hear him utter your praises — hear him vow his devotion — give him the occasion."

"Methinks — you take the occasion now," said she, in a voice scarce above the rustle of the air among the leaves.

"Nay — heaven's light! — I mean not myself!" he said, dismayed.

"Why, wha—? What then? What mean you?"

Her smile had fled in a breath, and in its place was a look of suddenly awakened horror that smote him like a whip's blow across the eyes.

"Oh, nothing," he stammered. "I mean — 'tis not myself that's worthy to praise you. I know not — I am out of my wits — forget — "

Just then a woman's voice was heard calling from the house, "Mistress Millicent, where art thou?"

"'Tis Lettice, my mother's woman," whispered the girl, quickly. "I must in. I have come out for this bunch of apple-blossoms. Some other time we'll talk — perhaps."

Without another word she ran from the garden.

The captain snapped his pipe in two, and flung the pieces to the ground; then turned toward the evening sky, in which a numerous company of stars now twinkled, a face bitter with self-loathing.

"I am a beast," he hissed; "a slave, a scavenger, a raker of rags, fit company for the dead curs in Houndsditch. Foh! but, by God's light and by this hand, I swear -- "

He raised his hand toward the stars, and finished his oath, whatever it was, in thought, not in speech. Then, suddenly resuming his former mien, he turned and walked rapidly into the house.

CHAPTER VIII.

SIR PEREGRINE MEDWAY.

"How the roses,
That kept continual spring within her cheeks,
Are withered with the old man's dull embraces!"
— *The Night-Walker.*

As the captain entered, he heard some little bustle, as of an arrival. In the lower passage, at the door leading to the kitchen, was a strange serving-man, already on terms of banter with the cook and maids. He was provided with a torch, as yet unlighted; evidently the guest he attended would stay till after dark. Ravenshaw climbed the narrow stairs to the withdrawing-room, of which the door was open.

This was a fine large room, with an oaken ceiling and oaken panelling; with veiled pictures and veiled statues in niches; with solid chairs, carved chests and coffers, tables covered with rich Eastern "carpets;" with a wide window bulging out over Cheapside, and with a great, handsome chimneypiece. The floor was strewn with clean rushes. Some boughs burning in the fireplace gave forth a pleasant odour. A boy was lighting the candles in the sconces.

Ravenshaw's glance took in these details at the same moment in which it embraced the group of people in the room. The goldsmith and his wife stood beaming, and the woman Lettice looked on at a respectful distance, while in the centre of the room was Mistress Millicent in the grasp of a tall, lean old gentleman in gorgeous raiment, who very gallantly kissed both her cheeks and then both her hands.

" Sweet, sweet," this ancient gallant lisped to her, "I can see how thou hast pined. But all is well now ; I am with thee again ; my leg is mended. Thou wert not fated to lose thy Sir Peregrine for all the ramping horses in England. So cheerily, cheerily now. Smooth thy face ; I see how thou'st grieved, and I love thee the better for it."

Mistress Millicent certainly looked far from happy ; but her dejection at that moment seemed to proceed less from any past apprehension for the visitor's safety than from a present antipathy to his embraces. She was pale and red by turns, and she drew back from him with much relief the instant he released her. Her eyes met those of Ravenshaw, and she blushed exceedingly, and looked as if she would sink out of observation.

" Come in, Master Holyday," said the goldsmith seeing the captain in the doorway. " Come in and be known to Sir Peregrine Medway. Master Holyday's father is an old friend of mine, that was my neighbour in Kent."

"Holyday, Holyday," repeated Sir Peregrine, with indifferent thoughtfulness, looking at the captain carelessly. "My first wife had a cousin that was a Holyday, or some such name, but not of Kent. Sir, I crave your better acquaintance," to which polite expression the old knight gave the lie by turning from the captain as if he dismissed him for ever from his consciousness, and offering his hand to Mistress Etheridge to lead her to a chair.

"What withered reed of courtesy, what stockfish of gallantry, may this be?" mused Ravenshaw, striding to a corner where he might sit unregarded.

"You should have come hither straightway, bag and baggage," said Master Etheridge to the old fop. "What need was there to go to the inn first?"

"Need? Oh, for shame, sir! Would you have me seen in the clothes I travelled in? Good lack, I trow not! Thinkst thou we that live in Berkshire know not good manners?" The knight spoke in pleasantry; it was clear he accounted himself the mirror of politeness. "What sayst thou, mother?"

"Oh, what you do is ever right, Sir Peregrine," replied Mistress Etheridge, placidly. But Ravenshaw, in his corner, was almost startled into mirth at hearing the wrinkled old visitor address the youthful-looking matron as mother. What did it mean?

Sir Peregrine bowed, with his hand on his heart; in which motion his eye fell upon a speck of something black upon the lower part of his stocking. Stooping further to remove it, and striving not to bend his knees in the action, he narrowly escaped overbalancing; and came up red-faced and panting. Ravenshaw thought he detected in Mistress Millicent's face a flash of malicious pleasure at the old fellow's discomfiture. She had taken a seat by the chimneypiece, where she seemed to be nursing a kind of suppressed fury.

The knight, after his moment of peril, dropped into a chair in rather a tottering fashion, and sat complacently regarding his own figure and attire.

The figure was shrugged up, and as spare as that of Don Quixote — a person, at that time, not yet known to the world. It was dressed in a suit of peach-colour satin, with slashes and openings over cloth of silver; with wings, ribbons, and garters. His shoes were adorned with great rosettes; a ribbon was tied in the love-lock hanging by his ear; and a huge ruff compelled him to hold high a head naturally designed to sink low between his sharp shoulders. His face, a triangle with the forehead as base, was pallid and dried-up; the eyes were small and streaky, the nose long and thin, the chin tipped with a little pointed beard, which, like the up-turned moustaches and the hair of the head, was

dyed a reddish brown. On this countenance reposed
a look of the utmost sufficiency, that of a person
who takes himself seriously, and who never dreams
that any one can doubt his greatness or his charms.

From the subsequent talk, it became known to
Ravenshaw that Sir Peregrine had, a few months
before, been thrown by a horse on his estate in
Berkshire, and had but now recovered fully from
the effects. The knight described the accident with
infinite detail, and with supreme concern for himself,
repeating the same circumstances over and over
again. He was equally particular and reiterative in
his account of his slow recovery. His auditors, making show of great attention and solicitude, punctuated
his narrative with many yawns and frequent nod-
dings; but on and on he lisped and cackled.

"Good lack," said he, "there was such coming
and going of neighbours for news of how I did!
I never knew so much ado made in Berkshire; faith,
I lamented that I should be the cause on't, such
disturbance of the public peace, and I a justice.
And what with the ladies coming in dozens to nurse
me! — troth, that they all might have a share on't,
and none be offended, I must needs be watched of
three at a time — What, sweet?" He was casting
a roguish look at Mistress Millicent. "Art vexed?
Art cast down? Good lack! see how jealous it is!
Fie, fie, sweetheart! Am I to blame if the ladies

would flock around me? Comfort thyself; I am all thine."

Mistress Millicent, despite her vexation, of which the cause was other than he assumed, could not help laughing outright. The captain began to see how matters stood. But old Sir Peregrine was untouched by her brief outburst of mirth, and continued to shake a finger of raillery at her.

"Sweet, sweet, ye're all alike, all womankind. My first wife was so, and my second wife was so; and now my third that is to be."

The girl's face blazed like a poppy with fury, and her blue eyes flashed with rebellion. She looked all the more young, and fresh, and warm with life, for that; and when Ravenshaw glanced from her to the colourless, shrivelled old knight — from the humid rose in its first bloom, to the withered rush — he felt for an instant a choking sickness of disgust. But the girl's parents remained serenely callous, and the old coxcomb, with equal insensibility, prattled on, putting it to the blame of nature that he should be, without intent, so much the desire of ladies and the jealousy of his wives past and to come.

Meanwhile Mistress Etheridge, having silently left the room with the woman Lettice, returned alone, and begged Sir Peregrine to come and partake of a little supper. From the knight's alacrity in accepting, it was plain he had honoured the family doubly, — first by tarrying to change his clothes for his call, and then by not tarrying to eat before coming to them, an additional honour that Mistress Etheridge had divined. With courtly bows and flourishes, he followed her toward the dining-chamber; whither he was followed in turn, for politeness' sake, by the goldsmith, who apologised to Ravenshaw for leaving him.

Whatever were the captain's feelings, Mistress Millicent seemed glad, or at least relieved, to be alone with him.

"I wish you joy of your coming marriage," said Ravenshaw, tentatively.

"You would as well wish me joy of my death," she replied, with a mixture of anger and forlornness.

He rose and walked over to the fireplace, near her.

"Why, 'tis true," quoth he; "when the bride is young, the arms of an old husband are a grave."

"Worse! When one is dead in one's grave, one knows nothing; but to be alive in those arms — foh!"

"Your good parents will have you take this hus-band, I trow, whether you will or no?"

"Yes; and I shall love them the less for it," she replied, sadly.

"Has a contract passed between you?"

"Not on my part, I can swear to that! Before
Sir Peregrine went back to Berkshire the last time,
they tried to have a betrothal before witnesses; but
I let fall both the ring he wished to force upon
me and the ring I was to give him; I would not
open my lips either to speak, or to return his kiss;
I held my hand back, closed tight, and he had to
take it of his own accord. And all this the witnesses noted, for they laughed and spoke of it
among themselves."

"Is the wedding-day set?"

"It may be any day, now that Sir Peregrine is
well and in London. No doubt they will get a
license, to save thrice asking the banns. I hope
I may die in my sleep ere the time comes!"

"'Twere pity if that hope came true," said Ravenshaw, smiling.

"I dare not hope for a better escape. I'm not
like to be favoured again as I was the other time
Sir Peregrine was coming to town for the marriage.
Then his horse threw him, and gave me a respite
— but for only three months. Now he is well
again, and safe and sound in London."

"What, were you in this peril three months
ago?"

"Yes. 'Twas that which made me try to run
away, the night you first saw me. The next day,
instead of him, came news of his accident."

"Whither would you have run?"

"To my Uncle Bartlemy's, in Kent. You know him of course; he lives near your father."

"Oh, yes, yes, certainly," replied the supposed Holyday.

"And you saw him that night; at least, you told me the watch had let him go."

"What, was that your Uncle Bartlemy?—the old gentleman you were to have met—the man my friends and I rescued from the watch!"

"I knew not 'twas you had rescued him; but 'twas he I went to meet at the Standard. Nay, then, if 'twas Uncle Bartlemy you rescued, you would have known him!"

"Oh, as for that," blundered Ravenshaw, realising how nearly he had betrayed himself, "no doubt 'twas your Uncle Bartlemy, now I think on't; but I recognised him not that night. For, look you, he took pains to keep unknown; and all was darkness and haste; and though we are neighbours, I see but little of him; and he is the last man I should expect to meet in London abroad in the streets after curfew."

"That is true enough," she said, with a smile; "and I hope you will not play the telltale upon him. If his wife knew he had been to London, there would be an end of all peace. Sure, you must promise me not to tell; for 'twas my pleading brought him to London."

"Oh, trust me. I give my word. So he came to help you run away from being married to this old knight?"

"Yes. You know there's no love lost betwixt Uncle Bartlemy and my father. But mine uncle hath doted upon me from the first, the more, perchance, because he hath no child of his own. And I think he loves me doubly, for the quarrel he has with my father."

"And so he had not the heart to refuse when you begged him to come and carry you away to his house," conjectured Ravenshaw.

"'Tis so. 'Twas the only way I could devise to escape the marriage. I thought, if all could be done by night, I might be concealed in mine uncle's house ; and even if my father should think of going there to seek me, he could be put off with denials."

"But what would your uncle's wife have said to this?"

"Oh, Aunt Margaret is bitter against my father ; she would delight to hoodwink him. The only doubt was how mine uncle might come and take me, without her knowing of his visit to London. For, of a truth, she would never consent to his setting foot inside London town ; and there was no one else I dared trust to conduct me. And so we had it that Uncle Bartlemy should feign to go to Rochester, and then, on 'his way home, to have happened upon me in my flight."

"And so your aunt be none the wiser? Well, such folly deserves to be cozened — the folly of forbidding her husband coming to London."

"Oh," replied Mistress Millicent, blushing a little as she smiled, "my dear aunt is, in truth, as jealous as Sir Peregrine would have us believe his wives were. There is a lady in London that Uncle Bartlemy played servant to before he was married, and Aunt Margaret made him promise never to come within sight of the town."

"I marvel how you laid your plans with him, without discovery of your people or his."

"There was a carrier's man that goes betwixt London and Rochester, who used to come courting one of our maids. We passed letters privately by means of him, till he fell out with the maid, and now comes hither no more. The last word I had of my uncle was after that night. He told me of his mishap with the watch, and of his getting free — though he said not how. And he vowed he must leave me to my fate, for he would never venture for me again as he had done. So I was left without hope. When I recognised you to-day as my preserver that night, and remembered that the Holydays were my uncle's neighbours, I thought — mayhap — you might have some message from him; but, alas — !"

"And that is why you followed me to the garden?" said the captain, carelessly, though inwardly he winced.

"Ay. Your look seemed to promise — but woe's me! And yet you spoke of my running away again?"

"Oh, I talked wildly. I know not what possessed me. Some things I said must have been very strange."

"Why, forsooth," said she, smiling again, and colouring most sweetly, "they seemed not so strange at the time, for I had forgot you are to be married; but now that I remember that — Belike you imagined for a moment you were speaking to the lady you are to marry?"

"Belike that is so. But touching this marriage: what is to hinder your running away to your uncle's now, with a trusty person to conduct you?"

"My uncle, in his letter, said he washed his hands of my affairs. He counselled me to make the best of Sir Peregrine's estate; he gave me warning he would not harbour me if I came to him."

"A most loving uncle, truly!"

"Nay, his love had not altered. But what befell him in London that night gave him such a fright of meddling in the matter."

"Perchance his warning was only to keep you from some rash flight. And, mayhap, now that his fears have passed away, he would receive you."

"I know not. If I might try! — hush, they are coming back!"

Ravenshaw could hear Sir Peregrine's cracked voice in the passage; but he ventured, quickly:

"I'd fain talk more of this — alone with you. When?"

"When you will," she replied, hurriedly. "I know not your plans."

"In your garden, then," he said at a hazard; "to-morrow at nightfall. Let the side gate be unlocked."

"I'll try. But do not you fail."

"Trust me; and meanwhile, if they turn sudden in the matter, and resolve to have the marriage forth-with, find shift to put it off, though you must e'en fall ill to hinder it."

"I'll vex myself into a fever, if need be!"

Ravenshaw was on his feet when the elder people came in; he advanced toward them as if he had waited impatiently that he might take his leave. As for Mistress Millicent, at sight of Sir Peregrine her face took on at once the petulant, rebellious look it had worn at his departure; no one would have supposed she had conversed during his absence.

When the captain had dismissed himself, he looked back for a moment from the threshold. The limping old coxcomb, more than ever self-satisfied after his supper, was bestowing a loverlike caress upon Mis-tress Millicent, who shrank from him as if she were

a flower whose beauty might wither at his touch.
With this vision before him, Ravenshaw was let out,
by the side door, into Friday Street, and made his
way eastward along Cheapside to meet the scholar
by appointment among the evening idlers in the Pawn
of the Exchange. He thought industriously, as he
went.

CHAPTER IX.

THE PRAISE OF INNOCENCE.

"He keeps his promise best that breaks with hell." — The Widow.

THE Royal Exchange, or Gresham's Bourse, formed an open quadrangle, where the merchants congregated by day, which was surrounded by a colonnade; the roofed galleries over the colonnade made up the Pawn, where ladies and gentlemen walked and lounged in the evening, among bazaars and stalls. Naturally the uses of such a resort were not lost upon Captain Ravenshaw and Master Holyday, who had reasons for knowing all places where a houseless man might keep warm or dry in bad weather without cost. When Ravenshaw entered, on this particular May evening, he found the Pawn crowded, and lighted in a manner brilliant for those days. The scholar was leaning, pensive, against a post.

"God save you, man, why look you so disconsolate? Is it the sight of so many ladies?"

"No. I heed 'em not, when I am not asked to speak to 'em," replied Holyday, listlessly. "How fared you?"

"Oh, — so so. The trick served. Faith, I e'en began to think myself I was Master Holyday. But what's the matter?"

It was evident the captain did not wish to talk of his own affair. The scholar was not the man to poke his nose into other people's matters. But neither was he one to make any secret of his own concerns when questioned.

"Oh, 'tis not much. I have been commissioned to write a play."

"What?" cried the captain, eagerly. "For which playhouse? — the Globe? — the Blackfriars? — the Fortune?"

"Nay," said the scholar, sedately; "for Wat Stiles's puppet-show."

"Oh! — well, is not that good news? Is there not money in it? Why should it make you down i' the mouth?"

"Oh, 'tis not the writing of the play — but I have no money to buy paper and ink, and no place to write in."

"What, did the rascal showman give you no earnest money?"

"Yes; but I forgot, and spent it for supper. I knew you would make shift to sup at the goldsmith's."

"Ay, marry, 'twould have gone hard else. Well, I am glad thou hast eaten. It saves our shifting for

thy supper. Troth, we shall come by ink and paper.
The thing is now to find beds for the night. Would
I had appointed to meet my gentleman this evening."
But suddenly, at this, the captain's face lengthened.

"When are you to meet him?"

"At ten to-morrow, in the Temple church," said
the captain, dubiously. After a moment's silence,
he added, "And to think that the fat of the land
awaits you in Kent whenever you choose to take a
wife to your father's house there! Well, well, it
must come to your getting the better of that mad
bashfulness — it must come to that in time."

"Why," quoth Holyday, surprised, "have you not
assured me that women are vipers?"

"Ay, most of them, indeed — but not all; not
all." The captain spoke thoughtfully.

"Well," said Holyday, after a pause, "I think I
shall lodge in Cold Harbour first, ere I take one home
to my father." Cold Harbour was a house in which
vagabonds and debtors had sanctuary; but the two
friends had so far steered clear of it, the captain not
liking the company or the management thereof.

Leaving the Exchange, they found the streets alive
with people; not only had the fine weather brought
out the citizens, but the town was full of countryfolk
up for the Trinity law term.

"'Odslid," a rustic esquire was overheard by the
captain to say to another, "I looked to lie at the

Bell to-night, but not a bed's to be had there. 'Twill go hard if all the inns — "

" Excellent," whispered Ravenshaw to the scholar. " We shall sleep dry of the dews to-night — else I'm a simple parish ass. Come."

They went at once to the sign of the Bell, where the captain applied, with an important air, for a chamber. On hearing that the house was full, he made a great ado, saying he and his friend wished to leave early in the morning in Hobson's wagon starting from that inn ; being late risers by habit, they durst not trust themselves to sleep elsewhere, lest they miss the wagon. Finally, going into the inn yard, the captain stated his case to one of Hobson's men, and suggested that he and his companion might lie overnight in the tilt-wagon itself, so as to make sure of not being left behind in the morning. The carrier, glad to get two fares for the downward journey at a season when all the travel was up to town, thought the idea a good one. And so the two slept roomily that night on straw, well above ground, sheltered by the canvas cover of the huge wagon. In the morning, pretending they went for a bottle of wine, they did not return ; and the carrier, whipping up his horses at the end of a vain wait of fifteen minutes, was provided with a subject of thought which lasted all the way to Edmonton.

Meanwhile, the captain and the scholar, postponing

their breakfast, whiled away the time till ten o'clock. At that hour, having left his friend to loiter round Temple Bar, Ravenshaw stepped across the venerable threshold of the church of the Temple.

This church, too, was a midday gathering-place, as was also Westminster Abbey. But ten o'clock was too early for the crowd, and the captain found himself almost alone among the recumbent figures, in dark marble, of bygone knights of the Temple in full armour. Not even the lawyers, in any considerable number, had yet taken their places by the clustered Norman pillars at which they received clients. The gentleman whom Ravenshaw had come to meet, to report the outcome of his attempt with the goldsmith's daughter, was not there.

Master Jerningham, indeed, had cause to be late. He had cause also for his mind to be, if not upset, at least tumbled about. In the first place, though he did not try to resist it, he cursed his unreasonable passion for this girl, which took so much time and thought from his final preparations for the voyage on which he had set so heavy a stake. He had been compelled to leave many things to his companion gentlemen-adventurers, which he ought to have overseen himself. And even as matters were, he was not clear as to what he would be about, concerning the girl. Suppose he won her to a meeting, could such a passion as his be cooled in the few hours dur-

ing which he might be with her before sailing? Or
should he indeed, as he had hinted to Sir Clement,
set himself to carry her off on his voyage by persua-
sion or force? He knew not; events must decide;
only two things were certain — he must behold her
a yielding conquest in his arms; and he must sail
at the time set or as soon after as weather might
permit.

Upon leaving Ravenshaw in St. Paul's, the day
before, he had gone to see a cunning man by whom
his nativity had been cast with relation to the voyage. The astrologer had foretold an obstacle to be
encountered at the last moment, and to be avoided
only by great prudence. This had darkened Master
Jerningham's thoughts for awhile, but he had forgotten it in the busy cares of the afternoon at Deptford, whither he had hastened to see the bestowal of
stores upon the ship. He had already got his men
down from London and Wapping, all taking part in
the work, some living aboard, some at the inns; so
as to risk no desertions. He had returned late to
Winchester House, passed a restless night, slept a
little after daylight, and set forth in good time before
ten for his appointment.

Just as he was going down the water-stairs, a
small craft shot in ahead of the boat his man Gregory
had hailed; a woman sprang up from the stern and,
gaining the stairs with a fearless leap, stood facing

"BADE HIS VISITOR BE SEATED UPON A STONE BENCH, AND
FACED HER SULLENLY."

him. She was a tall, finely made, ruddy-faced creature, in her twenties, attired in the shabby remains
of a country gentlewoman's gown, and wearing a
high-crowned, narrow-brimmed hat.

"Name of the fiend!" muttered Master Jerningham, starting back in anger and confusion. "What
the devil do you here?"

"Peace," said the woman, in a low voice. "Have
no fear. If your virtuous kinsman sees me, say I'm
old Jeremy's niece come to tell you what men he'll
need for the farm work." Her voice befitted her
tall and goodly figure, being rich and full; the look
upon her handsome countenance was one of mingled
humiliation and scorn.

"I am in haste," said Jerningham, in great
vexation.

"You must hear me first," she replied, resolutely.

Jerningham, stifling his annoyance, motioned Gregory to keep the waterman waiting; then led the
way up the stairs to the terrace, bade his visitor be
seated upon a stone bench, and faced her sullenly.

"Is this how you keep your promise?" he said,
rebukingly.

"Oh, marry, I put you in no danger. I might
have walked boldly to the doors and asked for you.
But I lay off yonder in the boat till you came forth;
it put me to the more cost, but you are shielded."

"Well, why in God's name have you come?"

"Because you would not come to the Grange, and I must needs have speech with you. You forbade messages."

"Then have speech with me, and make an end. But look you, Meg, I have no money. I have kept my word with you; I have given you a home at the Grange; 'twas all I promised."

"'Tis all I ask. But the place must be a home, not a hell. 'Tis well enough by day, and I mind not the loneness — troth, I'm glad to hide my shame. But by night 'tis fearful, with none but old Jeremy for protection, and he so feeble and such a coward. You must send a man there, you must! — a man that is able to use a sword and pistol, and not afraid."

"Why, who would go so far from the highroad to rob such a rotten husk of a house?"

"'Tis not robbers," she said, sinking her voice to a terrified whisper. "'Tis ghosts, and witches."

Jerningham laughed in derision of the idea.

"I tell you it's true. I know what I say," she went on. "Spirits walk there every night; there are such sounds — !"

"Poh!" he interrupted. "The creaking of the timbers; the moving of the casements in the wind; the flapping of the arras; the gnawing and running of rats and mice."

"'Tis more than that. There be things I see;

forms that pass swiftly; they appear for a moment, then melt away."

" 'Tis in your dreams you see them."

" I know when I am awake; besides, often I see them when I am not abed."

" They are the tricks of moonlight, then; or of rays that steal in at cracks and crevices; or they are the moving of arras and such in a faint breeze."

" I know better. Think not to put me off so. I'll not stay there alone with old Jeremy. I cannot bear it — such fright! Good God, what nights I've passed!"

Jerningham quieted her with a gesture of caution, as he looked fearfully around to see if her excited manner was observed.

" Then there are witches," she went on, more calmly. " They slink about the house and the garden in the shape of cats. Terrible noises they make at night."

" Why, they *are* cats, like enough; they seek the rats and mice. Troth, for horrible noises — "

" Nay, but I know better. T'other evening Jeremy was late fetching home the cow from the field, and so when I had done milking 'twas near nightfall. As I was crossing the yard with the milk, what did I see but an old woman leaning on her stick, by the corner of the house. She was chewing and mumbling, and looking straight at me. I saw 'twas old

Goody Banks, whom the whole countryside knows to be a witch."

"Foh! a poor crazy beldame, no doubt come to beg or steal a crust or a cup of milk."

"I thought so too, at first, after I had got over the fright of seeing her — for 'tis rare we ever see any one at the Grange. But as I was going to speak to her, she looked at me so evilly I remembered what the countryfolk say of her, and such a fright came over me again, I cried out, 'Avaunt in the name of Jesus!' and flung the pail of milk at her. I heard a kind of whisk, — for I had closed my eyes as I threw, — and when I opened them, there, instead of the old woman, stood a great cat, staring at me with the very same evil eyes! So I knew she must be a witch — turning into a cat before my very eyes!"

"But your eyes were closed, you say."

"Ay, she had bewitched me to close 'em, no doubt, so I might not see how she transformed herself."

"Why, 'tis all clear. The whisk you heard was of the old woman's running away from the milk-pail. The cat had been there all the while, belike, but you had not seen it for the old woman."

"I tell you I know what I saw," she replied, growing vehement again. "You need not think to fool me, and turn me off. Sith you have no other place for me to live, I am content to live at the Grange; but you must send a man there to guard the place

against ghosts and witches. You must do it, — a
stout, strong man afraid of nothing; no shivering old
dotard like Jeremy, who durs'n't stick his nose out of
his bedclothes between dusk and daybreak. You
promised to give me a home, and I to keep silent and
unseen; but a house of spirits and witches is no fit
home, and so what becomes of our agreement? So
best send a man."

"Why, if it be not possible?"

"Then I shall hold myself freed of my promise,
and if you cannot make one place a home for me, you
shall make another. I shall tell the bishop all that
is between us — oh, I shall get word to him, doubt it
not! — and I know what so good a man will do. He
will make you marry me, that is what he will! My
birth —"

"Oh, peace! I was jesting. I will send a man.
Is that all?"

"Ay, and little enough. There's much a man can
do there, for the good of the place itself. Will you
send him to-day?"

"Why, faith, if I can find him — a man fit for the
place, I mean. I have much to do to-day."

"But I cannot endure another night there, with
none but Jeremy in the house. You must send him
to-day; else I swear I will come —"

"Nay, give me a little time," pleaded Jerningham,
thinking that if he could but hold her off with prom-

ises for two days, her disclosure would matter little, as by that time he would be afloat — unless weather should hinder the sailing. At this "unless," he frowned, and remembered the fortune-teller's prediction. Without doubt, what Mistress Meg might do was the obstacle in the case. He entertained a morbid fear of an impediment arising at the last moment. The woman was capable of keeping her threat; and the bishop was capable of staying him at the very lifting of the anchor, capable even of having him pursued and brought back as long as he was in home waters. Meg knew nothing of his voyage. He must keep that from her, as well as satisfy her in the matter of her request. The wise man had said that "prudence" might avoid the obstacle; Jerningham must deal prudently with her. "I will send a man next week," quoth he.

"I will give you till to-morrow to find a fit man," she replied, resolutely. "To-night I can sit up with candles lit. But if your man be not there to-morrow at four o'clock in the afternoon, I shall start for London; if I come a-horseback I can be here by eight."

Jerningham fetched a heavy sigh. He knew this woman, and when she meant what she said, and how impossible it was to move her on those occasions. He thought what a close player his adverse fiend was, to set the time of her possible revelation upon the very eve of his departure. Durst he hazard some very probable hitch of her causing? No; that would not be "prudence." He must not only promise her; he must also send the man. After all, that was no difficult matter; once the master was safe away on the seas, destined to come back rich enough to defy bishop and all, or come back never at all, let the man look where he might for his wage. It was but palming off upon her the first ruffian to be hired, who might behave decently for a week or so.

Jerningham's face lightened, therefore; he gave his word, slipped the woman a coin to pay her boatman, saw her to the boat by which she had come, and then took his seat in the one awaiting him, and bade the waterman make haste to the Temple stairs.

As he and Gregory walked into the Temple church, he did not immediately know the man who hastened up to meet him; for the upturned moustaches, and the bareness of chin, except for the little tuft beneath the lip, gave the captain a somewhat spruce and gallant appearance, notwithstanding his plain attire.

"God save you, sir. I thought you had changed your mind."

"By my soul, sir — oh, 'tis Ravenshaw! 'Faith, 'tis you have changed your face. I was detained, against my will. Let's go behind that farthest pillar. Troth, this transformation — " He broke off and eyed the captain narrowly, with a sudden suspicion.

"A man's face is his own," said Ravenshaw, bluffly.

"One would think you had set yourself to charm the ladies."

"Fear not. I have no designs upon the lady you wot of. And now let me speak plain words. When I undertook your business yesterday, 'twas left in doubt between us whether your desire of this maid meant honestly."

"'Slight, it shall remain in doubt, as far as your knowledge is concerned," replied Jerningham, quickly, nettled at the other's tone.

"It was left in doubt, as far as speech went," continued Ravenshaw. "But there was little doubt in my mind. And yet I bound myself to the service because I was at war with womankind. I thought all women bad — nay, in my true heart I knew better, but I lost sight of that knowledge, and chose to think them so."

"Wherein does your opinion of the sex concern me?"

"But I was wrong," pursued the captain. "I have met one who proves they are not all bad. I were a fool, then, to hold myself at feud with the sex; and the greater fool to pay back my grudge, if I must pay it, upon one that is innocent."

"Why, thou recreant knave! Do you mean you have failed in the business and would lay it to your virtue?"

"Softly, good sir! I will tell you this: I can win the maid to meet you, if I will."

"Then what the devil — ? How much money — ? Come to an end, that I may know whether to use you or — "

"I will win the maid to meet you — if you will pledge yourself — "

"Go on; what price?"

"If you will pledge yourself to make her your wife at the meeting, and acknowledge her openly as such."

Jerningham stared for a moment in amazement. Then he gave a harsh laugh.

"A rare jest, i' faith! The roaring captain, desiring a city maid for his mistress, offers to get her a gentleman husband! A shrewd captain! Belike, a shrewd maid, rather!"

"By this hand, I ought to send you to hell! But for her sake, I will rather explain. She seeks no husband. But I conceived you might be a fit man for such a maid. You are young and well-favoured, — a fitter man than some that might be forced upon her. I thought a marriage with such a mate might save — But to the point: if you love her, why not honestly? And if honestly, why not in marriage?

You will behold few maids as beautiful, none more innocent. As to her portion, the marriage must needs be against her father's knowledge, by license and bond; but when he finds his son is so likely a gentleman, I warrant — "

"Come, come, an end of this; I am not to be coney-catched. Shall I meet the wench through your mediation, or shall I not?"

"You shall not. And I tell you this: she is not to be won to such a meeting as you are minded for; not by the forms of gods, the treasures of kings, or the tongues of poets!"

Jerningham shrugged his shoulders.

"It is the truth," said the captain. "Virtue beats in her heart, modesty courses with her blood, purity shines in her eyes, she is the mirror of innocence. Should you find means to try her, I swear to you the attempt would but mar her peace, and serve you nothing. Nay, even if that were not so, — if there were a chance of your enticing her, — black curses would fall upon the man by whose deed that stainless flower were smirched. Innocence robed in beauty — there's too little of it walks the world, that gentlemen should take a hand in spoiling it!"

"Man, you waste my time prating," said Jerningham, who had been thinking swiftly, and imagining many possibilities, and hence saw reason for calm speaking. "I see you are stubborn against the

business I bespoke you for. When I want an orator
to recommend me a wife, I may seek you. If I wish
to hear sermons out of church, I can go to Paul's
Cross any day."

The two looked at each other searchingly. The
captain sought to find why Jerningham, after his
exceeding desire, should show but a momentary
anger, and speedily turn indifferent. Had his desire
melted at a single disappointment? Perhaps; but
affairs would bear watching. On Jerningham's part,
he was wondering what the other would really be at,
concerning the maid; what had passed between
them, and how far the captain stood in the way of
Jerningham's possessing her by such desperate means
as might yet be used. If the man could only be
kept unsuspecting, and got out of London for a few
days! Jerningham had a thought.

" So let us say no more of this maid," he resumed,
"and if you forget her as soon as I shall, she will be
soon forgot. No doubt you remember I spoke of
other employments I might have for you. Of course
I meant if you served me well with the goldsmith's
wench. You proved a frail staff to lean upon in
that matter, but I perceive 'tis no fair test of you
where a woman is in the case. So, as you are a man
to my liking, I will try you in another business. By
the foot of a soldier, it cuts my heart to see men of
mettle hounded by ill fortune!"

So soft and urbane had Master Jerningham suddenly grown, so tender and courteous was his voice, so sweet a smile had transformed his melancholy face, that the captain was disarmed. All the gentleman in Ravenshaw seemed to be touched by the other's manner; he would have felt graceless and churlish to resist.

"If the business be one that goes less against my stomach, I will show my thanks in it," said he, in conciliated tones.

"'Tis a kind of stewardship over a little estate I have in Kent — if you mind not going to the country."

"Say on!" quoth the captain, opening his eyes at the beneficent prospect.

Master Jerningham depicted his small inheritance of neglected fields and crazy house in as favourable colours as he could safely use. The captain, dissembling not his satisfaction, averred he could wear the gold chain of stewardship as well as another man. An agreement was struck upon the spot; Jerningham imparted the general details, and said he would have the necessary writings made, and full instructions drawn up, within a few days; meanwhile, he desired the new steward to install himself in the house at once.

"Marry, a bite and a sup, and I am ready," cried Ravenshaw, gaily; then suddenly remembered his promise to meet the goldsmith's daughter that evening. "Nay, I forgot; I have some affairs to settle. I cannot go before to-morrow."

Jerningham, whose purpose had been so happily met by the captain's readiness, lost his gratified look.

"Oh, a plague on your affairs! You must go to-day," he said.

Ravenshaw shook his head. "I cannot go till to-morrow, and there's an end on't!"

Jerningham sighed with suppressed vexation. He dared not urge lest he arouse suspicion. It was too late to back out of the bargain without betraying himself. Moreover, to get the captain away on the morrow was better than nothing.

"Well, well; look to your affairs, then. But go early to-morrow."

Ravenshaw pondered a few moments. "I will start at noon, not before."

"But you must be at the Grange by four o'clock; I have given my word to the people there."

"I can do so, setting forth at noon. 'Tis eighteen miles, you say. I will go by horse."

"'Slight, man, have you a horse?"

"No, but you will give me one — or the means to buy one at Smithfield; and then may I die in Newgate if I be not at your country-house at four o'clock!"

After a little thought, Jerningham told him to call at a certain gate at Winchester House on the morrow at noon, where a horse would be in waiting; he then handed him a gold angel and dismissed him to his affairs.

The captain had no sooner strutted jauntily off than Jerningham quickly beckoned Gregory, and said earnestly:

"Dog his footsteps. Lose not his track till he comes to me to-morrow; and if he meets *her*— Begone! you will lose him. Haste!"

The jealous lackey, raised to sudden joy by this congenial commission, glided away like a cat.

"I will have her, 'gainst all the surly fathers and swaggering captains in London; and 'gainst her own will, and fiends and angels, to boot!" said Master Jerningham, in his heart.

About the same moment, Ravenshaw was saying in *his* heart, as he trod the stones of Fleet Street:

"Ere I leave London, I'll see her safe from the old man's hopes and the young man's devices. I'll pawn my brains, else!"

CHAPTER X.

IN THE GOLDSMITH'S GARDEN.

"Rather than be yoked with this bridegroom is appointed me I would take up any husband almost upon any trust." — Bartholomew Fair.

RAVENSHAW found Master Holyday leaning back against a door-post, with the unconscious weariness of hunger, and listening with a mild interest to the oration of a quack doctor who had drawn a small crowd.

"Come, heart," cried the captain, "the mountebank will never cure thy empty stomach; here's the remedy for that," and he showed his gold piece, and dragged the scholar to an ordinary. After dinner, they bought paper, ink, and pens, and took a lodging at the house of a horse-courser in Smithfield, — a top-story room, with an open view of the horse markets backed by gabled buildings and the tower of St. Bartholomew's Church.

Ravenshaw left the poet at work upon his puppet-play, of which the title was to be: "The Tragical Comical History of Paris and Helen; otherwise the King a Cuckold; being the Sweet Sinful Loves of the Trojan Gallant and the Fair Queen of Menelaus;

167

with the Mad, Merry Humours of the Foul-mouthed
Roaring Greek Soldier, Thersites."

The captain whiled away the afternoon in the
streets, where there were conjurers, jugglers, morris-
dancers, monsters, and all manner of shows for the
crowds of people in town for the law term. At
evening he took home a supper from a cook's shop,
and shared it with Holyday, who, being in the full
flow of inspiration, continued writing with one hand
while he ate from the other whatever the captain
offered him; the poet knowing not what food he
took, and oft staring or grimacing as he sought for
expression or felt the passion or mirth of what he
wrote. Ravenshaw presently placed a lighted candle
on the writer's deal table, and stole out to keep his
tryst with the goldsmith's daughter.

The day had gone eventfully at the goldsmith's
house. In the morning Master Etheridge announced that he would give a supper, with dancing,
that night, to show his pleasure at Sir Peregrine's
recovery and arrival. This was an age when rich
citizens missed no occasion for festivity. So there
was much bustle of sending servants with invita-
tions, hiring a band of musicians, cooking meats and
fowls and birds, making cakes and marchpane and
pasties, and other doings. Millicent uttered no
plaint or protest; the time of pleadings and tears
on her side, arguments and threats on her father's,

was past; many and long had been the scenes
between the two, such as were not uncommon in
that age, and such as Shakespeare has represented
in the brief passage between "Juliet" and her
parents, and these had left the goldsmith firm as
rock, Millicent weak and hopeless of resisting his
will.

As for Sir Peregrine, he had never thought it
necessary to urge; he took it for granted she adored
him — what lady had not? — and that in her heart
she counted herself supremely blessed in being
picked out for him. He attributed her aloofness
and sulkiness, even her outbursts of spoken detesta-
tion, to shyness, girlish perverseness, sense of un-
worthiness of the honour of his hand, and chiefly to
jealousy of his former wives and present admirers.
So he serenely ignored all signs of her feelings.

She bore her part in the day's preparations, a little
uneasy in mind lest the festivities might prevent her
appointed meeting at nightfall. She could not help
counting much upon this new acquaintance; he
seemed a man of such resource and ingenuity, and
such willingness to deliver her, even though he was
betrothed to another — what a pity he was betrothed!
She checked herself, with a blush; but all the same
she had an intuition that the other woman would not
be the best wife for him.

So it befell that, as Ravenshaw approached the

house at dark, he saw all the windows light, and from the open ones came forth the sounds of music, laughter, and gay voices. Nevertheless, he pushed gently at the Friday Street gate, which gave as he had hoped, and found himself alone in the garden. He softly closed the gate, went into the shadow of the apple-tree, and waited.

With his eyes upon the place where she must appear in coming from the house, he listened to the music of a stately dance, — the thin but elegant and spirit-like music of the time, produced on this occasion by violins, flutes, and shawms. When the strains died, they were soon followed by bursts of laughter from the open dining-room windows; then, presently, in the moonlight, he saw the figure he awaited. With a golden caul upon her head, and wearing the long robe and train necessary to the majestic pavan which she had recently been dancing, she glided across the turf, and stopped before him.

"You have come from great mirth," whispered the captain, looking toward the windows whence the laughter proceeded.

"It enabled me to escape," she whispered in reply. "They are listening to the tales of one Master Vallance; he has been telling of the rogueries of a rascal named Ravenshaw, a disbanded captain that swaggers about the town."

He stared at her, with open eyes and limp jaw; in a vague way he remembered one Master Vallance as a gallant who had insulted him one night in the Windmill tavern, the night he first met Master Holyday. Luckily, she did not notice his expression.

" As for me," she finished, " I think no better of gentlemen like Master Vallance for knowing such foul knaves."

" Ay, indeed," assented the captain.

" They are holding these little revels in welcome to Sir Peregrine," she went on. " You might have been invited, but I heard my father say he forgot where you lodged, if you told him."

" 'Tis better to be here, at your invitation."

" Then I bid you welcome," she said, smiling, and holding out her hand.

" Faith, a right courteous maid," said he, and took the least motion as if to touch the hand with his lips; but thought what he was, and stood rigid. " Well, we must talk now of your —"

" Good heaven! Stand close behind the tree," she whispered. " 'Tis Sir Peregrine, come after me."

Ravenshaw was instantly under cover. Sure enough, steps were shuffling along the sod, and a cracked old voice approached, saying:

" What, what, sweet? Wilt fly me still? wilt be still peevish? Nay, good lack, I perceive it now; thou knew'st I'd follow; thou wished to be alone with me, alone with thy chick. A pretty thought; I'll kiss thee for it."

Ravenshaw heard the smack of the old man's lips, and grated his teeth. She had stepped toward the knight, so as to meet him at a further distance from her secret visitor, of whom, manifestly, the old fellow's eyes had not caught a glimpse.

What was she to do? To send the interrupter back into the house upon a pretext was to be rid of him but a minute. She was not born to craft, or schooled in it; but her situation of late had sharpened her wits and altered her scruples. Ravenshaw, straining his ears, heard her say:

"I am angry with you, Sir Peregrine, and that is why I came away."

"What, angry, my bird, with thy faithfullest, ever-lovingest servant? Be I to blame if Mistress Felton smiled so at me?"

"Oh, Mistress Felton?—let her smile, I care not. I am angry because of thy gift. A goodly gift enough, and more than I deserve; but when you knew my heart was set upon the sapphire in your Italian bonnet—"

"Why, God's love, you never said you wished it! Sure, how—"

"Never said, with my lips, no doubt. But have I not said with my eyes, gazing on it by the hour? Troth, art grown so blind—?"

"Oh, good lack, say no more, sweet! The sapphire is thine own; I'll fetch it to-morrow."

" Nay, but I wish it to-night, long for it to-night, must have it to-night ; else I shall hate it, and never desire it, and throw it to a coal-carrier when you fetch it ! "

" God-a-mercy! thou shalt have it to-night. 'Tis at mine inn; I'll send one of my men straightway."

"What, trust it to thy man? Such a jewel, that I have set my heart on? If he were to lose it, or be robbed of it, I should ne'er —"

" Oh, fear not. Humphrey is to be trusted; he hath served me fifty — ah — twenty year, come Michaelmas ; he'll fetch it safe."

" Oh, well, then, if you fear to go alone for it after dark ! — if you choose not to make a lover's errand of it ! — if you are too old, why, then — "

" Oh, tush, I'll go for it ! Too old ! ha, ha ! Thou'rt a jesting chick, thou art. See how soon I shall fetch it."

He strutted to the gate, and was gone. In a moment, Millicent was by Ravenshaw's side ; neither of the two thinking to fasten the gate after the knight's departure.

" I see we must be quick," said Ravenshaw. " Your only escape from this marriage is to run away from it. Your only refuge, you once thought,

was your uncle's house.   But now that seems closed
to you."

"I am not sure.   My uncle wrote me so, when
he was fresh from his mishap in London.   But
if he found me at his door, he might not have
the heart to thrust me away."

"No doubt; but your father would seek you at
your uncle's.   You think you could be hid there;
but if your father is the man he seems, and your
uncle is the man *he* seems, your father would soon
have you out of hiding; he would have the house
down, else.   Is it not so?"

"Perchance you are right; alas!"

"Now there is a way whereby it may be possible
for you to find refuge elsewhere; or whereby you
may e'en go to your uncle's and defy your father
when he comes after you."

"In God's name, what is it?"

"Troth, have you ne'er thought on't?   If you
were already married — but not to Sir Peregrine or
any such kind of stockfish — might not your husband
take you to his own house? or if he took you to
your uncle's, what good were your father's claim
upon you against your husband's?"

She looked at him timidly but sweetly, and trembled a little.

"What?" quoth she, with pretended gaiety.   "Escape a husband by seeking a husband?"

"By accepting, not seeking, one — one less unfit-
one that a maid might find to her liking."

"Why, in good sooth — I hope I am not a bold
hussy for saying so — but rather than be bound to
that odious Sir Peregrine, I think I would choose
blindfold any husband that offered! And if he were,
as you say, to my liking —"

"I said he might be to the liking of some maids.
Have you ever considered what manner of man your
fancy might rest upon?"

He covered the seriousness of the question with
a feigned merriment. She, too, wore a smile; in
her confusion, she fingered the low-hanging apple-
blossoms, and avoided his eyes, but, watching him
furtively, she noticed how familiarly his hand reposed
on his sword-hilt; ere she bethought herself, she answered:

"Oh, a man of good wit, a better wit than face,
and yet a middling good face, too; a man that could
handle a rapier well — yes, certainly a good swordman; and as for —"

A voice was suddenly heard from the dining-
room window aloft:

"Millicent! What do you in the garden, child?
Sure 'tis thy train I see on the grass. What dost
thou behind the apple-tree?"

It was the girl's mother, — Ravenshaw dared not
look from behind the tree, but he knew the voice.

"Say you are with Sir Peregrine," he whispered.

With a trembling voice, she obeyed.

"Oh!" exclaimed Mistress Etheridge, satisfied; but then, as with a suddenly engendered doubt, "I should have thought Sir Peregrine would speak for himself."

"Oh, heaven!" whispered Millicent; "she will send down to see."

"Good lack, sweet mother!" cried Ravenshaw, in well-nigh perfect imitation of Sir Peregrine's cracked voice, "may not young lovers steal away for a tender minute or so? May not doves coo in a corner unseen? Must sweethearts be called from a quiet bower, and made to show themselves, and to give answers?"

"Peace, peace, Sir Peregrine! I am much to blame," replied Mistress Etheridge; and went away from the window, as Millicent observed in peeping around the apple-tree.

"Faith," whispered Ravenshaw, "lest we be overheard, I should speak love to you in his voice henceforth."

"Nay, I'd rather you spoke it in your own voice," said Millicent, ere she realised.

Ravenshaw's heart bounded.

"'Slight, what fool's talk!" she added, quickly, in chagrin. "I do indeed forget the other maid!"

"What other maid?" he asked, off his guard.

"The maid you are to marry, of course."

"Oh !— faith, yes, I forgot her, too !" he answered, truly enough.

"Fie, Master Holyday !" she said, pride bidding her assume the mask of raillery.

"Holyday, say you ?" called out an insolent, derisive voice, at which both Ravenshaw and Millicent started in surprise, for it came from within the garden. A moment later, a head was thrust forth from the shubbery by the gate, — the head of Master Jerningham's man Gregory, who had patiently hounded Ravenshaw all afternoon and evening, and had slipped in when Sir Peregrine had left the gate unclosed.

"Holyday, forsooth !" he went on, instantly alive to the opportunity of serving his master by shattering the falsely won confidence he saw between the maid and Ravenshaw. "You are cozened, mistress. The man's name is not Holyday ; 'tis Ravenshaw — and a scurvy name he has made of it, too !"

Astonishment and mortification had held the captain motionless ; but now, with a sharp ejaculation, he flashed out his rapier, and ran for his exposer. But the cat-footed Gregory had as swiftly darted along between shrubbery and wall, and Ravenshaw, on reaching the place where he had appeared, had to stop and look about in vain for him.

"What does he mean ?" demanded Millicent of

the captain, whom she had followed. " Is your name Ravenshaw ? "

He felt that his wrathful movement against his accuser had confirmed the accusation ; moreover, there was that in her look which made it too repugnant to deceive her longer.

" I cannot deny it," he said, humbly.

" What ! Not *that* Ravenshaw ? "

" The one of whom you heard Master Vallance speak ? — yes ! "

Here Gregory's voice put in again from another part of the shrubbery :

" 'Tis Ravenshaw, the roaring rascal, that calls himself captain, and lives by his wits and by blustering."

A slight sound told that this speech was followed by another prudent flight behind the shrubbery. Ravenshaw was minded to give chase and dig the fellow out at all cost, but was drawn from that intention, and from all thought of the spy, by the look of horror, indignation, and loathing that had come over Millicent's face. He took a step toward her ; but, with a gesture of abhorrence, she ran from him across the garden. Knowing not what he would say or do in supplication, he went after her.

" Not another step ! " she cried, turning upon him, and with the dignity of outraged trustfulness. " Go hence, villain, rascal, knave ! Go, or I will call my

father, to have his 'prentices throw you into the
street! Good God! to think I should have trusted
my secrets to such an ill-famed rogue! I know not
what your purpose was, but for once you shall fail
in your cheateries. I'd rather wed Sir Peregrine
Medway thrice over than be beholden to — "

At this instant, and as Ravenshaw stood shrinking
in the fire of her contempt, the unseen Gregory,
having seized his chance for a concealed dash from
the garden, reached the gate, and ran plump into the
arms of Sir Peregrine, who was returning with the
sapphire.

"Good lack, what the devil's this?" exclaimed
the ancient knight, knocked out of breath; and he
pluckily caught Gregory by the neck, and forced
him back into the garden.

"Let him go," said Millicent, as the knight came
forward in great amazement. "He is a knave,
doubtless, but deserves well for unmasking this other
knave."

"What, why, 'tis Master Holyday!" said Sir
Peregrine, quite bewildered. "Call'st thou him a
knave? And what dost thou here, Master Holyday? I knew not you were invited to the revels."

"'Tis no Master Holyday," said Millicent, "but
one Captain Ravenshaw, whose name is a byword of
the taverns; this man has declared him, and he
denies it not. What his designs were, in passing

upon my father by the name of Holyday, I know not."

"Good lack! here's wonders and marvels! And how comes he to be here to-night?"

Millicent hesitated. Ravenshaw spoke for the first time:

"I came through that gate, which you were so careless as to leave open, Sir Peregrine; I saw you go, as I stood without; and what my purposes were, you may amuse yourself in guessing. Yonder knave, I perceive, followed me — "

At this, Gregory, not liking the captain's tone, suddenly jerked from the old knight's grasp, and bolted out through the gate. Ravenshaw could not immediately pursue him, for he had been thinking swiftly, and had something yet to say:

"My designs being foiled, and to show that I am a man of pleasant humour, I will e'en give you a word of good counsel. When you tell Master Etheridge how he was fooled in his friend, young Holyday, let him suppose you were here when I entered this garden; for, look you, it will show ill in you to have left this lady alone, and the gate open; and it will appear careless in her, not to have made sure the gate was fastened. It will seem brave in you, moreover, to have been here and put me to rout when that knave betrayed me."

He paused, looking at Millicent to see whether

she inwardly thanked him for saving the secret of her dealings with him; but, though she seemed to breathe a little more freely, as if she realised her advantage in his suggestion, she exhibited nothing for him but contempt; doubtless she supposed he had deeper motives for his advice, or that he was jesting.

Receiving no reply from either her or Sir Peregrine, the captain, after waiting a moment, made a low bow, turned, and swaggered out through the gate.

"No doubt 'tis wise to do as he counselled," faltered Millicent, in a low tone, after Sir Peregrine had carefully closed the gate, and as he led her to the house.

"Ay, so I think. I would not have your father know you were careless, sweet. Take the sapphire, chick, and give me a kiss for it."

As she felt his arms around her, and his moustache against her lip, and meditated that her last hope had proved worthless, she gave herself up as lost, and accounted herself rather a dead than a living person for the rest of her days.

Meanwhile Captain Ravenshaw, after stumbling over the protruding feet of a figure that huddled drunkenlike in the next doorway, plunged rapidly on in search of Gregory; dogged at a safe distance by the drunkenlike figure, which, on rising from the doorway, proved to be that of Gregory himself, firm upon shadowing his enemy until the latter's meeting with Jerningham next day.

At last abandoning the quest, during which Millicent's whiplike words of dismissal lashed his heart all the while, Ravenshaw returned to a part of Friday Street where he could stand in solitude and see the light, and hear the sprightly music, that came from the goldsmith's windows.

"Though you loathe me and cast me off," he whispered, looking toward the room in which she might be, "yet, against your knowledge, and against your will to be served by me, I will keep my promise, and save you! You may fling me forth, but you cannot stop me from that! Hope be with you in these revels, sweet ; and sleep lie soft upon your eyelids afterward. Good night!"

After a little time, he made up his mind what to do, and took himself off through Cheapside, the keen-eyed, silent-footed serving-man still upon his track.

CHAPTER XI.

THE RASCAL EMPLOYS HIS WITS.

" What shall I do? I can borrow no more of my credit : there's not any of my acquaintance, man or boy, but I have borrowed more or less of. I would I knew where to take a good purse." — *The London Prodigal.*

RAVENSHAW had not the slightest thought that he was being followed, or had been followed during the day. He had recognised Gregory as Jerningham's attendant, but he supposed Jerningham had sent the man, for want of a better instrument, to attempt what Ravenshaw himself had withdrawn from, or perchance to carry a letter; he thus accounted for the serving-man's unexpected presence in the garden.

He knew that the knave would not succeed, even if he tried it, in communicating with Mistress Millicent that night. But doubtless further efforts would be made soon, and, while he felt she was proof against any manifest overtures against her honour, he feared some cunning proposal which might have a false appearance of honesty, and to which, in her desperate desire to escape from Sir Peregrine, she might therefore give ear. Here was additional reason why he must work swiftly to place her out of all danger, either on Jerningham's side or on Sir Peregrine's, if sufficient reason did not already exist in the fact that he had to leave London at noon the next day. The arrangement for his serving Master Jerningham in the country could not be at all affected by his passage with Jerningham's man in the garden. Gregory's action there must have been on the inspiration of the moment, and formed no cause of quarrel with Jerningham; while Jerningham, on learning that Ravenshaw had again visited the goldsmith's daughter, would be the more desirous to get him out of London.

Walking out Cheapside, the captain gave final order to the plans he had been evolving all the afternoon.

He first made search and question in sundry alehouses and such, about Pye Corner, for Cutting Tom; whom at last he found in a room filled with tobacco smoke, where a number of suburb rascals and sightseeing rustics were at the moment watching a fantastic fellow dance to a comrade's pipe and tabour. From this innocent amusement, Cutting Tom was easily drawn into the privacy of a little garden attached to the place.

"What cheer now?" queried Tom. "Fighting to be done? or coney-catching? You know I'm your man through sea-water and hell-fire, for a brace of angels or so."

"I have a small matter afoot to-morrow night," replied Ravenshaw, gruffly, "wherein I can employ a man like you, and three or four under him."

"Troth!" said Tom, becoming consequential, "I have some affairs of my own to-morrow night, and that's the hell of it."

"Then good night to you!"

"Oh, stay, captain!—I had some slight business; but to serve you, captain—"

"You bottle-ale rogue, think not to cozen me into a higher price. Affairs of your own!—no more of that. Shall we deal, or no?"

"Oh, I am all yours, captain. For you, I would put myself out any day. Say on."

"Then you are first to raise four stout fellows whom you can trust as you do your false dice or your right hand."

"They are near. Trust me for 'em."

"At sunset to-morrow, you and your men, all well armed, and furnished with lights, be in waiting before the White Horse tavern in Friday Street,—that is to say, loitering in a manner not to make people inquisitive. There will come to you anon a young gentleman—with a young woman. The gentleman is one you have seen. He was with me the night you turned tail to those counterfeit roaring boys."

"I have seen him with you since,—a lean, clerkly man."

"Ay; and he and the maid will pass the White Horse tavern, as soon after sunset as may be. Now, be sure you mistake not the man, — it may be nightfall ere they come."

"Never fear. I am a man of darkness. Mine eyes are an old tom-cat's."

"Without stopping them, you and your men will close around the couple as a guard, and accompany where the gentleman shall direct. If any pursue, or try to molest them, you are to defend, and help their flight, at all risks. But they are not like to be sought for till they are out of London. They will take to the water at Queenhithe, and you five with them, all in the same boat. And so down the river with the tide, how many miles I know not exactly, till you land, upon the Kentish side. The gentleman will give orders where."

"This should be worth ten pound, at the least, so far," said Cutting Tom, musingly, as if to himself.

"You will not get ten pounds at the most, and yet you will go farther," replied Ravenshaw, curtly. "After you are put ashore, will come your chief service, which is to protect my gentleman and maid to their destination inland. How far this journey will be, I am not sure, but 'twill be some walking, through woods and by lonely ways, and by night; and you are to guard them against the dangers and fears of the way, that is all. When they come to the place they are bound for, they will dismiss you, and you may fare home to London as you choose."

"Why, beshrew my body! 'tis an all-night business, then."

"It should be over something after midnight, if begun early and well sped; I count not the time of your return to London. And look you: I am not to be named in the affair, that is of the first import. If the lady knew — well, in short, I am not to be named. The lady is not to know of my hand in it; if she did all would go wrong, and I should make you sorry."

"I will remember. This should be worth, now, fifteen pound, at the smallest. I shall have to pay the men — "

"You can pay them a pound apiece, and have two pounds for yourself. That will be six pounds."

"Oh, jest not, I pray you! Ten pound and there's an end on't."

After some discussion, they met each other at eight pounds. Then arose another question.

"Since you are not to appear in the affair," said Cutting Tom, "and I know not the other gentleman save by sight, it behooves that you pay before we set forth."

"Half ere you set forth," conceded the captain, knowing his man, "half when the work is done."

"Then will the gentleman pay me the second half when we are at his destination?"

"No. He will have no money with him. I would not put you in temptation upon the journey, or afterward. Though I shall not appear in the matter, I shall pay." He thought for a moment. It was safest that Cutting Tom should know him alone as master, deal with him alone where gold was to be handled, and yet that he should not pay the first money till the last possible moment before leaving London. Finally he said: "For the first four pounds, thus: to-morrow, at fifteen minutes before noon, no later, be at the hither end of London Bridge; I will meet you there and pay. For the other four pounds, thus: when the journey is finished, pass the rest of the night at the gentleman's destination, — he shall find you room in some stable-loft, or such, — and there I will come the next day with the gold, for I shall be in that neighbourhood."

Cutting Tom grumbled a little; but Ravenshaw, after applying to him a few terms designed to make him think no better of himself, threatened to employ another man, and so brought him to agreement. The details having been repeated for the sake of accuracy, the captain left the place, and Tom returned to his amusements.

Ravenshaw's concern now was to raise the promised eight pounds and such other money as would be required in the exploit. He must needs bestir himself. At this late hour there was not time for any elaborate enterprise. Some bold, shrewd stroke must serve him. But might he expect to perform such a wonder now, when he had not been able to perform one, even at the pressure of dire want, during the past weeks? Yes; for he had the stimulus of a new motive; and the very shortness of the time at his disposal would put an edge to his wit, and sharpen his sight to opportunities to which he would commonly be blind.

The manifest thing to do first was to stake his few shillings at cards or dice. He entered the nearest dice-house; but here he was well known and no player would engage with him. He went into another place, where most of the gamesters were men from the country, whom a few hardened rooks of the town were fleecing. Here the captain got to work with the bones; but, as the dice were true, he soon, to his consternation, lost his last sixpence. In a desperate desire of getting some silver back in order to try for better luck elsewhere, he raised a howl of having been cheated with loaded dice, and proceeded to roar terror into his opponent. But the latter, frightened out of his wits, took bodily flight, and, though Ravenshaw pursued him out of the house, succeeded in losing himself in the darkness of Snow Hill.

What was the captain now to do? For a moment he thought of taking his stand on Holborn bridge, and crying " Deliver ! " to the first belated person who might be supposed to carry a fat purse. But there would be danger in that course, danger to his purpose, and he dared not risk that purpose as he would risk his own neck. He bethought himself with bitterness that there was not a human being in London, or in the world, who would lend him half the needed sum, to save his soul. Nerved by the reflection, he strode forward and swaggered into a tavern on the north side of Holborn, the door of which had just opened to let out three hilarious inns-of-court men who came forth singing :

> " For three merry men, and three merry men,
>   And three merry men we be."

He looked in at each open chamber door, and listened at each closed one. Neither eating, nor drinking, nor smoking, nor the music of begging fiddlers, had any attraction for him this time. But at last he came to a large upper room wherein money was passing, for he could hear the rattle of dice and the soft chink of gold amidst the exclamations of men, the voices of women, and the scraping of a couple of violins. Without knocking, he boldly flung open the door, and entered.

Candles were plentiful in the room, which was

hung with painted cloth. On a long table were
the remains of a supper; at one end of this table
the cloth had been turned back, and three gentlemen were throwing dice upon the bare oak. At the
other part of the table sat two women, with painted
cheeks and gorgeous gowns, and a fourth gentleman.
Upon the window-seat were two vagabond-looking
fellows a-fiddling. The women were dividing their
attention between the gamesters and a lean grey-
hound, for which they would toss occasionally a bit of
food into the air. Before each of the women there
was a little pile of gold, to which her particular game-
ster would add or resort, as he won or lost. All this
the captain took in with sharp eyes ere any one did
him the honour to challenge his entrance with a look.

"Oh, your pardon!" quoth he, when at last these
people showed a kind of careless, insolent surprise at
his presence. "I thought to find friends here; I
have mistaken the room." But instead of withdrawing he stepped forward, his glance playing between
the dice and the gold.

"Oh, Jesu!" said one of the women, a great lazy
blonde, with splendid eyes, and a slow voice; "'tis
that swaggering filthy rascal Ravenshaw, with his
beard cut off."

"'Tis Samson shorn of his strength, then!" said
the other woman, a little, Spanish-looking, brown
beauty, who spoke in quick, shrill tones. She was

dressed in brown velvet and scarlet satin. One of
her hands lay in the ardent clasp of a large gentleman, who, with his own free hand, held the dice-box.
He was handsome and simple-looking, and he now
broke into loud laughter at her jest.

"'Twould have needed a handsomer Delilah than
any here, to do the shearing," said the captain, rudely.
Having been a hater of women, he had been wont to
treat this kind with caustic raillery.

The large gallant roared at this, and said, "Faith,
ladies, you brought that on yourselves!" But
one of the other two gamesters, a lean, fox-faced,
eager-looking little man, he whose pile of winnings
lay before the indolent blonde, frowned with resent-
ment on her behalf. First his frown was directed
at Ravenshaw; but, deeming it prudent to aim it
elsewhere, he turned it upon the large gentleman,
saying:

"Your mirth is easily stirred, Master Burney."

The brunette shot a look of anger at the speaker
for the offensive tone he used toward her gallant.
The blonde noticed this, and took the little gentleman's hand in hers, to show where her allegiance
lay; and then she drawled out, with a motion which
might have come to a shrug of horror had she not
been too lazy to finish it:

"Oh, God! I pity Delilah, the poor woman, if her
Samson was such a bottle-ale rogue as this beast!"

Master Burney laughed at this sally, and somewhat reinstated himself in the favour of the little gallant.

Ravenshaw bowed low. "I salute your most keen, subtle, elegant, biting wit, Lady Greensleeves ! It cuts ; oh, it cuts !"

"'Lady Greensleeves !' Ho, ho, ho !" bawled Master Burney, and forthwith essayed to sing, with a tunelessness the worse for the opposition of the fiddlers, some lines of the familiar ballad :

> "Greenselves was all my joy,
> Greensleeves was my delight;
> Greensleeves was my heart of gold,
> And who but Lady Greensleeves ? "

The point of the nickname lay in the fact that the pink silk gown which encased the large, shapely figure of the lady — a gown so cut as to reveal an ample surface of bust — was fitted with sleeves of light green.

"Christ ! what caterwauling !" quoth Lady Green-sleeves, with a smile, not ill-naturedly.

"'Tis not as bad as his laughing, at worst," said her gallant.

"What is amiss with his laughing ?" spoke up the brunette, pressing Master Burney's hand the more tightly.

"Oh," replied the little gallant, "I find no fault that he laughs ; but 'tis the manner of his laugh. If he but laughed like a Christian, I should not mind. But he laughs like a — like a — "

" Like a what ? " persisted the brunette, defiantly.

" Like a pig," said Lady Greensleeves, placidly.

The brunette's eyes flashed at the fair woman, but the latter's amiable, half-smiling look disarmed wrath, or seemed to put it in the wrong, and so for a moment nobody spoke. Meanwhile Ravenshaw had made these swift deductions : Here was one gentleman prone to laugh at anything ; there was another gentleman quick to take offence at that laughter if it was directed against his mistress ; neither gentleman was afraid of the other, but both were afraid of Ravenshaw, whose name gave him a fine isolation, making it as hard for him to find adversaries in fight as in gaming ; and each gentleman was adored by his lady. In a flash, the captain saw what might be made out of the situation.

" How is it you knew who I was, Lady Greensleeves ? " he asked. " I think, if I had ever met you, I should have remembered you."

" Oh, lord ! I would not for a thousand pound rub against all the scurvy stuff that's in your memory ! I was in Paris Garden the day you killed the bear that got loose among the people, and that is how I learned who you were. And oft since then I have seen you hanging about tavern doors, as I have gone about the town in my coach. I think I have seen

you at prison windows, hanging down a box for
pennies, but I'm not sure."

This time Master Burney's laugh was upon the
captain, and all joined in it.

"No doubt," said Ravenshaw; "and I think you
once put a penny in the box, but when I drew it
up I found it was a bad one."

"Troth, then," she said, "here's a good coin to
make up for it." And she took up the smallest piece
of gold from the pile in front of her, and threw it
toward him. "Take it, and buy stale prunes to keep
up your stale valour!"

"Nay," he retorted, throwing it back; "keep it,
and buy stale paint to keep up your stale beauty!"

Master Burney's shout of mirth was cut short by a
curse, and a slap in the face, both from Lady Greensleeves's lover, who had leaped to his feet and was
the picture of fury. The struck man, with a loud
roar of anger, sprang up instantly; and both had
their rapiers in hand in a moment.

The two other gentlemen and the brunette rushed
in to keep the angry gallants asunder; Lady Greensleeves sat like one helpless, and began to scream like
a frightened child; the fiddlers broke off their tune
of a sudden; the hound fled to the empty fireplace,
and barked. The two opponents struggled fiercely
to shake off the would-be peacemakers, and were for
killing each other straightway.

"Gentlemen, gentlemen," shouted Ravenshaw above the tumult; "not before ladies! not indoors! There be the fields behind the tavern, and a good moonlight."

With this, he caught the brunette by the wrists, and drew her from the fray. Holding her with his left arm, he pushed Master Burney's enemy violently toward the door.

"To the fields, then!" cried the little gentleman. "To the fields an he dare follow!"

Master Burney's reply was drowned by the cries of the ladies, as he dashed after the other. The two neutral gentlemen, yielding to the trend of the incident, accompanied the angry ones forth. The captain, instead of following, slammed the door after them, released the brunette, and stood with his back to the closed door to stop any one else from leaving the room. The brunette, shrieking threats, tried again and again to pass him, but he pushed her back each time until she sank exhausted on a chair by the table; and all the while poor Lady Greensleeves wailed as if her heart would break.

"'Tis not for ladies to interfere in these matters," said Ravenshaw, when he could make himself heard. "A blow has been struck, and men of honour have but one course. Their friends will see all fitly done. Despair not, mistress: your gallant has great vantage in size and strength."

"Then you think he will win ?" cried the brunette. "Heaven be praised!"

"Oh, God! oh, God!" moaned Lady Green-sleeves. "Then my dear servant is a dead man. Woe's me! woe's me! I'll turn nun ; nay, I'll take poison, that I will!"

"Why, madam," said Ravenshaw, "your gentle-man will acquit himself well, be sure of it. He is so quick ; and the other's bulk is in your man's favour."

It was now the brown beauty's turn to be dismayed.

"Oh, thank heaven!" cried Lady Greensleeves, smiling gratefully through her tears. "Yes, indeed, he is quick ; he will give that big Burney a dozen thrusts ere the great fellow can move."

At this the dark woman started up for another struggle with Ravenshaw, but he stayed her with the words :

"Nay, the small gentleman is too light to thrust hard. Think of Master Burney's weight ; when he does touch, 'twill go home, no doubt of that."

All this time the captain was on tenter-hooks lest the fight had really begun ; a moment's loss of time would be fatal to his purpose ; he must bring matters to a point.

"In very truth," he said, "as a man acquainted with these things, if I were to wager which of the two is like to be killed —"

"Which?" cried the women together, as he paused. "Both!"

Even Greensleeves sprang up this time, and Ravenshaw found himself confronted by two desperate, sobbing creatures.

"Back, ladies!" he shouted, quickly. "I will stop their fighting!"

They stood still, regarding him with wondering inquiry.

"If you will stay in this room," he continued.

"We will not stir a step," cried Lady Greensleeves. "Make haste, for God's sake!"

"And if you will give me a handful of those yellow boys yonder," he added.

With a cry of joy, Greensleeves swept up a handful of the two little piles of gold, and held it out to him.

"Stay," said the brown lady, closing her palm over the gold in the other's hand. "He shall have it — when he brings the two gentlemen back to us, friends and unscathed."

"That's fair," said Ravenshaw; "so that you give it to me privately, ere they take note."

"Yes, yes!" panted the brunette; and "God's name, haste!" cried Greensleeves; and the captain, without another word, dashed out of the room, and down the stairs.

He ran through the garden behind the tavern, and

so by a gate, which the gentlemen had left open,
to the fields, which stretched northward to Clerkenwell and Islington. He descried the four gallants
near at hand, where they had chosen a clean, level
piece of turf. Fortunately, the many noises in the
tavern, noises of music, laughter, gaming, and singing, had kept attention from being drawn to the
tumult of this affair, and so no one had followed
the four gentlemen out. The two who had tried
to make peace had now fallen naturally into the
place of seconds, and were finishing the preliminaries
of the fight, while the adversaries stood with their
doublets off, waiting for the time to begin. Just
as their weapons met, with a musical ring of steel,
the captain dashed in and struck up the rapiers with
his own.

"Gentlemen, I am defrauded here," he said, as
the combatants stood back in surprise. "I was the
first to offend, in the house yonder, and the first to
be offended. 'Tis my right to fight one of you first
— I care not which — and, by this hand, you shall
not proceed till my quarrel is settled!"

"Oh, pish, man!" said the little gallant; "we
have no quarrel with you. Our fight is begun; I
pray, stand aside, and let us have it out."

"Upon one condition, then," said Ravenshaw.

The two gallants raised their points, to rush at
each other.

"That the survivor shall fight me afterward," he finished.

The two gallants lowered their points, and hesitated.

"Troth, I have taken no offence of you, sir," said Master Burney; "and given none, I think."

"But your ladies yonder gave me offence; and to whom shall I look for reparation, if not to you two?"

"Faith," said the small gallant, "a man who undertook to give reparation for every foolish word a woman spoke, would have no time to eat, drink, or sleep."

"I see how it is," said Ravenshaw, with a shrug. "I may not hope for satisfaction unless I force you to self-defence; and that would be murder. But, by the foot of a soldier, if I must go without reparation, I'll not be the only one! If I forego, so must you both. How like you that, Master Burney?"

"How can I? He struck me a blow."

"Well, no doubt, if I pray him, he will withdraw the blow. Will you not, sir?"

"I do not like to," answered the little man; "but if he will withdraw his laughter —"

"Why, forsooth, a man of known courage may withdraw anything, and no harm to his reputation," said the captain. "To prove it I will withdraw all offence I have given, and will take it that you two,

on behalf of the ladies, withdraw all offence they
have done me. Saviolo himself, I swear, could
not adjust a quarrel more honourably. What say
you, shall we go back now in peace and friendship
to bring joy to the hearts of the ladies who are
dying of fear? Come, gentlemen, my sword is the
first to be put up, look you."

Somewhat sheepishly, the adversaries followed
his example, to the amusement of the seconds, who
would doubtless have acted with similar prudence
had they been exposed to the risk of having to fight
Captain Ravenshaw. The captain then took Master
Burney and the little gentleman each by an arm, and
started for the tavern, followed by the other two.
The song of the three inns-of-court men returned to
his mind, and he and the two fighters marched back
to the ladies, singing at the top of their voices:

> " For three merry men, and three merry men,
>   And three merry men we be."

Lady Greensleeves folded the little gentleman in
her arms till he grimaced with discomfort; the
brown beauty leaped up and clung around Master
Burney's neck; but, as she did so, she dangled behind his back a purse, in the face of Captain Ravenshaw, to whose hand she relinquished it a moment
later. The captain stepped out into the passage,
made sure that the purse really contained a handful

of gold, and then fled down the stairs ere any but the brunette knew he was gone.

The fiddlers, who had waited through all the suspense of the women, now struck up a merry love tune, and Master Burney bawled for a drawer to bring some more wine, declaring he must drink the health of Captain Ravenshaw; but the captain was hastening to his lodging in Smithfield, grinning to himself, and fingering the heavy round pieces in the purse.

"ONE HAND GESTICULATING, WHILE THE OTHER HELD HIS
NEW-WRITTEN MANUSCRIPT."

CHAPTER XII.

MASTER HOLYDAY IN FEAR AND TREMBLING.

*" If I know what to say to her now
In the way of marriage, I'm no graduate."
— A Chaste Maid in Cheapside.*

As Ravenshaw climbed the narrow stairs to his
room in darkness, he heard the voice of his fellow
lodger in loud and continued denunciation. Wondering at this, for the scholar was wont to speak
little and never vehemently, the captain hastened
his upward steps, thinking to rescue Master Holyday from some quarrel with the landlord or other
person. But when he burst into the chamber he
found the poet alone, pacing the floor in the flickering light of an expiring candle, his hair tumbled, his
eyes wild, one hand gesticulating, while the other
held his new-written manuscript.

At sight of Ravenshaw the poet stopped short a
moment, then finished the passage he had been
spouting, dropped the manuscript on the table, and,
coming back to the present with a kind of tired
shiver, sank exhaustedly upon a joint stool.

" Excellent ranting," said the captain, " and most
suitable to what I have to say." He threw his hat

and sword-girdle on a bed in a corner of the room, filled and lighted a pipe of tobacco, and took up his stand before the chimney as one who had weighty matters to propound.

"How suitable?" queried Master Holyday, with a languor consequent upon his long stretch of poetic fervour.

"As thus," replied the captain, with a puff. "Your play there concerns the carrying away of a lady."

"Of Helen by Paris; yes. But that is only a little part —"

"'Tis a part that you have conducted properly and well, no doubt."

"Why, without boasting, I profess some slight skill in these matters."

"Well, now, look you. Your carrying away this lady in the spirit is well; 'tis a fit preparation for your carrying away a lady in the flesh."

Master Holyday broke off in the middle of a yawn and stared.

"You shall carry away this goldsmith's daughter to-morrow night. Now mark how all is to be done —"

"God's name, are you mad?" cried the scholar, roused from his lassitude into a great astonishment.

"No more mad than to have planned all this for the saving of that maid from dire calamities, and the making of your joy and fortune."

"My joy?"

" Ay, indeed ; for to possess that maid — "

" Oh, the maid — hang all maids ! " exclaimed Holyday, with a kind of shudder, and falling into perturbation. " I'll none of 'em ! "

" And as to your fortune, how often have you told me what welcome and comfort wait you at your father's house the day you come to him with a wife ? "

" Wife ! " echoed Master Holyday, and first paled with horror, and then gave forth a ghastly laugh.

" Ay," said the captain, "and such a wife, your father will bless the day that made her his daughter ! E'en though she come without dowry, he cannot choose but take her to his heart. Her father will not hold out for ever, perchance, when he finds her married to his old friend's son. But if he does, she hath an uncle who is like to make her his heir, I take it. And so, man, there's an end to this beggary for you. And now mark what is to be done — "

" No, no, no ! I have not the stomach for it. I have not ! "

" We must be stirring early in the morning," went on the captain, " for all must be arranged ere I leave London at noon. And first, how you are to call upon the goldsmith's family, and secretly get the girl's consent."

"Get her consent ! Never, never ! I'll do no wooing ; not I ! "

"By God, and you will that, and 'tis I that say so!"

The scholar looked wildly at the captain a moment, then rose and made for the door, as if to escape a fearful doom. Ravenshaw quickly caught up the manuscript of the puppet-play, and held it ready to tear it across. The poet stopped, with a sharp cry of alarm, and came back holding out his hand for the freshly covered sheets of paper. But the captain pushed him to a seat, and retained the manuscript.

"I'll tear it into fifty pieces, and burn 'em before your face," said Ravenshaw, "if you listen not quietly to what you must do."

Poor Holyday, keeping his eyes anxiously upon the precious work, gave a piteous groan, and sat limp and helpless.

"At daybreak," began Ravenshaw, "we shall go together and bespeak the boat that shall carry you and the maid, and your attendants, down the river in the evening. It shall be your business next to visit the goldsmith as if you came newly to London from your father in the country. Tell Master Etheridge you intend to marry a lady in Kent, and that you will be purchasing jewels and plate."

"But, God's sake!" objected the scholar, dismally, and as if he partly doubted the captain's sanity,

"have you not passed yourself off to him as me?
And how, then, will he believe that I am I?"

"Troth, I have been discovered to him as my true
self."

"Well, then, as he has been once imposed on, he
will treat me as an impostor, too," urged Holyday,
desperately ready to find impediments.

"No, for if he makes any question, you need but
stand upon your likeness to your mother. And then
you can mention a thousand things that his memory
must share with yours, where I could mention but
the few you told me. And there was a mistake
I made, saying it was a terrier that bit him in
the leg the last time he was at your house, whereas
it was a water-spaniel, as you had told me. If you
speak of the spaniel biting him, you will prove yourself the true Holyday, and confirm it that I was
a false one."

"Ne'ertheless," moaned the scholar, in despair at
the whole matter, "'twill seem a dubious thing, two
men appearing within three days' time, both calling
themselves Francis Holyday's son."

"'Tis easily made clear. Say that, travelling to
London three days ago, you fell in with that rascal,
Ravenshaw, but knew not what a knave he was.
Say that he won upon your confidence, you being free
of mistrust, so that you told him many things of
yourself, and your intended marriage, and your pur-

pose in coming to London, and of Master Etheridge. And say that you both took lodgings for the night at an inn in Southwark ; when you woke in the morning you found yourself ill, and two nights and a day had passed while you slept, so that Ravenshaw must have given you a draught in your wine, and gone to counterfeit you in the goldsmith's house, thinking to make some use of his freedom therein. Oh, they will swallow that without a sniff ! And, look you, call me a thousand ill names, and say 'tis your dearest wish to kill the scurvy rogue that cozened you so."

Holyday uttered a deep sigh, and shook his head lugubriously.

"And note this," pursued Ravenshaw, "no word to any but the maid that she is the lady you came to marry. They are hot upon tying her to an old withered ass, a knight of Berkshire. That she may escape him, I have planned this good fortune for you ; but all must be done to-morrow, for he is already in town for the wedding, and there is another danger threatens her, too, if she tarries in London. So, when you have been admitted to the family, you must find, or contrive, some time alone with Mistress Millicent, and speedily open the matter to her."

Holyday visibly trembled, and was the picture of woe. "Good God ! " he exclaimed ; "how I shall find voice to speak to her, and words to say, I know not!"

"One thing will make all easy in a trice. Her Uncle Bartlemy, whom you know, would serve her an he saw the way; and even to the last she has looked for some secret help from him. You shall therefore begin by saying you come from her Uncle Bartlemy, who bids her accept you as a husband. Say that his description of her beauty, and of her unhappy plight, hath so wrought upon your mind that you were deep in love ere you e'en saw her. And then say the reality so far outshines the description, your love is a thousand times confirmed and multiplied. She cannot but believe you are from her uncle, knowing you live in his part of the country. After that, if you have time for a few love speeches of a poetical nature, such as, no doubt, this work is full of " (he held up the manuscript) —

"Troth," said the poet, "'twere easier for me to write whole folios of love than speak a line of it to a real maid!"

"Oh, heart up, man!" said Ravenshaw. "'Twill be smooth sailing, once a start is made. But you will not have to say much. Your youth and figure will speak for you when she contrasts them with Sir Peregrine. In her present mind, any man were a sweet refuge from that old kex. I remember she said she would prefer a good swordman; tell her you are a good swordman, therefore. And then bid her meet you at her garden gate in Friday Street at dusk, ready for a journey. Not earlier, look you, for the men who will attend you may not be in waiting at the White Horse till sunset, and 'twere dangerous to miss them."

The scholar breathed fast and hard, as if a burden were being forced upon him, under which he must surely faint, and his eyes roved about as if seeking a way of evasion.

"Now all this must be agreed upon betwixt you and the maid a full hour before noon," proceeded Ravenshaw, "so that you may come to me with the news ere I set out from London. I wish to go to my new affairs with an easy mind. The place I go to is not far from that to which you and the maid shall go, and I will meet you in proper time. But take note of one thing. She is not to know that I have the least hand in this business; if she did, she would not stir a step in it, for she abhors the very name of Ravenshaw. Therefore, when you are with her, if my name comes up, be sure you vilify me roundly."

"I could vilify you now, for pushing me into this business!"

"Very like; and think not to get out of it till it's done; for, mark well, I shall not be far from you while you are in the goldsmith's house. I shall bring you in sight of the house, and shall wait in sight of it till you come out; and if you come not out by eleven o'clock, and with word that all is planned, then, by these two hands, I know not what will happen!"

The poor scholar shrank at the captain's fierce manner.

"And now, for your flight and marriage," resumed Ravenshaw, after an impressive pause; and he set forth particulars as to their being joined by Cutting Tom and his men, their taking boat, their trip down the river with the vantage of tide and moonlight, their landing at whatever point Holyday, in his knowledge of the country, should deem best. "You will then find your way as fast as may be," he continued, "to the house of your friend Sir Nicholas, the parson. Prevail upon him to keep you hid there till he can marry you by license, which can be quickly had of the bishop's commissary of Rochester. Being so much your friend, Sir Nicholas will wink at little shortcomings, — such as the consent of the girl's parents being omitted, and that of her friends sufficing. The maid can swear she is not precontracted; there is truly no consanguinity, and for names to a bond, the parson can scrape up another besides your own. And so, safely tied, you shall bear her to your father's house, and defy the world."

Master Holyday looked as if he fancied himself bound to the seat of a galley for life.

"The parson must lodge your attendants till the next day," added Ravenshaw, "when I will come and dismiss them. Stable room will do. Belike I will see you when I come; but she must not set eyes on me. When all's done, you may tell her what you will. Her uncle will stand your friend, I think. And so, a rascal's blessing on you both!"

The poet was silent and miserable. But after a time he looked up, and, stretching forth his hand, said, in a supplicating way:

"Give me back my puppet-play, then. 'Tis my masterwork, I think."

"You shall have it back when you are married," replied Ravenshaw, placing it carefully inside his doublet.

Master Holyday groaned, as one who gives himself up for lost.

CHAPTER XIII.

"Down with them! Cry clubs for prentices!"
— *The Shoemaker's Holiday.*

WAN and tremulous, after a night of half-sleep varied by ominous dreams, Master Holyday was led by the captain, in the early morning, to the wharf where was to be found the waterman whom Ravenshaw knew he could trust. The scholar attended in a kind of dumb trance to the interview between Ravenshaw and the boatman, who was a powerful, leather-faced fellow, one that listened intently, scrutinised keenly, and expressed himself in quick nods and short grunts. Even the unwonted sight of gold in the captain's hands did not stir the unhappy poet to more than a transient look of faint wonder.

Ravenshaw pulled him by the sleeve to a cook's shop in Thames Street, but the wretched graduate had difficulty in gulping down his food, and scarce could have told whether it was hot pork pie or cold pease porridge. It went differently with the ale which the captain caused to be set before them afterward. Holyday poured this down his throat with feverish avidity, and pushed forth his pot for more. At last Ravenshaw, considering it time for the goldsmith's family to be up, grasped his companion firmly by the crook of the arm, and said, curtly :

"Come ! "

The poor scholar, limp and sinking, turned gray in the face, and went forth with the look of a prisoner dragged to execution. The captain had to exert force to keep him from lagging behind, as the two went northward through Bread Street. They stopped once, to buy a cheap sword, scabbard, and hanger ; which Holyday dreamily suffered the shopman to attach to his girdle. Nearing Cheapside, the doomed bachelor hung back more and more, and when finally they turned into that thoroughfare, his face all terror, he suddenly jerked from Ravenshaw's hold, and made a bolt toward Cornhill.

But the captain, giving chase, caught him by the collar, in front of Bow church, seized his neck as in a vice, turned him about toward the goldsmith's house, took a tighter hold of his arm, and impelled him relentlessly forward. From his affrighted eyes, ashen cheeks, and dragging gait, people in the street supposed he was being taken to Newgate prison by a queen's officer.

"Now, look you," said the captain, with grim earnestness, as they approached Master Etheridge's shop, "I durst not go too near the place. I shall leave you in a moment; but I shall go over the way, and take my post behind the cross, where I can watch the house in safety. Mark this : my hand shall be upon my sword-hilt, and if you try flight, or come forth unsuccessful, you shall find yourself as dead a poet as Virgil — what though I swing for you, I care not! Come forth not later than the stroke of eleven ; walk toward the Poultry, and I will join you. Keep me not waiting, or, by this hand — Go ; and remember ! "

He gave the scholar a parting push, and strode across the street ; a few seconds later he was peering around the corner of the cross, and Master Holyday was lurching into the goldsmith's shop.

The shop, as has been said, extended back to where a passage separated it from domestic regions of the house ; but it was, itself, in two parts, — a front part, open to the street, and a more private part, where the master usually stayed, with his most valuable wares.

In entering the outer shop, Holyday had to pass the end of a case, at which a flat-capped, snub-nosed, solid-bodied apprentice was arranging gold cups, chains, and trinkets.

"What is't you lack?" demanded this youth, squaring up to the scholar.

"God knows," thought Holyday. "My wits, I think." And then he found voice to say that he desired speech of Master Etheridge.

The shopman pointed to the open door leading to the farther apartment, and thither Holyday went. The place was mainly lighted by a side window; the poet could not fail to distinguish the master, by his rich cloth doublet and air of authority, from the journeymen who sat working upon shining pieces of plate.

"What is it you lack, sir?" inquired Master Etheridge.

"Sir," replied Holyday, in a small, trembling voice, "I must pray you, bear with me if I speak wildly. I am sick from a sleeping-drug that a villain abused me with three days ago, — one Captain Ravenshaw — "

At this name the goldsmith, who had received elaborate accounts from Sir Peregrine of last night's incident in the garden, suddenly warmed out of his air of coldness and distrust, and began to show a sympathetic curiosity which made it easier for Holyday to proceed with his tale. When the scholar announced who he was, the goldsmith lapsed for a moment into a hard incredulity; but this passed away as Holyday, not daring to stop now that he had so good an impetus, deftly alluded to his father, — "whom, they say, I scarce resemble, being all my mother in face," quoth he parenthetically, — and hoped that Master Etheridge had forgiven him his water-spaniel's bite the last time the two had met.

"Aha! I knew it was a water-spaniel," said Master Etheridge, triumphantly. "The rogue would have it a terrier." This hasty speech required that the goldsmith should relate how the impostor had played upon him and his household; at which news Master Holyday had to open his eyes, and feign great astonishment and indignation. He found this kind of acting easier than he had supposed, and was beginning to feel like a live, normal creature; when suddenly his mind was brought back to the real task before him by Master Etheridge, saying:

"Well, the rascal failed of his purpose here, whatever it was; and now 'twill please the women to see the true after the counterfeit. This way, pray — what, art so ill? Tom, Dickon, hold him up!"

"Nay, I can walk, I thank ye," said poor Holyday, faintly, and accompanied his host into the passage, and up the stairs to the large room overlooking Cheapside. No one being there, the goldsmith went elsewhere in search of his wife, leaving the scholar to a discomfiting solitude. He gazed out of the window at the cross, and fancied he saw the edge of a hat-brim that he knew, protruding from the other side. He cursed the hour when he had fallen in with Ravenshaw, and wished an earthquake might swallow the goldsmith's house.

When he heard Master Etheridge returning, and the swish of a feminine gown, he felt that the awful moment had come. But it was only the goldsmith's wife, and she proved such a motherly person that he found it quite tolerable to sit answering her questions. Presently Master Etheridge was called down to the shop, and his wife had some sewing brought to her, at which she set to work, keeping up with Holyday a conversation oft broken by many long pauses.

Each time the door opened, the scholar trembled for fear Mistress Millicent would enter. But as time passed and she came not, a new fear assailed him, — that he might not be able to see her at all, and that the dread stroke of eleven should bring some catastrophe not to be imagined. He was now as anxious for her arrival on the scene as he had first dreaded it. His heart went up to his throat when the door opened again; and down to his shoes when it let in nobody but Sir Peregrine Medway.

The old knight inspected Holyday for a moment with the curiosity due to genuine ware after one has been imposed upon by spurious; and then he dropped the youth from attention as a person of no consequence, and asked for Mistress Millicent.

"Troth," said Mistress Etheridge, "the baggage must needs be keeping her bed two hours or so; said she was not well. She has missed her lesson on the virginals. I know not what ails her of late. I'm sure 'twas not so with me when I was toward marriage, — but she sha'n't mope longer in her chamber. Lettice!" she called, going to the door, and gave orders to the woman.

Holyday breathed fast, and stared at the door. After a short while Millicent entered, with pouting lips, crimson cheeks, and angry eyes; she came forward in a reluctant way, and submitted to the tremulous embrace of the old knight. Not until she was free of his shaking arms did she take note of Master Holyday, and then she looked at him with the faintest sign of inquiry.

As for the scholar, a single glance had given him a sweeping sense of her beauty; daunted by it, he had dropped his eyes, and he dared not raise them from the tips of her neatly shod feet, which showed themselves beneath the curtain of her pink petticoat.

"'Tis my daughter, Master Holyday," said Mistress Etheridge, "and soon to be Sir Peregrine's lady." Holyday bowed vaguely at the pretty shoes, and cast a vacuous smile upon the old knight.

"What, another Master Holyday?" said Millicent, in an ironical manner suited to her perverse mood.

"The true one," replied her mother; "that rogue cozened him as he did us. Well, 'twas a lesson, Master Holyday, not to prate of your affairs to strangers."

"The rogue shall pay for giving me the lesson," ventured Holyday, bracing himself to play his part.

Mistress Millicent looked as if she doubted this.

"I know he is a much-vaunted swordman," added Holyday, catching her expression; "but I have some acquaintance with steel weapons myself."

His small, unnatural voice was at such variance with his words, that Millicent looked amused as well as doubting. He felt he was not getting on well, and was for sinking into despair; but the thought of Ravenshaw waiting behind the cross, hand on hilt, acted as a goad, and raised the wretched poet to a desperate alertness.

Master Etheridge came in, holding out his hollowed palm. At sight of its contents Mistress Millicent turned pale, and caught the back of a chair. Sir Peregrine bent his eyes over them gloatingly, and took them up in his lean fingers.

"The wedding-ring, sooth," he said. "Good lack, 'twas speedy work, father. But which of the two is it?"

"Which you choose," replied the goldsmith. "They are like as twins. I had the two made to the same measurement; 'tis so small, one of them will be a pretty thing to keep in the shop for show. Belike there may be another bride's finger in London 'twill fit."

"Troth now, my first wife had just such another finger," said the knight. "I know not which to take; 'tis a pity both cannot be used."

Master Holyday was suddenly inspired with an impish thought, the very conception of which brought courage with it.

"An you please, Master Etheridge," he said, "the lady I wish to marry hath such another hand, in size, as your sweet daughter here can boast of. It were a pleasant thing, now, an I might buy one of these rings."

"Nay, by my knighthood," quoth Sir Peregrine, with a burst of that magniloquent generosity which went with his vanity, "buy it thou shalt not, but have it thou shalt. I buy 'em both, father; see 'em both put down to me. Here, young sir; and let thy bride know what 'tis the mate of." And he tossed one of the rings to Holyday, not graciously, but as one throws a bone to a dog.

"She will hold herself much honoured," said Holyday, coolly, picking up the little circlet from among the rushes, and inwardly glad to make a fool of such a supercilious old fop. Noticing that Millicent observed his irony and approved it, he went on: "Of a truth, though, I am somewhat beforehand in the matter; the maid's consent yet hangs fire." And he cast her a look which he thought would set her thinking.

"Troth, then," said the goldsmith, good-humouredly, "you go the right way to carry her by storm. Show her the wedding-ring, and tell her 'tis for her, and I warrant all's done."

"I will take your counsel," said Holyday, glancing from the ring to Millicent's finger. "She might be afflicted with a worse husband, I tell her."

"Ay, young man," put in Sir Peregrine, for the sake of showing his wisdom in such matters, "be not afraid to sound your own praises to her. If you do not so yourself, who will? — except, of course, your merits were such as show without being spoken for." The knight unconsciously glanced down at himself.

"Oh, I have those to recommend me that have authority with her," said the scholar. "She hath an uncle will plead my suit; and truly he ought to, for 'twas he set me to wooing her, and from his account I became her servant ere ever I had seen her."

"Hath the lady no parents, then?" queried Master Etheridge.

"Oh, yes; they are well inclined to me, too; I spoke of the uncle because 'twas his word made me first seek her out."

"And did you find her all he had said?" asked Mistress Etheridge.

"Oh, even more beautiful. 'Tis her beauty makes me bashful in commending myself to her."

"Oh, never be afraid," said Mistress Etheridge. "You have a good figure, for one thing, and a modest mien."

"So her mother says," acquiesced Holyday, innocently.

"Your father hath a good estate," said Master Etheridge, "and that speaks louder for you than modesty or figure."

"That is what her father hath the goodness to say for me. I hope she will take her parents' words to mind. But I doubt not, in her heart she thinks me better than some."

"Well, her parents are the best judges," said Master Etheridge. "I must go down to the shop; you will eat dinner with us, friend Ralph?"

"I thank you, sir; but I must meet a gentleman elsewhere at eleven o'clock."

If Mistress Millicent had taken his meaning, he thought, she would now see the necessity of speedily having a word with him alone.

After the goldsmith had left the room, Sir Peregrine directed the conversation into such channels that Holyday was perforce out of it. The old knight evidently thought that enough talk had gone to the affairs of this young gentleman from Kent.

The scholar, wondering how matters would go, agitated within but maintaining a kind of preternatural calm without, ventured to scan Millicent's face for a sign. She was regarding him furtively, as if she apprehended, yet feared to find herself deceived; in truth, her experience with Captain Ravenshaw had made it difficult for her to hope, or trust, anew.

But surely fate could not twice abuse her so; this must indeed be Ralph Holyday, — her father was not likely to be deceived a second time, — and the Holydays were neighbours of her uncle, from whom she had not entirely ceased to look for aid. In any case, there, in the shape of Sir Peregrine, was a horrible certainty, to which a new risk was preferable. With a swift motion, therefore, she put her finger to her lip; and Master Holyday felt a great load lifted from his mind.

While Sir Peregrine was entertaining Mistress Etheridge with a minute account of how he had once cured himself of a calenture, Millicent suddenly asked:

"What is the posy in your wedding-ring, Master Holyday?"

The scholar screwed up his eyes to see the rhyme traced within the circlet.

"Nay, let me look," she demanded, impatiently. "I have better eyes, I trow."

He handed her the ring; she walked to the window, to examine it in good light; the casement was open, to let in the soft May air. Suddenly she turned to the others, with a cry:

"Mercy on me! I have dropped Master Holyday's ring into the street."

"Oh, thou madcap child!" exclaimed Mistress Etheridge.

"Oh, 'tis nothing," said Holyday, confusedly, not yet seeing his way. "I can soon find it."

"Nay, I saw where it fell," said Millicent, quickly. "'Tis right I fetch it back."

Ere any one could say nay, she ran from the room. Holyday, understanding, called out, "Nay, trouble not yourself!" and hastened after her as if to forestall her in recovering the ring. He was upon the stairs in time to see that she went out, not through the shop, but through the door from the passage into Friday Street. He followed, wondering what Ravenshaw would think on seeing the two. When they came into Cheapside she began to search a little at one side of the open shop-front, so as not to be seen from within. Glancing up, however, Holyday saw that Mistress Etheridge and Sir Peregrine were look-. ing down from the window above. He dared not turn his eyes toward the cross, for fear of meeting those of Ravenshaw. Both he and the maid searched the cobble paving, within whispering space of each other.

"'Tis safe in my hand," she said; "so we may be as long finding it as need be. What mean you with this talk of a maid's uncle?"

"I mean thine Uncle Bartlemy," said he, heartened up at the easy turn his task had taken. "He sent me to save you from wedding this old knight. The only escape is by wedding me instead. If you are willing, be at your garden gate in Friday Street this nightfall, ready for a journey by boat. The rest is in my hands."

Thank Heaven, she reflected, it needed but a word from her to settle the matter. She could have swooned for joy at the unexpected prospect of escape. But she was not flattered by this young stranger's unloverlike manner. The word could wait a moment.

" What, does my uncle think I will take the first husband he sends, and go straight to marriage without even a wooing beforehand ? "

" Why," said Holyday, thrown back into his agitation, " there's no time for wooing before this marriage. It must wait till after."

" Troth, how do I know 'twill be to my liking, then, without ever a sample of it first ? "

" Did I not say within," he faltered, feeling very red and foolish, " that your charms overpower my tongue ? "

" Well, if you think a maid is to be won for the mere asking, even though to save herself at a pinch, I marvel at you."

Her tone was decidedly chill. He felt she was slipping from him, and he thought of the relentless man behind the cross; he must rouse himself to a decisive effort.

" Stay," he said, as the perspiration came out

upon his face. "If you must have wooing — god
'a' mercy! — Thy charms envelop me as some sweet
cloud Of heavenly odours, making me to swoon."

She threw him a side-glance of amazement, from
her pretended search of the ground.

"Wooing!" he thought; "she shall have it,
of the strongest." And he went on: "And wert
thou drownèd in the floorless sea, Thine eyes would
draw me to the farthest depths."

"Why," quoth she, "that sounds like what the
players speak. Do you woo in blank verse?"

"'Tis mine own, I swear," he said, truly enough,
for it was from his new puppet-play of Paris and
Helen. "I'll give you as many lines as you desire,
— only remember that time presses. I must away
before eleven o'clock. Best agree to be waiting
at the gate at nightfall, ready for flight."

"If I wed you, shall I be your slave, or my
own mistress?"

"Oh, no — yes, I mean — as you will. You
shall have all your own way," he said, glibly.

"No stint of gowns, free choice of what I shall
wear, visits to London at my pleasure, my own
time to go to the shops, milliners of my own
choosing?"

"Yes, yes!"

"My own horses to ride, and a coach, and what
maids I like, and what company I desire, and no

company I don't desire, and all the days to be spent after my liking ? "

" Yes, anything, everything ! "

" Why, then, this marriage will not be such a bad thing. But I cannot think you love me, if you give me so many privileges."

" Oh," said he, petulantly, worn almost out of patience, " 'tis the vehemence of my love makes me promise all rather than lose you ! " At the same time, he said in his heart : " I shall be happier, the more such a plague keeps away from me ! "

" How you knock your sword against things ! " she complained. " One would say you were not used to it."

" 'Tis my confusion in your presence," he answered, wearily. " I can use the sword well enough."

" Well, — " She paused a moment, trembling on the brink ; then said, a little unsteadily : " I will be at the gate at nightfall."

A coach was lumbering along at the farther half of the street. A large lady therein, masked, blonde-haired, called out toward the other side of the cross :

" How now, Captain Ravenshaw ? Hast spent all that money ? Art waiting for a purse to cut ? "

Millicent gave Holyday a startled look, and exclaimed :

"She said Captain Ravenshaw!—the rogue that cozened you. He must be yonder."

"Impossible!" gasped the scholar, turning pale.

"It must be he. She is laughing at him. What, are you afraid?—you that would make him pay for the lesson!"

In desperation, the fate-hounded poet grasped his sword-hilt, and strode to the other side of the cross, coming face to face with the captain.

"I'm not to blame," said the terrified scholar, in an undertone. "She heard your name; I had to seek you—"

"Then feign to fight me," answered Ravenshaw, whipping out his rapier. "All's lost else."

Holyday drew his sword, and began to make awkward thrusts.

"Has she consented?" whispered Ravenshaw, parrying and returning the lunges in such manner as not to touch the other's flesh.

"Yes," said the poet, continuing to fence, but backing from his formidable-looking antagonist in spite of himself, so that the two quickly worked away from the cross into full view of the gold-smith's house.

Meanwhile, Lady Greensleeves's coach had passed on; Mistress Etheridge and Sir Peregrine, from their window, had observed Holyday's movement, and now recognised the captain; Millicent had run to the shop entrance, and her father, seeing her there, had come forth wondering what she was doing in the street, a question which yielded to his sudden interest in the fight. Shopkeepers hastened thither from their doors, people in the street quickly gathered around, but all kept safely distant from the clashing weapons.

"Give way, and take refuge in the shop," said Ravenshaw to his adversary, in the low voice necessary between the two, "else somebody will come that knows us; if our friendship be spoken of, they'll smell collusion."

The scholar, making all the sword-play of which he was capable, rapidly yielded ground.

"But not too fast," counselled the captain, using his skill to make his antagonist show the better, "else she'll think you a sorry swordman."

Poor Holyday, panting, perspiring, weak-kneed, light-headed, but upheld by the mysterious force of Ravenshaw's steady gaze, did as he was bid. A murmur of excited comment arose from the crowd; the windows of the high-peaked houses began to be filled with faces. Ravenshaw perceived there must soon be an end of this; so, nodding for the scholar to fall back more rapidly, he advanced with thrusts that looked dangerous.

Millicent, who had stood in bewilderment since the beginning of the fight, suddenly realised the folly of any ordinary man's crossing swords with Captain Ravenshaw. If Holyday were slain or hurt, what of her escape?

"Good heaven!" she cried, in a transport of alarm. "Master Holyday will be killed! Father, help him!"

"Murder, murder!" shouted the goldsmith. "Constables! go for constables, some of ye!"

Even at that word, the captain's rapier point came through a loose part of Master Holyday's doublet, and the scholar, for an instant thinking himself touched, stumbled back in terror.

Millicent screamed. "Constables?" cried she; "a man might be killed ten times ere they came. Prentices! Clubs! clubs!"

With an answering shout, her father's flat-capped lads rushed out from where they had been looking across the cases. With their bludgeon-like weapons in hand, they took up the cry, "Clubs! clubs!" and made for the fighters, intent upon getting within striking distance of Ravenshaw.

The captain turned to keep them off. Holyday, quite winded, staggered back to the shop entrance. Millicent caught him by the sleeve, and drew him into the rear apartment, scarce observed in the fresh interest that matters had taken in the street. He put away his sword, panting and trembling. She led him into the passage, and then to the Friday

Street door, bidding him make good his flight, and saying she would be at the gate at nightfall. She then returned to the front of the shop.

As he ran down Friday Street, Holyday heard an increased tumult in Cheapside behind him; he knew that apprentices must be gathering from every side; Ravenshaw's position would be that of a stag surrounded by a multitude of threatening hounds. A thrown club might bring him down at any moment. The scholar, with a sudden catching at the throat, ran into the White Horse tavern, and, seizing a tapster by the arms, said hoarsely in his ear:

"The noise in Cheapside — the prentices — they will kill Ravenshaw — for God's sake, Tony! — the friend of all tapsters, he — but say not I summoned ye."

He dashed out and away, while Tony was tearing off his apron and bawling out the name of every drawer in the place.

Meanwhile, in the middle of Cheapside, in the space left open by the swelling crowd for its own safety, a strange spectacle was presented: one man with sword and dagger, menaced by an ever increasing mob of apprentices with their clubs. It was a bear baited by dogs, the shouts of the apprentices dinning the ears of the onlookers like the barking of mastiffs in the ring on the Bankside. When the first band of apprentices rushed forth, two stopped short as his sword-point darted to meet them, and the others ran around to attack him from behind. But with a swift turn he was threatening these, and they sprang away to save themselves. Ere they could recover, he was around again to face the renewed oncoming of the first two. But now through the surging crowd, forcing their way with shouts and prods, came apprentices from the neighbouring shops, in quick obedience to the cry of "Clubs." Ravenshaw was hemmed in on all quarters. By a swift rush in one direction, a swift turn in another, a swift side thrust of his rapier in a third, a swift slash of his dagger in a fourth, he contrived to make every side of him so dangerous that each menacing foe would fall back ere coming into good striking distance.

He had once thought of backing against the cross, so that his enemies might not completely encircle him; but he perceived in time that they could then fling their clubs at him without risk of hitting any one else. As it was, the first club hurled at his head, being safely dodged, struck one of the thrower's own comrades beyond; a second one, too high thrown, landed among some women in the crowd, who set up an angry screaming; and a third had the fate of the first. Some clubs were then aimed lower, but as many missed the captain as met him, and those that met him were seemingly of no more effect than if they had been sausages. As those who threw their clubs had them to seek, and knew their short knives to be useless except at closer quarters than they dared come to, the apprentices abandoned throwing, and tried for a chance of striking him from behind.

But he seemed to be all front, so unexpected were his turns, so sudden his rushes. Had any of his foes continued engaging his attention till a simultaneous onslaught could be made from all sides, he had been done for ; but this would have meant death to those that faced him, and not a rascal of the yelling pack was equal to the sacrifice. So they menaced him all around, approaching, retreating, running hither and thither for a better point of attack. But the man seemed to have four faces, eight hands ; steel seemed to radiate from him. They attempted to strike down his sword-point, but were never quick enough. With set teeth, fast breath, glowing eyes, he thrust, and turned, and darted, maintaining around him a magic circle, into which it was death to set foot. Well he knew that he could not keep this up for long ; the very pressure of the growing crowd of his foes must presently sweep the circle in upon him, and though he might kill three or four, or a dozen, in the end he must fall beneath a rain of blows.

And what then ? Well, a fighting man must die some day, and the madness of combat makes death a trifle. But who would be at London Bridge before noon to pay Cutting Tom, and what would become of all his well-wrought designs to save the maid, her whose contumely against him it would be sweet to repay by securing her happiness? To do some good for somebody, as a slight balance against his rascally, worthless life — this had been a new dream of his. He cast a look toward the goldsmith's house. She was now at the window, with her mother and Sir Peregrine, and she gazed down with a kind of self-accusing horror, as if frightened at the storm she had raised. God, could he but carry out his purpose yet! His eyes clouded for an instant; then he took a deep breath, and coolly surveyed his foes.

More apprentices struggled through the crowd. Their cries, thrown back by the projecting gables of the houses, were hoarse and implacable. Pushed from behind, a wave of the human sea of Ravenshaw's enemies was flung close to him. He thrust out, and ran his point through a shoulder; instantly withdrawing his blade, he sprang toward another advancing group, and opened a great red gash in the foremost face. A fierce howl of rage went up, and even from the spectators came the fierce cry, "Down with Ravenshaw! death to the rascal!" Maddened, he plunged his weapons into the heaving bundles of flesh that closed in upon him, while at last the storm of clubs beat upon his head and body. The roar against him ceased not; it was all "Death to him!" Not a voice was for him, not a look showed pity, not a —

"Ravenshaw! Ravenshaw! Tapsters for Ravenshaw!"

What cry was this, from the narrow mouth of Friday Street, a cry fresh and shrill, and audible above the hoarse roar of the crowd? Everybody turned to look. Some among the apprentices, tavern-lads themselves, stood surprised, and then, seeing Tony and his fellow drawers from the White Horse beating a way through the crowd with clubs and pewter pots, promptly took up the cry, "Tapsters for Ravenshaw!" and fell to belabouring the shop apprentices around them. The new shout was echoed from the corner of Bread Street, as a troop of pot-boys from the Mermaid, apprised by a back-yard messenger from the White Horse, came upon the scene. The prospect of a more general fight, against weapons similar to their own, acted like magic upon Ravenshaw's assailants. Those who were not disabled turned as one man, to crack heads more numerous and easier to get at. Ravenshaw, with an exultant bound of the heart, made a final rush, upsetting all before him, for the goldsmith's shop; ran through to the passage, turned and gained the door leading to the garden, dashed forward and across the turf, unfastened the gate, and plunged down Friday Street with all the breath left in him.

A few of the apprentices pursued him into the shop, knocking over a case of jewelry and small plate as they crowded forward. The goldsmith, appalled at the danger of loss and damage, flung himself upon them to drive them back. Those who got to the passage ran straight on through to the kitchen, instead of deviating to the garden door. After a search, they observed the latter.

But by that time Captain Ravenshaw, registering an inward vow in favour of Tony and all tapsters, and knowing that the fight must soon die out harmlessly in the more ordinary phase it had taken, was dragging his aching body down Watling Street to meet Cutting Tom at London Bridge.

"A fit farewell to London," said he to himself. "The town will deem itself well rid of a rascal, I trow."

CHAPTER XIV.

JERNINGHAM SEES THE WAY TO HIS DESIRE.

" Stands the wind there, boy? Keep them in that key,
The wench is ours before to-morrow day."
— The Merry Devil of Edmonton.

MASTER JERNINGHAM, upon setting Gregory to dog
the steps of Ravenshaw, had made all haste from the
Temple Church to Deptford, where he passed the
afternoon in busy superintendence, and where he lay
that night. But whether at work, or in the vain
attitude of sleep, he housed a furnace within him,
the signs of which about his haggard eyes were
terrible to see, to the experienced observation of
Sir Clement Ermsby when that gentleman greeted
him upon the deck of the anchored ship in the
morning.

"Death of my life, man! thou hast the look of
Bedlam in thy face. And thou wert formerly the
man of rock! The wench is not to be thine,
then?"

"She is, or I am to be the devil's!" replied
Jerningham.

"But we sail to-morrow. Or do we not?"

238

"Ay, we sail to-morrow. Is not the bishop to come and bid us Godspeed, and see us lift anchor? But the maid shall sail with us."

"Oho! Without her consent?"

"I cannot wait for that longer. I have been some time coming to this mind; in bed last night I resolved upon my course. Unless my man Gregory hath, by some marvel, put the matter forward in the meantime, I will take a band of those Wapping rascals" (he nodded toward some of his sailors who were drawing up casks alongside, singing at the work) "to the goldsmith's house to-night, force an upper window, and carry her off, though murder be done to accomplish it. We sail to-morrow; the deed will not be traced till we are far afloat, if ever."

"'Twill be luck if you get her safe from the house. Will you bring her straight to the ship, for the bishop to find when he comes to bless our venture?"

"I am not yet a parish fool. I will take her by boat to Blackwall; the Dutchman there will lock her up in his inn over night. To-morrow, when the bishop has seen us sail, we shall but round the Isle of Dogs, and then lay to at Blackwall and fetch the maid. A sleeping draught will make easy handling of her, and we can bring her aboard in a sack. Then ho for the seas, and the island; we shall set up our own kingdom there, I trow."

"If we might give the bishop the slip, and not

tarry for his prayers, you'd be spared trusting the Dutchman."

"Oh, he thrives by keeping secrets; he is a safe, honest rogue. I durst not give the bishop the slip; he would be so fain to know the reason, he would send post to the warden of the Cinque Ports; and we should have a pinnace alongside as we came into the narrow seas. Especially as he would have heard of this maid's kidnapping. Such news flies."

"You were not always wont to be so wary; you think of every possibility."

"I have been warned, in my fortune, of an obstacle at the last hour. I must be watchful."

"Well, God reward your vigilance, and your enterprise with the wench," said Sir Clement, lightly. He would face anything, and yet cared little for anything, save when a whim possessed him.

Jerningham returned to Winchester House by horse, in good time before noon, to see Ravenshaw set out for the Grange, and to receive Gregory's report of the captain's doings.

Dismissing the servant who opened the gate at which he arrived, Jerningham tied his horse just within the entrance, and waited. He would be much disappointed if the captain came not, for he could not help thinking that the success of his project would be the less uncertain, the farther from London that man should be. If news of the maid's disappearance reached Ravenshaw's ears ere the ship was away beyond recall, things might go ill, for Ravenshaw knew whom to suspect. But to the lonely Grange, half-way between main road and river, reached by a solitary lane that led nowhere else, visited by no one, news never found its way. Once lodged there, Ravenshaw would stay till he gave up hope of receiving the further instructions which Jerningham had said he would send; and by that time Jerningham and the maid would be far beyond the swaggering captain's sword and his roar. The only fear was that Ravenshaw might have caught Gregory dogging him, and have thrown over the stewardship.

But at length a quick step was heard, there was a tapping at the gate, Jerningham drew it open, and the captain stood before him.

"Well, you have kept your word. Here is the horse."

"A trim beast," quoth Ravenshaw, looking at the animal with approval, and not failing to note the good quality of the saddle.

"He will scarce have a trim rider," said Jerningham, staring at Ravenshaw's face and clothing. "You look as if one horse had already thrown you. What's the matter?"

"Oh, there has been a riot, which I must needs leave, that I might not be late with you," said Ravenshaw, carelessly.

The two gazed at each other a moment in silence, as they had done at a former interview. Jerningham looked for any sign of Ravenshaw's having detected Gregory's espionage, and found none. Ravenshaw waited for Jerningham to mention Gregory's encounter with him in the goldsmith's garden, assuming that Gregory must have reported it the previous night. It was not for Ravenshaw to introduce the subject; so it was not introduced at all, and the captain mounted the horse.

"You remember all I told you yesterday, no doubt?" said Jerningham. "Touching the place you are going to, I mean."

"Yes; I shall find it easily enough. Ay, four o'clock, I know. And particular instructions will come in a few days. I can wait for instructions while provisions last. But one thing — a steward's chain — good gold, look you!"

"It shall be of the best," replied Jerningham, with his strange smile. "When it comes," he said to himself, as the captain rode out of the gate.

And the captain was saying to *himself:* "Either his knave has not told him, or he counts it of no matter. Ten to one, from his look, he is forging some plot against her; but she will be safe from all plots this time to-morrow, I think." And he headed his horse for the Canterbury road.

Jerningham went to his own chamber in Winchester House, a fair room looking toward the church of St. Mary Overie. He had not been there a quarter of an hour, when to him came Gregory, dusty and tired, but eager-eyed.

"What news?" inquired the master, with simulated coldness.

"An't please you, sir, I have stuck to his heels since you bade me. Twice they led me to that goldsmith's house."

"Ah! What happened there? Make short telling of it, knave!"

"The first time was last night. The maid talked with him alone in the garden. I could not hear what they said, until she called him by the name of Holyday."

"A false name. The rascal! — then he has his plot, too!"

"Ay, sir; and, thinking to nip it in the bud, I came forth and denounced him to her, saying he was Ravenshaw. Belike he spoke of it to you awhile ago."

"Go on. What did the maid then?"

"She spurned him as he were kennel mud, and he came away like a whipped hound. But I had already given him the slip, to save my skin."

"Troth, then, all betwixt her and him must have come to naught."

"So one would think. And yet — But you must

know that I still dogged him, to carry out your full command. He kept me waiting outside many taverns, but at last went into a house in Smithfield which I took to be his lodging for the night. Bethinking me of the danger if he chanced to see me by daylight, I went to a friend of mine in that neighbourhood — a horse-stealer, if truth must be told — and borrowed a false beard and a countryman's russet coat. In these I followed the man when he set forth at daybreak with his companion, that lean young gentleman you saw with him in Paul's."

"Oh, fewer words. What hath the lean young gentleman to do — ?"

"Much, I trow, an it please you. The end of their going about was, that the lean companion, under some pressure from the captain, went to the goldsmith's house, while the captain waited behind the cross in Cheapside, e'en as I waited at the corner of Milk Street."

Gregory then described the occurrences in front of the goldsmith's shop. What to think of the fight between Ravenshaw and the scholar, he knew not, whether it marked a falling out between them or was part of a plot. Jerningham was of opinion it was part of a plot. The serving-man told of Ravenshaw's flight into the shop from the apprentices.

"They that ran after him," he continued, "came out presently, saying he must have fled by the back way. I pushed through to Friday Street, and saw the gate indeed open. Methought he would now fain come to you, for shelter and protection; and so I started hither. And lo! at t'other end of London Bridge, whom did I set eyes on but my captain, counting over money to another fellow of his own kind, but more scurvy. I kept out of sight till they parted, and then, while the captain crossed the bridge, I accosted the scurvy fellow and said there was one would deal with him as fairly as the captain had, if he chose."

"Well, well, and what said he?"

"He was for killing me, at first, but the end of it was that he is now waiting for a word with you yonder at the bridge. We have seen the captain ride away, and all is safe. I took off my beard and russet gown in the lane without, and hid them in the stable." And the faithful rascal, with bowed head, watched narrowly for the look of approval to which he felt entitled.

"You have done well, Gregory; and you shall eat, drink, and sleep, to pay for your abstinence, — but first come to the bridge and show me this man. And remember, if my Lord Bishop's servants are inquisitive, you lay at Deptford last night, as I did."

A few minutes later Master Jerningham was in converse with Cutting Tom at the Southwark end of London Bridge, beneath the gate tower, on top of which was a forest of poles crowned with the weatherbeaten heads of traitors.

"Oh, but sell secrets, that is too much!" Cutting Tom was saying, in an injured tone. "A poor soldier hath little but his honour. Belike I am ill-favoured with wounds, and ragged with poverty through serving my country, but my honour, sir! my trust! my loyalty! Troth, 'tis mine only jewel, and if I sold it — well, I should want a good price, and there's the hell of it!"

But even when a price was fixed, Cutting Tom, dazzled on one side by his lifetime's chance of obtaining so excellent a patron, on the other side fearful of Ravenshaw's vengeance, temporised and mumbled and held back, until Jerningham assured him of protection and of Ravenshaw's long absence from London. The rascal then told all he knew of what was planned to be carried out that night.

Jerningham listened with apparent passivity, though at the last he averted his eyes lest his exultation should gleam out of them. Here was all trouble, all desperate and well-nigh impossible venturing, made needless on his part. He studied the matter for a minute, and then said, musingly:

"His companion and a maid — the White Horse — 'tis the nearest tavern — sooth, there can be no question it is she. Look you, sirrah, I must know to what place they are bound."

" I would I knew. 'Tis somewhere on the Kentish side of the river."

" What, would the rascal dare? — think you 'tis the place he is now riding to?"

" He said he would be in the neighbourhood of our destination, and he would come to-morrow to pay and dismiss us."

" If he is to come to you to-morrow, it cannot be to the Grange, — he will be there already. He knows more of that neighbourhood than he would have me think; he used the name Holyday — there's a Holyday family in that country. Well, I know not; but 'tis certain you will be near my house of Marshleigh Grange."

A grim smile flitted over Jerningham's face, as he saw another difficulty removed — for he could now dispense with the use of the Dutch innkeeper at Blackwall, and with the risk of putting his captive aboard from so public a place.

" Now mark," said he, while he held Cutting Tom with fixed eyes, " you will indeed have four men with you when you meet the gentleman and maid at the White Horse; but one of those four shall be a man I will send there betimes. You will easily know him; he is the man that brought you to see me. His beard, you must know, is false, and you will warn your men; else, detecting it, they might snatch it off in mirth. Without disguise, he would be known to the maid and gentleman, — then our business were undone. And so, to the journey."

Proceeding, he gave orders full and concise, to which Cutting Tom lent the best attention of his cunning mind. Then, being curtly dismissed, the rascal, between elation at his great windfall, and perturbation at the temerity of betraying Captain Ravenshaw, shambled off through the darkish lane that the rows of high shop-houses made of London Bridge.

Master Jerningham, returning to Winchester House, was rejoined by Gregory at the place where the serving-man had waited.

"You have five hours wherein to fill your stomach and sleep; and then you must be off upon a night's work that shall make you your own man, if it turn out well."

The zealous hound, a little staggered at the opening words of this announcement, took fresh life at its conclusion, and looked with new-lighted eyes for commands.

Having given these with the utmost particularity, Jerningham presented himself, in all docility and humbleness, to the bishop in the latter's study, where he made a careful tale of his readiness for sailing on the morrow.

He then took horse for Deptford; upon arriving, he related his good fortune, and set forth his new plan to Sir Clement Ermsby, on the deck of the ship.

" But how at the Grange, man, if Ravenshaw be there?" Sir Clement asked.

" I shall go there betimes, and send him straight upon some errand — some three days' journey that will not wait for daylight."

" He will think it curiously sudden. Besides, if he thinks to meet and pay his men in that neighbourhood to-morrow, he will not be for any three days' journey to-night."

" Most men will defer paying money, when their interests require. I can but try sending him."

" And if he refuse to stir? What will you then?"

" Kill him! There will be enough of us, in good sooth."

" Ay, no doubt," acquiesced Sir Clement, carelessly. " Methinks the weather bodes a change," he added, looking at the sky. " It may rain to-night."

" Rain or shine, storm or fair," replied Master Jerningham, his eyes aglow, " I feel it within me, this is the night shall give me my desire."

CHAPTER XV.

RAVENSHAW FALLS ASLEEP.

"Thou liest. I ha' nothing but my skin,
And my clothes; my sword here, and myself."
— *The Sea Voyage.*

CAPTAIN RAVENSHAW headed his horse for the
Canterbury road, and, having soon left the town
behind him, began to feel a pleasant content in the
sunlight and soft air. The fresh green of spring,
the flowers of May, the glad twitter of birds, met his
senses on every side. Never since his boyhood had
the sight and smell of hawthorn been more sweet.
He conceived he had, for once, earned the right to
enjoy so fair a day. He was tired and bruised, but
he looked forward to rest upon his arrival. Peace,
comparative solitude, country ease, seemed so inviting that he had not a regret for the town he left
behind.

His road, at the first, was that which Chaucer's
pilgrims had traversed blithely toward Canterbury.
He had a few villages to ride through, clustered
about gray churches, and drowsy in the spring sunshine; a few towered and turreted castles, a few
gabled farmhouses, to pass in sight of. But for the

"SUDDENLY THE NARROW WAY BEFORE HIM BECAME
BLOCKED WITH HUMAN CREATURES."

most part his way was by greenwood and field and common, up and down the gentle inclines, and across the pleasant levels, of the wavy Kentish country. Often it was a narrow aisle through forest, with great trunks for pillars, and leafy boughs for pointed arches, and here and there a yellow splash where the green leaves left an opening for sunlight. And then it trailed over open heath dotted with solitary trees or little clumps, and along fields enclosed by green hedgerows. It was a good road for that time, wide enough for two riders to pass each other without giving cause for quarrel; ditchlike, uneven, rutted, here so stony that a horse would stumble, there so soft that a horse would sink deep at each step.

Ravenshaw had already turned out of the Canterbury road to the left, and was passing from a heath into a thick copse, when suddenly the narrow way before him became blocked with human creatures, or what seemed rather the remnants of human creatures, that limped out from among the trees at the sides.

He drew in his horse quickly to avoid riding over any one, while the newcomers thronged about him with outstretched palms and whining cries :

" Save your good worship, one little drop of money ! " " A small piece of silver, for the love of God ! " " Pity for a poor maimed soldier ! "

"A few pence to buy bread, kind gentleman!"
"Charity for the lame and blind!"

"Peace, peace, peace!" cried the captain. "What be these the greenwood vomits up? Hath the forest made a dinner of men, and cast up the pieces it could not stomach?"

Pieces of men in truth they looked, and of two women also. All were in rags; the men had unkempt beards and hair; those that did not go upon crutches showed white eyes, or an empty sleeve, or great livid sores upon face and naked breast, or discoloured bandages; one of the women, fat and hoarse-voiced, went upon a single leg and a crutch; the other woman, a gaunt hag, petitioned with one skinny hand, and pointed with the other to her colourless eyeballs.

"Let go; I am in haste; I have no money," said Ravenshaw, for one of the men — a white-bearded old fellow poised on his only foot — had taken firm hold of the bridle near the horse's mouth.

But, so far from the man's letting go, some of his companions seized upon Ravenshaw's ankles, and the chorus of whines waxed louder and more urgent. With his free hand he reached for his dagger; but the lean woman, having already possessed herself of the handle, drew it from the sheath ere he knew what she was doing. He clapped his other hand to his sword-hilt; but his fingers closed around the two hands of a dwarf on a man's shoulders, who had grasped the hilt, and who now thrust his head forward and caught the captain's knuckles between his jaws.

"Oho!" exclaimed Ravenshaw, changing to a jovial manner. "I see I have walked into Beggars' Bush. Well, friends, I pray you believe me, I am a man wrung dry by war and ill fortune, and little less a beggar than any of ye. I have chanced upon a slight service will keep my body and soul together; if I lose time here I shall lose that. I have nothing but my weapons, which I need in my profession, and my clothes, which would not serve you in yours. The horse I require for my necessary haste, and —"

"He lies, he lies!" shrieked the lean hag, striking the pocket of Ravenshaw's breeches. "Hearken to the chinking lour! A handful!"

"A piece of gold for a poor maimed soldier!" cried the white-bearded man, whipping out a pistol from his wide breeches, whereupon other of the rogues brandished truncheons and staves. At sight of the clubs, Ravenshaw made a wry face, and his bruised body seemed to plead with him. He had one hand free, with which he might have seized the dwarf's neck, but he thought best to use it for holding the rein and guarding his pocket.

"Ay, there's money in the pocket," he said; "but I spoke truth when I said I had none. This is not mine ; 'tis another man's, to whom I must pay it to-morrow."

" Let the other man give us charity, then ! " cried the fat woman.

" Ay, we'd as lief have another man's money as yours," said the white-bearded rogue, aiming the pistol. The lean hag tried to force her hand into Ravenshaw's pocket, and men caught his clothing by the hooks at the ends of their staves.

" Nay, maunderers ! " cried Ravenshaw ; " shall not a gentry cove that cuts ben whids, and hath respect for the salamon, pass upon the pad but ye would be foisting and angling ? " —

" Marry, you can cant," said the white-bearded beggar, his manner changing to one of approval, which spread at once to his associates.

" As ben pedlar's French as any clapperdudgeon of ye all," replied the captain.

" Belike you are a prigger of prancers," said the beggar, looking at the horse.

" No, my upright man, a poor gentry cuffin, as I have said, but one that hath passed many a night out-of-doors, and now fallen into a little poor service that I am like to forfeit by my delay. As for the lour in my pocket, I am a forsworn man if I deliver it not to-morrow. So I beg, in the name of all the maunders I have stood friend to in my time — "

" A ben cove," said the upright man. " Mort,

take off your fambles; brother rufflers, down with
your filches and cudgels. By the salamon, the cant-
ing cuffin shall go free upon the pad."

Released on every side, no more threatened, and
his dagger restored to its sheath, the captain looked
gratefully down upon the grotesque crew. As he
did so, his nose became sensible of a faint, delicious
odour, borne from a distance. He sniffed keenly.

"Cackling-cheats," said the chief beggar. "Our
doxies and dells are roasting 'em in a glade yonder.
Plump young ones, and fresh. We filched 'em but
last darkmans. We be toward a ben supper, and
you are welcome, — though we lack bouze."

The captain sighed. He had not dined; the fresh
air of the country had whetted his stomach; roast
chickens were good eating, hot or cold; and he had
gathered, from the vague replies Jerningham had
made to his inquiries about provisions, that his diet
at the Grange would be a rather spare one of salt
meat, stockfish, milk, and barley-cakes.

"Alas, if I durst but tarry!" He looked to see
how far behind him the sun was, and then shook his
head and gathered up his reins. "I must hasten on
— tis a sweet smell of cookery, forsooth! — how
soon, think you, will they be roasted?"

"Oh, half an hour, to be done properly."

"Then I must e'en thank ye, and ride on. I
durst not —" He broke off to sniff the air again.

"Marry, I have a thought. You lack bouze, say you? Now at the place whither I am bound, there is ale, or my gentleman has lied to me. I shall be in a sort the master there, with only a country wench and an old doting man — Know you Marshleigh Grange?"

"Ay," spoke up a very old cripple; "the lone house 'twixt the hills and the marshes; there hath been no ben filching there this many a year; the wild rogues pass it by as too far from the pads; neither back nor belly-cheats to be angled there."

Ravenshaw addressed himself again to the bearded chief of the beggars, received answer, passed a jovial compliment, and rode on alone in cheerful mood. In due time he turned into the by-road which accorded with Jerningham's description; and at length, emerging from a woody, bushy tract, he came upon a lonely plain wherein the one object for the eye was a gray-brown house, huddled against barn and outbuildings, at the left of the vanishing road, — a house of timber and plaster, warped and weather-beaten, its cracked gables offering a wan, long-suffering aspect to the sun and breeze. This was the Grange.

A short canter brought Ravenshaw to the rude wooden gate, studded with nails, in the stone wall that separated the courtyard from the road, which here came to an end. Ere the captain had time to knock, or cry "Ho, within!" the gate swung inward on its crazy hinges, and a thin, bent old man, with sparse white hair and blinking eyes, shambled forward to take the horse. At the same time, as further proof that Ravenshaw had been looked for, a woman appeared in the porched doorway of the house, and called out :

"Jeremy will see to your horse. Come within."

Ravenshaw looked at her with a little surprise ; this robust, erect, full-coloured, well-shaped creature, upon whom common rustic clothes took a certain grace, and whose head stood back in the proud attitude natural to beauty, was scarce the country wench he had expected to meet. But he said nothing, and followed her into the hall. This was a wide, high apartment of some pretension, its ceiling, rafters, and walls being of oak. Bare enough, it yet had the appearance of serving as the chief living-room of the occupants of the house. Upon an oak table, at which was an old chair, stood a flagon of wine and some cakes. Meg offered Ravenshaw this repast by a gesture, while she scrutinised him with interest.

"Wine?" quoth he, promptly setting to. "'Tis more than I had thought to find."

"There is some left since the time when — when Master Jerningham used to come to the Grange oftener," said Meg. "Ale serves for me and old Jeremy."

"Troth — your health, mistress ! — I am glad you

have ale in store. Would there be enough to entertain a few guests withal — some dozen or score poor friends of mine, if they were travelling this way? To tell the truth, I should not like to waste this wine upon such."

"Travellers never pass this way," said Meg, plainly not knowing what to make of him.

"Oh, we are some way from the highroad here, indeed; but a foolish friend or so might turn out a mile for the pleasure of my company."

"I know not what you'd set before 'em to eat, if there were a dozen."

"Marry, they would have to bring eatables with 'em, — my reason for having 'em as guests. Only so there be ale enough."

"Oh, there is ale," said Meg, without further comment.

Ravenshaw, munching the cakes, and oft wetting his throat, looked around the hall. The front doorway faced a wide fireplace at the rear, now empty. At the right was a door to a small apartment, a kind of porter's room, lighted by a single high narrow window; farther back in the hall was the entrance to a passage communicating with other parts of the house; and still farther back, a door leading to the kitchen. At the left hand were, first, a door to a large room, and, second, the opening to a passage like that on the right.

By way of this left-hand passage, and a narrow staircase which led from it, the captain was presently shown by old Jeremy to his chamber. It was large and bare, hung with rotten arras, and contained a bed, a joint-stool, and a table with ewer and basin; its window looked into the courtyard.

He flung his bruised body on the bed, and soon sank deliciously to sleep.

Meanwhile old Jeremy, returning to the hall, found Meg sitting with her chin upon her hands, and gazing into the empty fireplace.

"A sturdy fellow," whispered the old man, pointing backward with his thumb, and taking on a jocular air. "Cast eyes on him; a goodly husband mends all; cast eyes on him!"

"Thou'rt a fool; go thy ways!" quoth Meg; but she did not move.

CHAPTER XVI.

THE POET AS A MAN OF ACTION.

" O father, where's my love? were you so careless
To let an unthrift steal away your child?"
— The Case Is Altered.

MILLICENT, after the riot had ceased and dinner had been eaten, passed the day with a palpitating heart but a resolved mind. Under cover of her usual needlework, she fashioned a sort of large linen wallet, in which to carry the few things she wished to take with her. Her emotions were, in a less degree, similar to those which had affected her in the hours preceding her former attempt to run away. At supper she looked often with a hidden tenderness at the composed, unsuspecting face of her mother. When the light of evening faded she slipped to her chamber, and put a few chosen objects into the receptacle she had made, wrapped this in a hooded cloak, and dropped it from her window into the concealed space behind the garden shrubbery. She then waited, watching from the window that part of Friday Street in which Master Holyday must appear.

At last his slender figure lurched into view in the dusk, and came to a stop outside the gate.

Millicent sped across her chamber. At the door she turned, with fast-beating heart, and cast an affectionate, tearful look at the place in which she had spent so much of her childhood and youth, and which seemed to share so many of her untold thoughts. It appeared for an instant to reproach her sorrowfully; but when in her swift thought she justified her action, its aspect changed to that of wishing her Godspeed, and counselling her to hasten.

She hurried through the house as if upon some indoor quest, found herself alone in the garden, recovered her cloak and parcel, and went to unfasten the gate.

"'Tis I, Master Holyday," she said, in a low tone, as she loosened the bolt.

"Good! good! excellent!" came the scholar's reply from outside the gate, in a voice rather parched and excited.

Having slid back the bolt, she made to pull the gate open, but it would not move.

"What is the matter?" quoth she. "I cannot open it. Push it from your side."

She heard his hands laid against it, then his shoulder, then his back. But it would not budge. She examined it closely in the dusky light, and suddenly gave a little cry of despair.

·

"Oh, me! There is a new lock on the gate, and God knows where is the key!"

During the afternoon, in fact, Master Etheridge, alarmed by the easy entrance obtained by Ravenshaw and Gregory the previous night, and by Ravenshaw's exit from the garden that day, — an exit after which the gate had been left open, — had caused an additional lock to be put on, a lock to be opened by means of a key which the goldsmith thought best to keep in his own care.

"Oh, what shall I do?" she cried, after a futile tug at the lock.

"Is there no other way to come out?" queried Holyday, in perturbation.

"Alas, no! There's the street door from the gallery, but my father locks it himself at supper-time and keeps the key. I durs'n't go through the shop; if it isn't closed, my father may be in the back shop and the apprentices will surely be in front."

"God's name, I know not what—" began the poet, agitated with perplexity and fear of failure, but broke off to "Can't you make another pretext to go out? — drop another wedding-ring into the street, or something?"

"Nay, they would sure stop my going or follow me out at this hour. Oh, would I could leap the wall! By St. Anne, 'tis too bad — Ha! wait a minute."

Under the impulse of her thought she sped away without listening for answer, unconscious that her last words had been spoken too low to go beyond the gate.

Hence she did not know that Master Holyday, attacked by an idea at the same moment, and expressing himself with equal inaudibility, had as suddenly made off toward the White Horse Tavern.

She was in the house ere it occurred to her that she ought to have rid herself of her burden by throwing it over the wall. She thought best not to retrace her steps. So she ran up-stairs and along the passage to a small window that looked down on Friday Street. She pushed open the casement, saw that no one was passing below, and dropped the parcel, trusting it to the darkness. She had a moment's idea of calling to Holyday to come and take it, but a second thought was wiser; she cast a single glance toward the gate, but was uncertain whether she made out his form or not in the decreasing light. Then she went down-stairs, and boldly into the back shop. Her father sat at his small table counting by candle-light the day's money.

"Eh! what is it?" he asked, looking sharply up. "What dost thou here, baggage?"

"I have an order for George," she replied, quietly, forcing her voice to steadiness, and praying that her throbbing heart and pale face might not betray her.

George was an apprentice whom, for his cleverness, Mistress Etheridge was wont to employ on errands. Millicent could see him now in the outer shop, busy with other apprentices in covering the cases and closing up the front.

"'Zooks!" grumbled the goldsmith; "thy mother would best take the lad for a page, and be done with it."

Millicent passed on to the front shop.

"George," said she, when out of her father's hearing, but in that of one or two of the other apprentices, "you are to come with me to Mistress Carroll's next door; there is something to fetch back. Nay, wait till you have done here; I'll run ahead, 'tis but a step."

Upon the hazard that her father, in the rear shop, would not lift up his eyes from his money for some little time, she passed out to Cheapside. In a breath she was around the corner, from the crowd and the window-lights, into the dusk and desertion of Friday Street. She stooped and picked up her cloak and bag; then ran on, to the gate.

"Speed! speed! there's not a moment to lose!" she whispered, catching the elbow of the man who stood there, and who had not heard her coming swiftly up behind him.

He turned and stared, putting his eyes close to hers on account of the darkness; she saw that he had a great, scarred, bearded face, and that his body was twice the breadth of Master Holyday's.

"Oh, God!" she exclaimed, drawing back. "I thought you were Master Holyday."

"Master Holyday, eh?" growled the man. "What of him?"

"I — I was to meet him here," she faltered, looking around with a sinking heart.

"Oh! — God's light! — you are the maid, belike? Well, troth, beshrew me but that's the hell of it!" And the fellow grinned with silent laughter.

"What mean you? What maid? Know you aught — ?"

"Of Master Holyday? Sooth, do I! He's on t'other side of this gate."

She stared at the closed gate in bewilderment. "What? In the garden?"

"Ay, in the garden." The man raised his voice a little. "Sure thou'rt there, Master Holyday?"

"Ay," came the reply in the scholar's unmistakable voice. "But the maid is not. Hang her, whither is she gone?"

"Here I am," answered the maid, for herself. "In God's name, how got you in there?"

"In God's name, how got you out there?" said Holyday, vexatiously. "A minute ago you were here, and I was there. You could not come out, so

I went for this gentleman, who lifted me to the top of the wall — "

"Which was a service not included in the contract," remarked Cutting Tom.

"And here I dropped, thinking to find you," continued Holyday, in exasperation, "and to help you out as he helped me in. And now — "

"Well, I am out, nevertheless," she replied, quickly. "So come you out, pray, without more ado; my father may discover at any moment — "

"Why, devil take me!" cried Holyday, in despair. "I cannot climb the wall; there's none here to give me a shoulder."

"Is there nothing there you can climb upon?" queried Cutting Tom.

"Yes," cried Millicent, taking the answer upon herself; "there are benches. Oh, pray, make haste, Master Holyday!"

Soon Master Holyday could be heard dragging a bench across the sward; in its ordinary position it would not give him sufficient height, so he seemed to busy himself in placing it properly for his purpose. "*Nomine patris!*" he exclaimed as he bruised his fingers. Finally a thud against the upper part of the gate indicated that he had fixed the bench slantwise. Mounting the incline chiefly by means of hands and knees, he stood trembling at the top, high enough to get a purchase of his elbows on the gate, and so to wriggle his body over.

Millicent breathed more freely as soon as his head and shoulders appeared; but, as he was righting himself on the gate-top in order to drop safely outside, there came a voice from within the garden:

"Hey? How now? Good lack, more comings and goings!"

"Oh, God! that meddling Sir Peregrine!" cried Millicent. "We are found out. Hurry, Master Holyday!"

The poet, startled, was still upon the gate, staring back into the garden. With a revival of earlier agility, the old knight came up the sloping bench at a run, took hold of the gate's top with one hand, and of Master Holyday's neck with the other. His eyes fell upon the pair waiting outside. It was not too dark for him to recognise a figure which he had oft observed with the interest of future ownership.

"What! Mistress Millicent! And who's this? Master Holyday, o' my life! 'Zooks and 'zounds! here's doings!"

The poet, suddenly alive, jerked his neck from the old knight's grasp, and threw himself from the gate without thought of consequences. Luckily, Tom caught him by the body, and saved his neck, though both men were heavily jarred by the collision.

"Come!" cried Millicent, seizing Holyday by the

sleeve ere he had got his balance. She darted down Friday Street, the poet staggering headlong after her, Cutting Tom close in the rear.

"What, ho!" cried Sir Peregrine, astonished out of his wits. "Stop! stay! The watch! constables! Master Etheridge! Runaways, runaways, runaways!"

His voice waned in the distance behind Millicent as she hastened on. She still held the poet's sleeve; he breathed fast and hard, but said nothing. In front of the White Horse, four men, at a gruff word from Cutting Tom, fell in with the fugitives, and the whole party of seven ran on without further speech. For a short time, tramping and breathing were the only sounds in Millicent's ears; but soon there came a renewed and multiplied cry of "Runaways! stop them!" whereby she knew that Sir Peregrine had given the alarm, and that her father and his lads had started in pursuit.

"God send we get to the boat in time!" she said, as she halted for a single step so that Master Holyday might take the lead. She cast a swift look over her shoulder, and saw two or three torches flaring in the distance.

Holyday led across Knightrider Street obliquely, then down the lower part of Bread Street, along a little of Thames Street, and through a short passage to Queenhithe. This wharf enclosed three sides of a somewhat rounded basin, wherein a number of craft now lay at rest in the black water that lapped softly as stirred by the tide and a light wind. Houses were built close together on all three sides.

The poet made straight along the east side of the basin, and down a narrow flight of stairs to a large boat that lay there. A man started up in the boat, and held out his hand to help the maid aboard, lighting her steps with a lantern in his other hand, — for a veil of clouds had swept across the sky from the west, and the only considerable light upon the wharf was from a lantern before one of the gabled houses, and from the lattice windows of a tavern. Other boatmen steadied the vessel, so that Millicent boarded without accident; Holyday, coming next, and setting foot blindly upon the gunwale, rather fell than stepped in. Cutting Tom and his men huddled aboard, and the whole party crowded together astern, to leave room forward for the rowers.

"Whither?" asked the waterman in command.

"Why, down-stream, of course," replied Holyday. "Know you not — how now? Where is Bill Tooby?"

"Bill Tooby? He is yonder in his boat, waiting for some that have bespoke him." The man pointed across the basin.

Holyday was stricken faint of voice. "Oh, *miserere!*" he wailed. "He is waiting for us. We have come to the wrong stairs."

"Hark!" cried Millicent.

Cries of "Runaways! Stop them! Stop the maid!" were approaching from, apparently, the vicinity of Knightrider Street.

"We must e'en change to the other boat," said Holyday, despairingly.

"Oh, heaven, there is not time!" cried Millicent.

"If you be in haste," said the waterman, "stay where ye are. Whither shall we carry ye?"

"Nay, nay, I durst not!" cried Holyday, and yet stood in helpless indecision.

"Come, then!" said Millicent, and leaped from the boat to the stairs. Reaching back for Holyday's hand, she pulled him after her, dragged him up the steps, and led him around the three sides of the basin, their five protectors following close.

A larger boat, manned with a more numerous crew, was in waiting at the western stairs. The waterman with whom Ravenshaw had bargained in the morning, making sure of Holyday's face in the light of a lantern, guided the fugitives aboard with orderly swiftness. But already the noise of pursuit was in Thames Street; ere the last man — a slim fellow with a thickly bearded face, which he carried well forward from his body — was embarked, the cries, swelling suddenly as the pursuers emerged from the narrow passage, were upon the wharf, and the red flare of torches came with them.

The party in chase was headed by the gold-smith himself, no covering on his head, his gray hair standing out in the breeze; then came his apprentices, and sundry persons who had joined in the hue and cry; the rear was brought up by Sir Peregrine, lamed and winded. Master Etheridge made out the party in the boat at once, and, with threatening commands to the waterman to stop, led his people around to the stairs.

"Cast off!" growled Bill Tooby, the waterman, pulling the slim fellow aboard. The order was obeyed, and Millicent, who had sat more dead than alive since her father had come into sight, saw the wharf recede, and a strip of black water spread between the boat and the torch-lit party that stood gazing from the stairs.

"Oh, wench, I'll make thee rue this day!" cried the goldsmith, shaking his arms after the boat. As for Sir Peregrine, he looked utterly nonplussed.

Then her father spoke hurriedly to his followers, and called loudly for a boat. The waterman to whom Holyday had first led his own party was quick to respond. Meanwhile Tooby's craft headed down-stream. Millicent, looking anxiously back over the water, saw the other boat, or its lantern and one of the torches, shoot out from the stairs.

"Think you they will catch us?" she asked Mas-ter Holyday.

"I think nothing," said the poet, dejectedly, really thinking very small of himself for the mistake which had enabled the goldsmith to come upon their heels.

Surprised at the apparent change in Master Holyday since the forenoon, she turned to Tooby. "What think you, waterman?"

"Why, mistress, an they make better speed than we, belike they'll catch us; but, an we make better speed than they, belike they'll not catch us," growled Tooby.

"And that's the hell of it!" quoth Cutting Tom.

CHAPTER XVII.

DIRE THINGS BEFALL IN THE FOREST.

> "' Mistress, it grows somewhat pretty and dark.'
> ' What then ? '
> ' Nay, nothing. Do not think I am afraid,
> Although perhaps you are.' " — *Beggars' Bush.*

THE two large boats were not alone upon the river. Here and there, in the distance, moved the tiny lights of a wherry carrying a benighted fare ; and up toward the palaces and Westminster more than one cluster of lanterns and torches swept along, where some party of ladies and gentlemen were rowed to a mask or other revels. From one such company the western breeze brought the strains of guitars ; Bill Tooby and his comrades, infected with the spirit of melody, began to sing " Heave and ho, rumbelow," in deep voices, in time with the movement of their bodies.

Along the northern bank of the river, where the dwellings and warehouses of merchants rose like a wall from the water's edge, the dim lights of windows ran in a straggling, interrupted line. Farther west, where the river washed the stairs to the gardens of the great Strand residences and of the Temple, there were scarce any lights at all. On the south bank, a few glowing windows marked the row of taverns and other houses — many of them of questionable repute — which, set back a little from the river, concealed the bear-gardens and playhouses in the fields behind. But soon, as the boat sped down-stream, the buildings on that bank were flush with the shore, save where Winchester House showed a few lighted windows beyond its terrace. Little did Millicent imagine that anything bearing upon her destiny had ever been spoken or thought on that terrace or in that house. In front, spanning the river, another irregular row of window lights indicated the tall, close-built houses of London Bridge; and the roar of the water, first dammed by the piers and then falling in a kind of cataract through the twenty arches, was already loud in the ears.

Millicent kept her eyes on the lights of the boat behind, — only two lights, a lantern at the prow, and a torch held by some one near the stern. They came steadily on, seeming neither to lose nor gain. Suddenly she lost sense of them; but that was when her own boat plunged into one of the arches of the bridge, and seemed to be gulped down by a blacker night, a chill air, and a thunderous noise. Forward and slightly downward the boat flung itself, as if into some gulf of the underworld, but all of a sudden it was out again in the soft air and the calm water, and Millicent, looking up, saw the lit windows of the eastern side of the bridge. She continued gazing back, and very soon the two lights, the little yellow one and the trailing red one, came into view between the piers, still in pursuit at the same distance.

"They don't gain upon us," growled Cutting Tom, with a desire of making himself agreeable to the maid.

"But they do not lose," said Millicent, in a troubled tone.

"Why, sooth, an they still gain not, 'tis sure they'll ne'er catch us."

"But they can see where we land," said she, "and they can land there, too, and so follow us to the end."

"Then we can e'en teach 'em better manners," said Tom, grandly. "I'd as lief split a throat this night as another."

"Oh, no; in heaven's name, no!" she cried. "We must escape them without that. No blows, I beg of you, whate'er befall!"

"Yet you see how they stick to our heels. How is it, waterman? Shall we not give 'em the slip soon?"

"Belike, and belike not," replied Tooby. "We can do our best, no more."

Suddenly Master Holyday, thinking in some manner to redeem himself, had an inspiration.

"How if they couldn't see to follow us?" he asked, abruptly. "How if we put out our lights and went on in the dark?"

"Not for ten pound a minute," said Tooby, "would I row without lights, a night like this. 'Tis bad enow as it is, with all the ships and small boats lying in the Pool here. E'en with our lanterns, we shall do well an we bump not our nose."

There was a silence, broken only by the plash of the oars, the creak of the rowlocks, the strange noises of the river, the lessening sound of what an obscure dramatist of those days describes as

> "The bridge's cataracts, and such-like murmurs
> As night and sleep yield from a populous number."

"But I will e'en try something better," added Tooby, presently, and forthwith gave an inaudible order to his men.

They instantly stopped rowing, and even proceeded to stay the boat's movement with the current, so that it remained almost stationary.

Millicent cried out in alarm as the lights behind came rapidly nearer.

"Peace, mistress," said Tooby. "There will be no blood spilled." He then spoke in a low tone to the men in the bow, and himself strode to the stern, where he stood with his long arms slightly crooked at the elbows as if to be in readiness for action.

Swiftly the other boat came alongside. Millicent, holding her breath, wondering what was about to occur, made out her father bending forward in the attitude of one ready to grasp and punish. The torch revealed Sir Peregrine also, limply huddled up so that his beard was between his knees, and two of the apprentices, one of whom held the torch.

"Ay, thou dost well to yield, wench!" spake the goldsmith, in tones so wrathful as rather to contradict his words.

"Ay, chick," called out Sir Peregrine, reassuringly, "no need to run away from me; I'll give thee no cause for jealousy, I promise thee."

Master Etheridge stood up to reach out for his daughter. She had a fearful thought that Tooby had chosen to betray her. But at the same instant Tooby, leaning over to the other boat, violently struck the torch-bearing apprentice's hand, and deftly caught the torch away. She heard a slight crash forward; and then her own boat shot through the water, leaving the other in complete darkness, one of Tooby's men having knocked the lantern from its prow with an oar.

Millicent gave a quick breath of relief and put on her cloak; but then she thought of the other boat's danger of running into something, or of being run down itself, and of this she spoke.

"Never fear," said Tooby. "He'll no more ven-

ture in the dark than I would. We'll fast put yon
ship's hull 'twixt them and us, and be out of their
ken ere ever they can get a light. And now pull,
hearts, for the honour of watermen ! "

Soon the lights on the left bank, becoming fewer,
took such height and shape that Millicent knew her
boat was passing the Tower. Somewhere there the
water plashed against the underground stairs of
Traitors' Gate, that arched cavern which had lifted
its iron door often in nights as dark as this, to admit
some noble prisoner whose face, redly pale in the
torchlight, betokened a heart chilled with a feeling
that those damp walls formed a vestibule of death.
Master Holyday, for all that was upon his mind,
thought of these things, and of much else in the
night-clad surroundings ; but Millicent kept her eyes
fixed on the darkness behind, alert for any moving
light that might appear in chase.

None such appeared ; and by the time the boat
had traversed the city of great ships, and had come
to where the lights upon the banks were few, and
the mysterious noises of the town had given place to
those of the country, she had cast away all fear of
danger from behind.

At Deptford they passed one ship, of which Millicent took no more note than she took of any other of
the countless vessels whose lights dotted the gloom
around her that night ; but on which she might have

bestowed a second look had she known all that was to be known.

The tide, the current, and the wind being with the rowers, it seemed not long till Tooby hinted that Master Holyday would do well to keep his eyes open for the place of landing. The scholar, scanning the blue-black darkness in perplexity, said that he could not for his life see anything of the shore. Tooby asked him whether he knew the different landmarks by name. The scholar was acquainted with those in the neighbourhood of where they should land. Thenceforth the waterman called out the name of each village, wharf, riverside tavern, hill, tributary, or well-known country-seat, the contents of the darkness being known to him perhaps by his sense of distance, perhaps by reference to some far-off light, perhaps sometimes by the smell of marsh or wood. Holyday began to recognise the names; and at last told the waterman to put ashore at the mouth of a certain creek.

The boat glided along a low bank and stopped. Tooby, standing up, held out his lantern to show where there was safe footing. Master Holyday, leaping out too hastily, alighted up to his knees in water. Millicent, aided by the waterman's hand, stepped ashore. Cutting Tom and his men lost no time. Ere it seemed possible, the lights of the boat were moving swiftly away. Its departure, and espe-

cially that of Tooby, left Millicent with a sudden
pang of loneliness and misgiving. But she reflected
that the last stage of her flight was reached; taking
new heart, she grasped Holyday's sleeve, and waited
to be led.

The party had two lanterns and a torch, all which
had been lighted in the boat. Cutting Tom assigned
one lantern to Holyday, the other to the slim fellow
with the projecting head, the torch to himself. The
poet, with a deep sigh, and craning his neck to
peer into the mysterious blackness beyond the little
area of feeble light, started forward; Millicent
clung to his elbow; Cutting Tom placed himself at
her other side, and the four men followed close.

The walkers proceeded slowly, Master Holyday
having often to stop to ascertain his way. At first
the turf under them was springy, then it became
softer, and sometimes one's foot would sink into a
tiny pool; then the ground became higher, and presently they entered a wood. This seemed intermi-
nable; not only was poor Master Holyday compelled
to pause every minute to identify his whereabouts
but also the protruding roots, fallen boughs, and
frequent underbrush made every step a matter of
care.

As they moved their torch and lanterns, so the
light and shadow constantly moved about them;
trunks and boughs, bush and brake, would suddenly

appear and as quickly vanish as the yellow rays
swung here and there. The breeze rustled unceas-
ingly among the leaves, and the air was pleasant with
forest odours. Millicent's fancy peopled the shades
with sleeping giants, goblins, witches, dragons, and all
the creatures of the old tales of fairies and knights
errant. She thought a similar terror must have
come upon the others; her companion hesitated so
when he strove to pierce the shadows with wide-open
eyes; and Cutting Tom kept so close to her; while
one of the men had stepped up to the other side of
Holyday and tightly grasped his arm.

"'Tis a weary journey, mistress," complained the
poet.

"Nay, I find it pleasant sport," said she, feeling
that one of the two must show a light heart. Holyday's manner all evening had been so at variance
with his readiness to fight a dangerous man some
hours earlier, that she made no attempt to understand
the alteration; she merely attended to the need of
keeping up his spirits, though her own heart faltered.
But she could not help adding: "Is there much more
of this wood to go through?"

"More than I wish there were," replied Holyday.

They went some distance farther in silence. Then
the slim fellow with a lantern suddenly gave two
coughs. Instantly Cutting Tom gripped Millicent's
arm, stood still, and said to Holyday:

"A plague on your eyes, sir! you are leading us the wrong way."

Holyday, stopping perforce with all the rest, replied, in amazement: "'Tis the right way; I have come by this path to fish in the Thames a hundred times."

"Poh! fish me no fish, sir!" cried Cutting Tom, while the slim lantern-bearer strode around to the front. "Am I to be led astray, and this maid here, for your designs? You have dragged us too long through this cursed wood — and that's the hell of it!"

"'Tis the right way, I tell you," said Holyday; "and how can you say otherwise, when you know not whither we are bound?"

"But I do know whither we are bound — and that's the hell of it!"

"I begin to think you are an impudent fellow," quoth Holyday, momentarily reckless through loss of patience; "and *that's* the hell of it, in your Bedlam gibberish!"

"Death!" bellowed Cutting Tom; "'hell of it' belongs to me; no man in England dare steal my speech!"

He handed his torch to one of the men, ran at the scholar, dealt him a blow between the eyes, seized his lantern, and dragged Millicent away, motioning the slim knave to lead on. The knave took a direction leftward from their former one.

"What mean you?" cried the maid, trying to release herself. "I'll not leave Master Holyday."

One of the men caught her by the free arm, and she was borne away by him and Cutting Tom. Glancing back, she saw that the two remaining men, one of whom had quickly stuck the torch in the ground, were grappling with Holyday, who was struggling between them.

"In God's name, what would you do?" Millicent cried, as her captors hastened on at the heels of the new guide.

The men vouchsafed no answer. After a little while, at a word from Cutting Tom, they stopped and waited. Tom gave a whistle, which was answered from the direction whence they had last come, — evidently by one of the men who had remained with Holyday. Being at intervals repeated, and answered at lessening distances, the whistle proved to be for the purpose of guiding these two men. Soon they appeared with the torch, but without Holyday.

"Oh, heaven! what have you done with him?" cried Millicent, turning cold.

"Only lightened him of these, lady," said one of the twain, indicating a bundle of clothing under his arm.

"And left him tied safe to a tree, lest he roam about i' the dark and do himself an injury," quoth the other.

"Come," said Tom, tightening his grasp on the girl's arm. The guide moved on, and the party made haste through the forest.

"Whither are you taking me?" Millicent asked, tearfully, but got no reply. Wondering and appalled, scarce believing she was herself, oft doubting the reality of this strange journey, she walked as she was compelled.

At last they came out of the wood and made their way over a flat, heathy plain. It seemed to Millicent that they had worked back to the neighbourhood of the river. Cutting Tom grew impatient, muttered to himself, and presently asked: "How far now?"

"'Tis straight before us," said the guide, in a voice muffled as if by the heavy beard that covered his face.

A narrow rift in the clouds let through a moment's moonlight; Millicent had a brief vision of lonely country, with a little cluster of gables ahead; then all was blotted out in thicker darkness.

CHAPTER XVIII.

" Captain, rally up your rotten regiment, and begone." — *A King and No King*.

MASTER JERNINGHAM, having communicated his good hopes to Sir Clement Ermsby on the deck of his ship, considered that, as the maid was not to leave London till nightfall, and, as he was now between London and the Grange, he had ample time to reach his country-house and send away the captain ere she could be brought there by her escort. He therefore resolved to proceed with leisure and order. And first, as he had long fasted, and as he had a night's business before him, he went ashore to his accustomed tavern at Deptford, and had supper with Sir Clement in a room where they were alone.

" We shall take one of our own boats and four of our men," said Jerningham, "and row down to the old landing at the Grange. 'Tis but a short walk thence to the house. You and two of the men would best wait without the house, whilst I go in and send away Ravenshaw. If he saw you and so many men he might smell some extraordinary business, and have the curiosity to set himself against my orders."

"If he should do so, nevertheless," said Ermsby, "then, as you said awhile ago — You may want our help in that."

"Then I must e'en call you. But I shall try to have him without his weapons."

"What would Mistress Meg say to another ghost in the house?"

"Hang her, mad wench! Ay, she would be howling of murder and blood. I know not — she might fly to my lord bishop with the news. Well, I can tie her up and lock her in a chamber, at the worst. Yet she is a very devil. I think I'd best breed no more trouble at the last. I'll not have the knave killed unless he cannot be got away otherwise."

"An you send him away, will you leave some one in his place?"

"Ay, to keep Meg quiet till we are safe at sea. I'll leave Meadows, and charge him not to tell her of our sailing. He is a trusty fool."

"But what will she say to this goldsmith's wench being housed overnight in the Grange?"

"Why, I'll have a tale ready when we arrive: that I am saving the maid from a runaway marriage, to take back to her father; or that the maid is for you; or some such story."

"Best say the maid is for me. Women who

have gone that road are ever ready to push others into it."

"Not always. But I shall contrive to make Meg tolerate the other's presence for a few hours, e'en if I must do it with promises. I can offer to find her a husband, — this Ravenshaw, an she like his looks, or another that may be bought. I think she has grown out of her sulks, and into the hope of rehabilitation, by this time. As for the Cheapside maid, first I will try wooing; she may be compliant of her own accord. But if she hold out, there's nothing for it but the sleeping potion. Gregory will fetch that with him ; I bade him get it in Buck-lersbury on his way to Friday Street."

"May it give her pleasant dreams!"

"When she is fast asleep," continued Jerningham, "I'll leave Gregory to watch her, and we'll come back to welcome my lord bishop in the morning. And to-morrow, when my lord has seen the last of us, and the tide is bearing us down the river, we need only put the ship to at the old landing, walk to the house, and carry her aboard. There will be none to see but Meg and old Jeremy, and they shall not know the ship is ours, or that we are farther bound than Tilbury."

Sir Clement's appetite, which had been less neglected of late, was satisfied before Jerningham's, and the knight proposed that he should go and get the boat in readiness while the other finished eating. Jerningham consented, naming the men who were to be taken from the ship's crew upon the night's business.

" I will join you very soon," said he, as Sir Clement left the room.

Jerningham brought his supper to an end, and bade a drawer fetch the reckoning. Waiting for the boy's return, he flung himself on his back on a bench that stood against the wall. The knowledge that all was provided for, that his course was fully thought out, and that only action lay before him, brought to his mind a restfulness it had not lately known. The effect of his heavy meal acted with this to snare his senses ; so long it was since sleep had overtaken him, he was not on guard against it. When the tavern lad came back with the score, the gentleman's eyes were closed, his breathing was slow and deep. Knowing by experience that sleeping gentlemen sometimes resented disturbance, the drawer went away more quietly than he had entered ; Master Jerningham was a good customer, and might as well pay last as first.

Sir Clement saw the boat ready, and then busied himself in the study of maps and charts by candlelight in the cabin, pending Jerningham's appearance. In his preoccupation, he lost thought of the night's affair, in which Jerningham bore all the responsibility. He took no observance of the increasing darkness outside, until at last he became wonderingly sensible of Jerningham's delay. Hastening ashore, he found the sleeper in the tavern.

"Good God!" cried Jerningham, springing up at his friend's call; "what's the hour? How long have I slept? Death! is all lost?"

"Nay, there is time, if we bestir ourselves."

"Then we must fly. My plans are all undone if she be there before I send away that captain."

Learning what o'clock it was, Jerningham found he had yet time to write a short pretended letter, to serve as pretext for Ravenshaw's journey. This done, he hastened to the boat.

Not until he was being rowed past Blackwall, did it occur to him that, in the haste of departure, he had not looked to the thorough arming of the party, and that there was not a firearm with the whole company.

"Oh, pish! there is steel enough among us to cut eight captains' throats with a clean blade apiece, an it comes to throat-cutting," said Ermsby.

"'Twould come to that soon enough, but for the storm Meg would raise. Plague take her! would I had the heart to quiet her the sure way! But I cannot steel myself to that. I must be led by circumstance; 'tis for this captain's doings to say whether his throat need be cut. He had no pistol when he

left me. As for his sword and dagger " — here Jerningham raised his voice and called to one of the men
rowing : " Goodcole, thou hast some skill in sleights,
and cutting purses, and the like, I have heard."

" Ay, sir," was the confident reply. " In my time
I have been called the knave with the invisible
fingers. My friends used to say I could filch a
man's shirt off his back while he stood talking to
me in the street."

" Poh ! " growled another of the men ; " I much
doubt whether you can pick a pocket."

" Here's a handful of testers I picked from yours,"
said Goodcole, resting his oar for a moment that he
might return his comrade the coins.

There was a brief stoppage from rowing while the
other men hastily investigated the condition of their
own pockets.

" Excellent Goodcole ! " quoth Sir Clement Ermsby.
" Thou art a proficient in a most delicate craft."

" Thou couldst take away a man's sword and
dagger ere he knew it, belike," said Jerningham.

" I could take away his teeth, or the thoughts in
the centre of his head," promptly answered Goodcole.

" Perchance I shall put thee to the test by and
by," said Jerningham.

In good time they found the landing with their
lights, made the boat fast, and hastened through the

darkness to the country-house. The gate of the courtyard was not fastened. Jerningham first led the way to a small penthouse in one corner of the yard, where he desired that Sir Clement and two of the men should remain until he saw how the captain took the new commands.

"And e'en when the maid is brought," he added, with a sudden afterthought, "best you be not seen at the first; wait till I try whether she is to be won softly. If she saw you she might remember that night, and be thrown into greater fear and opposition. I'll call when I have need of you."

He then went with Meadows and Goodcole to the door within the porch; finding it made fast inside, he gave two rapid double knocks, then two single ones. Soon a tiny wicket opened behind a little grating in the door. Jerningham held a lantern close to his face so that he might be quickly recognised. The door opened, and Jerningham found Mistress Meg alone in the hall, where the light of a single candle struggled with the darkness. The lantern and torch brought in by the newcomers were a welcome reinforcement. Jerningham set the lantern on the chimney shelf, and had the torch thrust into a sconce on the wall.

"Did the new steward come?" he asked.

"The new steward?" quoth Meg, with faint derision at the title. "Yes; am I not still here?"

"Where is he?" asked the master, ignoring the allusion to her threat.

"In his chamber. He arrived, ate, drank, went thither; and I have not seen him since."

A sudden light came into Jerningham's eyes. "Ten to one he sleeps. He had a laborious day of it ere he came hither. What weapons had he when he came?"

"Rapier and dagger," answered Meg, looking surprised at the question.

"'Twere a good jest now," said Jerningham, pretending amusement, "to take them from him in his sleep, then come away and send Jeremy to wake him."

"Is he the kind of man to see the mirth of that jest?" inquired Meg, with little interest.

"We shall see if he be. Goodcole, a chance to prove your mettle. Where's Jeremy? Pray send him to me, mistress, and I'll thank you."

While Meg was at the kitchen door calling the old man-servant, Jerningham spoke quietly to Goodcole. Jeremy appeared, blinking and bowing; as he passed Meg, he chuckled, and said, in undertone, "A husband mends all, sooth!" Master Jerningham, ascertaining from Meg what chamber the captain lay in, bade the old man show Goodcole the way. The pair took a lantern, of which Goodcole concealed all but a small part in his jerkin.

During the absence of the two, Jerningham directed Meg's attention to Meadows : "This is the man shall abide here for a time ; I must send t'other on business that bears no delay, — him that lies upstairs, I mean. 'Tis partly for that reason I have come here. And partly 'tis that I may, for an hour or so, play the host to a visitor that must perforce lodge here to-night, — a young woman."

He paused ; but Meg merely paid attention to him with eyes and ears, and displayed no emotion.

"She is daughter to a merchant I much esteem in London ; she has been in some manner bewitched, or constrained, or seduced, to fly from her home to this neighbourhood with an unthrift knave. By chance the plot came to my ears, and for her father's sake, and her honour's, I have caused her to be stayed in her flight and fetched hither. To-morrow I will come and put her aboard a vessel that shall carry her to Tilbury, where her father hath gone upon his affairs. If it fall to you to comfort or serve her while she is here, take heed you talk nothing of the matter, for all she may say to you. And not a word of this before Captain Ravenshaw when he comes down."

Whatever were Meg's thoughts, she kept them to herself. Though she might fear ghosts and witches, she was not to be thrown out of composure by surprises and visits, even if they came

thick in a few hours, after months of the still
and solitary life that was the rule at the Grange.

Goodcole and Jeremy returned, the former carrying the rapier and dagger with a nonchalant, even
contemptuous, air, as if his task had been too easy.
Jerningham smiled approval; he took the weapons,
thrust the dagger in his girdle, and laid the rapier
behind him on the table, as his own scabbard was, of
course, occupied.   He then sent Jeremy back with a
candle to summon the captain down to the hall.

When the captain came, it was he that held
the candle; while with one hand he dragged Jeremy
by the collar.

"Hell and furies!" he roared; "what nest of
rogues, what den of thieves, what — what — "   He
paused, and stared open-mouthed at Jerningham,
who was standing with folded arms and a look of
amusement.

"How now, captain?   What is ill with you?"

"My weapons, sir — my rapier, my dagger —
angled, filched, stolen in my sleep!   God's death,
is this the kind of a house you keep here? —   Ah,
you have them, I see."

But Jerningham pleasantly raised his hand, so
that the captain in mere courtesy stopped in the
midst of a stride forward, and waited for the
other's words.

"A slight piece of mirth, captain, and a lesson

for you, too. Coming hither upon a sudden business, and learning you were so sound a sleeper,
I saw my chance of disarming you, and showing
you what danger a man may be in asleep."

"Why, sooth, I am not wont to sleep so sound,"
said Ravenshaw, a little shamefacedly; "but, being
come to this quiet and lone place, I allowed myself
to slide, as one might say, and — so 'twas. But
to take my weapons from me awake, that were
a different business, sir, I think I may say."

"All the world knows that, captain."

"By your leave, sir, I'll have them back again,
I feel awkward without 'em."

"A mere moment, I pray you, captain," said Jerningham, with a smile of harmless raillery. "I
would have you hear first the business I have
come hither so late to send you upon. As it is
so sudden a matter, and hath some discomfort in
it, you might take it in choler; and then 'twere best
you had no steel to your hand."

Ravenshaw thought that his master's wit was
of a very childish quality; but said, merely, as he
summoned patience :

"What is the business?"

"Oh, a slight, simple matter in itself, but needing
absolute sureness in the doing, and instant speed
in the starting. This letter is to be carried to
Dover, to him that is named upon it, and an

answer brought to me at Winchester House. That is all."

"Oh, pish! a slight, paltry journey; nothing to make me choleric. With the horse I rode to-day, I'll go and come in four days."

Which was very good time upon the horses and roads of that period.

"But there's the pinch," quoth Jerningham, "I must have the answer Monday morning ere the Exchange opens. You must know I take a gentleman's part in a merchant's venture or so, and if certain cargoes now due at Dover — In short, you must ride forth immediately, as soon as horse can be saddled."

Ravenshaw, remembering his promise to pay Cutting Tom at the parson's on the morrow noon. slowly shook his head.

"How now, captain? Would you shirk at the outset? Will you be continually failing me? This is no such matter as the other, man."

"I do not shirk; but I will not start to-night. I will set forth to-morrow, and make what speed man and beast can."

"Look you, captain; my commands are that you set forth now. If you choose to throw yourself out upon the world again — "

Jerningham paused. Now, in truth, Ravenshaw had felt he could be very comfortable for a time

on this quiet estate; his body and his wits, both
somewhat overtaxed in the struggle for existence
he had so long maintained, plead for repose. He
sighed, and fell back upon obvious objections, not
aware that Jerningham already knew of his engagement for the morrow with Cutting Tom.

"Why, bethink you, the darkness —" he blundered.

"A man may go a steady pace by lantern-light.
I've ridden many a mile so," said Jerningham.

"But how is a man to keep the right road, with
none awake to tell him?"

"You must know the way to the highroad,
for you came over it to-day; and you must know
the highroad as far as to Canterbury, for you told
me so when I directed you to this place. It will be
daylight long before you come to Canterbury."

The captain shook his head again.

Jerningham felt that time was passing rapidly.
"If you are for disobedience, you are no longer
for my service," he said. "Take yourself from
my house and my land forthwith."

Ravenshaw laughed; and stood motionless, which
was what Jerningham wished, in case the captain
was determined against an immediate start for
Dover, for it would not do to have him free in the
neighbourhood, perchance to learn of the treachery
concerning the maid in time to give trouble. It had

occurred to Jerningham that a threatening step on the captain's part, by affording excuse for a deed of blood, would lessen its horror and create in Meg, with less fear of retribution upon the house, less mood for turning accuser. So he resumed, with studied offensiveness of tone :

"Begone from my house, I bid you!" With which, he drew the captain's dagger as if he forgot it was not his own.

Jerningham's back was to the table; Ravenshaw faced him, three or four paces away; by the front door stood Meadows, with a long knife in his girdle; Goodcole, before the fireplace, was similarly armed. Meg and Jeremy, wondering spectators, were near the kitchen door. Ravenshaw noted all this in a single glance right and left; noted in the looks of the two men the habit of instant readiness to support their master.

"Pray, consider the hour," said Ravenshaw, feeling it was a time for temporising.

"'Tis for you to consider; I command," said Jerningham, taking the captain's sword from the table behind him.

"You should give me my weapons before you bid me depart," said the captain, in as light a tone as he could assume.

"When you are gone, I will throw them after you."

Ravenshaw dashed forward with a growl; but stopped short in time, with the point of his own sword at his breast. He had an impulse to grasp the blade; but he knew, if he were quick enough for that, there was yet the dagger to be reckoned with, besides the two men, who drew their knives at that moment. Jerningham seemed to brace himself for a spring; he held the captain's sword and dagger as in sockets of iron; a dark gleam shone in his eyes. Ravenshaw knew the look; time and again he had worn it himself; he knew also when, as player in a game, he was within a move of being checkmated.

"Well," quoth he, with a grin of resignation, "you hold all the good cards. I will carry your letter." He suddenly bethought him of a friend or two in Rochester, which he would pass through early in the morning if he made the journey, by whom he might send Cutting Tom's money to the parson. Contemplating the life of ease he had promised himself in his new service, he was not sorry a good pretext had occurred for withdrawing his refusal.

"You will set out immediately?" asked Jerningham.

"The sooner the better, now."

Jerningham sent the old man out with a lantern to saddle the captain's horse and bring it to the door. He then handed the letter to the captain, and gave particular instructions, such as would be necessary in

a genuine errand. Jeremy reappeared, at the front
door, and announced that the horse was ready. Jerningham surrendered the captain's rapier and dagger
with grace, and gave him money for the journey.
Ravenshaw then examined the lantern which Jeremy
brought him, waved a farewell to Jerningham and
Meg, and strode to the door.

Jerningham breathed softly, lest even a sigh of
satisfaction might betray his sense of triumph. "She
is mine!" sang his heart.

The door, left slightly ajar by the old man, opened
wide as if by a will of its own, just as the captain
was about to grasp it. A white-bearded, ruddy-faced
man, dressed in rags and upheld by one leg and a
crutch, stood grinning at the threshold.

"God save your worship!" said he to the captain.
"We come late; but first our affairs hindered us,
and then we mistook the way. By good chance, we
find you awake; else had we passed the night under
some penthouse or such, hereabouts, and come to
drink your health in the morning."

Ravenshaw having mechanically stepped back, the
old beggar hobbled in, followed by several other
maimed ragamuffins, with whom came the two
women Ravenshaw had seen in the afternoon, and
a pair of handsome frowsy young hussies who had
not appeared in the road. The legless dwarf still
rode upon a comrade's shoulders. As the motley

gang trooped in, there was a great clatter and thud of crutches, wooden legs, and staves.

"God's death! who are these?" cried Jerningham, in petulant astonishment.

"Some poor friends of mine I met on the way hither," said Ravenshaw, apologetically. "I asked them to sup with me here. I had well-nigh forgot."

"Sup with you! By what right — well, no matter for that. Where did you think to find provender for all those mouths?"

"I was to find drink only; they were to find meat."

"Ay," said the chief beggar, "chickens; and here they be, young and plump." He thrust his hand into a sack another fellow carried, and drew out a cold roast pullet. The captain gazed at this specimen with admiring eyes, and unconsciously licked his lips.

"By your leave," said he to Jerningham, "I'll tarry but a half-hour to play the host to my invited guests; and then away. I can make up the time; a half-hour, more or less —"

"'Tis not to be thought of!" cried Jerningham. "There has been too much time lost already."

"Nay, I'll make it up, I tell you. I am bound to these people by my invitation; they have come far out of their way."

"Oh, as for that, they need not go away thirsty.

Jeremy, take these — good people — to the kitchen, and broach a cask." Master Jerningham, in his desire for Ravenshaw's departure, could force himself to any concession; he considered that, left to themselves, these beggars would be no obstacle to his design; they could be kept at their ale in the kitchen.

"Why, to tell the truth," interposed the captain, "'tis not so much their thirst troubles me; 'tis my hunger." And he leaned a little toward the fowl, sniffing, and feasting on it with his eyes.

"Take it with you, man, and eat as you ride," said Jerningham, still restraining his impatience.

"Why, that's fair enough," replied Ravenshaw. "I'll just drink one cup with these my guests, and then leave 'em to your hospitality." Without more ado, he walked to the kitchen door, where Jeremy was standing, and motioned the beggars to follow. They filed into the kitchen, seven men and four women, not a whole body in the gang save the two robust wenches.

"A bare minute or so, sir," said ·Ravenshaw to Jerningham, and went after them, taking the lantern with him. Soon there came from the kitchen the noise of loosened tongues chattering in the gibberish of the mendicant profession.

Master Jerningham, knowing that opposition would only cause further delay, controlled himself as best

"THERE . . . WAS THE MAID OF CHEAPSIDE, PALE AND
BEWILDERED."

he could, and waited in silence, pacing the hall, while the captain had his humour. Meg, with housewifely instinct, betook herself to the kitchen to keep an eye on matters there. Presently the captain reappeared, with a pullet in one hand, his lantern in the other, Meg having meanwhile lighted candles in the kitchen.

"And now to horse!" cried he, closing the kitchen door after him.

"And God save us from any more delays!" said Jerningham, with a pretence of jocularity.

"So say I," quoth Ravenshaw, stalking forward.

In the centre of the hall he stopped, with a cry of astonishment, which made Jerningham turn swiftly toward the open front door.

There in the porch, which was suddenly lighted up with rays of torch and lantern, was the maid of Cheapside, pale and bewildered, held on either side by Cutting Tom and one of his comrades.

CHAPTER XIX.

KNAVE AGAINST GENTLEMAN.

"Who shall take your word?
A whoreson, upstart, apocryphal captain,
Whom not a Puritan in Blackfriars will trust
So much as for a feather."   *— The Alchemist.*

CUTTING TOM was struck motionless at sight of
the captain; but, after a moment, reassuring himself
by a look at Jerningham, he led his captive into the
hall. His men followed. The group came to a halt
ere any one found voice.

Ravenshaw, recovering a little from his surprise,
was about to hurl a question at Cutting Tom, when
his tongue was stayed by his seeing the maid's eyes
turn with blazing indignation upon himself, and her
lips open to speak.

"So, then, it is your work!" she said.

"My work?" quoth the captain, in a maze, dropping his chicken.

"No doubt you spied upon poor Master Holyday,
and corrupted these rogues he trusted in," she went
on; and then, giving way, she wept: "Oh, God! into
whose hands have I fallen!"

Ravenshaw quailed at her tears; but suddenly

stiffened himself, set down his lantern, and said wrathfully to Cutting Tom:

"What means this, knave? Why came you here? Where is — the gentleman you serve? Speak, thou slave, or by —"

But Millicent, coming swiftly out of her tears, cried, scornfully:

"Think not to blind me, thou villain! The gentleman is where you bade these wretches leave him, — in the woods, robbed, — mayhap slain! Alas, having seen his fate, what may I expect for myself!" And again she fell into lamentations.

"I understand this not," said Ravenshaw. "Cutting Tom, thou blundering hound, why bring you this maid to this place, and to me?"

"Oh, out upon pretense!" cried Millicent. "Thinkst thou I am so great a fool as not to see? God send I were Sir Peregrine's wife rather than such a villain's captive!"

"Mistress, I know not why you are here, nor what hath befallen Master Holyday. There is some mistake or falseness, which I shall worm out of this tongue-tied knave; but first assure yourself you are not my captive."

"Oh, peace! As if this fellow, whom you call by name, and who cringes before you, had not turned treacherous!"

"Ten to one he hath turned treacherous, and dear

he shall pay for it; but he hath not turned so at my instigation."

"Oh, no more, I pray. Even this fellow is not bold-faced enough to deny it is for you he has betrayed us. God knows what is to become of me, a prisoner in your hands, without a soul that knows my whereabouts to protect me!"

At this, Master Jerningham, who had kept still while an inspiration perfected itself in his mind, stepped courteously forward, and said, with grave sympathy:

"Not so, mistress. I, the master of this house, will protect you in it."

She looked at him in surprise. His was a face she recalled vaguely as having seen, or faces more or less resembling it, in the streets of London, or in churches, or other public places; but it was not a face she had ever had reason to note carefully. Whatever were the forgotten occasions upon which she may have observed it, as she had observed ten thousand faces worth a careless second glance, the night of her adventure in February was not one of them; for on that night, besides keeping himself in shadow, and leaving all talk to Sir Clement Ermsby, Jerningham had hidden his countenance under the brim of a great Spanish hat. So his face at this moment, appearing as that of a stranger, awakened in her mind no association either pleasant

or unpleasant; in itself, it wore so serious and sweet
a smile, and the manner of its owner was so quietly
chivalrous, that Millicent's feelings promptly declared
in its favour. A sudden sense of safety came over
her, depriving her for a moment of speech. Then
she murmured, unsteadily:

"Master of this house, say you?"

"Ay, mistress, but no conspirator in your being
brought here. I am not often at the place; this
man hath newly arrived as steward; I came to-night
without warning, no more expecting to see strangers
in my house than he expected to see me. I know
not what hath been afoot; but Heaven must have
sent me here, if my coming has saved you from
a mischief."

He offered her his hand. Cutting Tom had
already released her arm. After a moment, she
took the hand, and allowed Jerningham to lead
her to a seat by the table. As she scanned his
features, an increasing trustfulness appeared in her
own.

"Sir," she faltered, deeply relieved and grateful,
"I must thank Heaven for my deliverance. To
find a gentleman — after these rascals — "

She cast a glance at Ravenshaw, and trembled
to think what manner of man she had escaped;
for indeed at that instant the captain looked like
the very devil.

"He deliver you!" exclaimed Ravenshaw, as soon as his feelings permitted him to speak calmly. "Why, he is of all men the one you most need deliverance from!"

Jerningham smiled with tolerant contempt. "I scarce think you will believe that, mistress," said he, lightly, "seeing how completely I am a stranger to you."

"Believe him?" she replied, scornfully. "He is the prince of cozeners; he is all made of lies and shifts. I know not how he hath come to be steward to a gentleman; belike you know not of him; perchance he hath passed upon you by another name, as he did upon us; he is Captain Ravenshaw."

"To say truth, mistress, I knew him; but I little thought —"

"Knew me?" said Ravenshaw, with a laugh. "Ay, indeed. Well enough for me in turn to know his designs against yourself, mistress; from which, as from marriage with that old dotard, I had hoped to see you saved. As for your being brought here, ask these men. Find your tongue, Cutting Tom, and explain this."

"Why, of a truth," said Cutting Tom, slowly, finding courage in a significant glance from Jerningham, "I know not what you would have me explain. I am but a dull-witted man; if you had only told me beforehand what to say —"

"'Tis too clear these knaves acted by your orders, captain," interrupted Jerningham.

"Why, yes, so we did, and that's the hell of it," said Cutting Tom.

"Liar and slave!" cried Ravenshaw, half drawing his sword; but he controlled himself, and said: "'Tis plain that you, Master Jerningham, have bought this knave, though 'tis beyond my ken how you learned what he was to be about to-night. Mistress, I swear to you, the man who intends you harm is he that you put your trust in; the man who would save you is he that you revile and disbelieve."

"Mistress," said Jerningham, ignoring this speech, "wherever you have come from, wherever you would go, 'tis now too late in the night to leave this house. Shall I conduct you to a chamber where you will be safe and alone? Your ears need not then be assailed by the rude talk of this man. Surely you will not doubt me upon his wild words?"

"Nay," said she, rising compliantly, "I heed not his words."

"For proof of them," said the captain, "let me tell you that this gentleman employed me to be his go-between with you."

She blushed. Jerningham said: "Oh, villain! You have the devil's invention, I think. You would make yourself out a worse knave, that you might make her distrust me. Mistress, if you have the smallest fear — "

"Sir, God forbid I should doubt a gentleman on the word of a known rascal!"

Jerningham led her by the hand toward the corridor at the right. But the captain, not delayed by his momentary reflection upon the occasional inconvenience of a bad reputation, sprang ahead of them, and took his place at the corridor entrance, grasping his sword. Master Jerningham instantly drew back with the maid, in a manner implying that the captain's threatening action was as much directed against her as him. He hastened with her toward the opposite passage, but Ravenshaw was again beforehand. Jerningham thereupon conducted her to the front part of the hall. It was not his desire to release her hand, as he must needs do if he himself fought Ravenshaw at this juncture. He did not wish to call in Ermsby yet, fearing the effect her recognition of that gallant might have upon her confidence in himself. His own two followers in the hall were armed only with knives. Cutting Tom, the disguised Gregory, and their three companions, were his men in reality; but he must seemingly win them over before using them, lest she perceive they indeed acted for him in giving this direful turn to her elopement.

"Thou whom he calls Cutting Tom," said Jerningham, " thou and thy fellows, — ye have done a dangerous thing for your necks in conveying this lady hither against her will."

" Sir, I know it," replied Tom. " But I was led by my needs, and these my followers knew nothing of the business. I take you to be a gentleman that has power in the world. I beg of you, now that the villainy has failed, deal not too hardly with us."

" It lies with yourselves. If you be minded to undo the villainy, to serve me in my protection of this maid — "

" We will, we will! and thank your good worship!" said Tom, quickly, and turned to his men with a look which elicited from them a chorus of confirmatory " ayes," supported by a variety of oaths.

" Then seize that man, till I pass with this lady," said Jerningham, in a decided tone. " To him, all of ye, — Meadows and Goodcole, too ! "

Cutting Tom and his men drew their swords ; having first attached their lanterns and torch to wall-sconces, and dropped the bundle of Holyday's clothes. The party advanced upon Ravenshaw, being joined by Meadows and Goodcole, which twain preferred wisely that the bearers of longer weapons should precede them into the captain's immediate neighbourhood. Tom himself went rather shufflingly, doubtless willing to give opportunity for any more impetuous comrade to be more forward in the matter. But the other men were no more eager than he to be first; and so the movement, beginning with some show of a fearless rush, deteriorated in a trice to a hesitating shamble. At two steps from the captain, the party came to a stop.

"Ho, dogs, will ye come dancing up to me so gaily?" cried Ravenshaw. "Dance back again as fast!" His rapier leaped out, and sang against three of their own blades in the time of a breath.

All seven of the men, appalled at his sudden on-slaught, stepped hastily back. The captain strode forward. The fellows increased their backward pace. He followed. They turned in a kind of panic, and ran pell-mell for the front door. Laughing loudly at their retreat, Ravenshaw stopped, as he was in no mind to be drawn outside while Millicent remained within. At sound of his laugh, the fellows turned and stood about the doorway with their weapons in defence.

"Sir," said Ravenshaw, turning to Master Jer-ningham, "I pray you, look upon this maid; consider her youth and her innocence. Will you mar such an one a lifetime, to pleasure yourself an hour? As you are a gentleman, I ask you, give her up."

"Do not give me up to him!" she said, af-frightedly, clinging closer to Jerningham.

Ravenshaw shook his head in sorrow. "Ah, mistress, that you should think I would harm you!

If you but knew — but for what you think of me, no matter. 'Tis a cruel twist of circumstance that you should oppose him that would save you, and cleave to him that would destroy you. You would know how the affair stands, if there were a spark of truth to be found among these knaves and traitors. Oh, for a gleam of honesty! How foul falsehood looks when it has the whole place to itself!"

A whinny of impatience was heard from the horse waiting outside.

"'Tis high time you were in the saddle, captain," said Jerningham. "Come, man; I will forget your attempt upon this maid, since no harm has followed. And she, too, will forget it, if she take my counsel. Will you trust your welfare in this matter to me, mistress?"

"Entirely," answered Millicent, in a low voice.

"Oh, mistress, how you are deceived!" said Ravenshaw. "What can I do to save you?"

She shrank back from his look.

"Fear not, mistress," said Jerningham, softly. "Come, come, captain, an end, an end! Time is hastening. I pray you, be off upon your ride to Dover."

"Dover!" echoed the captain, with a strange laugh. "Ride to Dover! By God's death, things have changed in the past ten minutes! I shall not ride to Dover, thank your worship! not this night! I shall stay here to save this lady in spite of herself! — in spite of herself and of you all, good gentlemen!"

"Is this your promise, you rascal?" exclaimed Jerningham. "You gave your word to ride forthwith."

"And being a rascal, I claim a rascal's privilege to break his word!" cried Ravenshaw. "Away from that lady, or by this hand —"

He did not finish his threat, but made straightway for Jerningham. The latter ran with the maid to the farther side of the table, and whipped out his sword. Ravenshaw, in pursuing, turned his back to the fellows at the doorway. "Upon him, men!" shouted Jerningham, and then, raising his voice still higher, called out: "Ho, Ermsby, to the rescue!"

Ravenshaw, trusting his ears to warn him of what threatened in the rear, kept Jerningham's sword in play rather cautiously, for fear of too much endangering or frightening Millicent, who was pale as death. The girl, clinging to Jerningham, was thus rather a protection than an encumbrance to that gentleman. Very soon the captain heard the bustle of newcomers entering at the front door, and then a general movement, led by a more resolute tread than he had noticed before. He turned and faced Sir Clement Ermsby, whom he recognised but vaguely as a per-

son with whom he had been in collision sometime
in the past. He parried the knight's thrust, and
guarded himself with his dagger from a lunge of
Cutting Tom's. He then spun around on his heel,
lest Jerningham might either pierce his back, or
profit by the opportunity to take the maid away.

Jerningham had chosen the latter course, but he
was hindered by the rush of some of his own men,
who had run around the table in order that the
captain might be surrounded. Thus checked for an
instant, and in some way made sensible of Ravenshaw's last movement, Jerningham turned back, and
again engaged the captain. Ravenshaw was thus
between two forces, one headed by Jerningham, the
other by Sir Clement. He leaped upon the table,
jumped to the floor on the other side, while half a
dozen blades darted after him; dragged the table to
a corner, and turned to face his enemies from the
little triangular space behind it. Led by Ermsby,
they rushed upon him, thinking to find the table of
short use as a bulwark against such numbers.

But Jerningham stood back out of the rush, still
holding Millicent by the hand, and shouted:

"Some keep him busy above the table; some
thrust under at his legs. Let the knave die, 'tis
good time! I'll look to the comfort of the lady."
And he started again toward the right-hand passage.

Ravenshaw bent forward across the table, and

swept aside the points of steel with sword and dagger; but they threatened him anew, and he heard men scrambling under the table to stab his legs; he saw, between two heads of his foes, Jerningham's movement toward the passage, and he shouted:

"Ho, rufflers, maunderers, upright men! a rescue! a rescue!"

Jerningham halted, somewhat wondering. The kitchen door flew open, and, with a hasty thumping of crutches, the beggars hobbled in, men and women, most of them with pewter cans, from which they had been regaling themselves. At sight of these maimed creatures, with their frowsy hair, their gaunt looks, the red blotches and bandages of some, the white eyeballs of others, Millicent started back in horror. As the door by which they came in was near the passage toward which Jerningham was leading her, and as they spread into a wide group in entering, they blocked the way of her departure.

"Stop the gentry cove!" cried Ravenshaw. "In the name of the salamon, stand by a brother!"

The captain's assailants had drawn away a little to see who the newcomers were. Having satisfied himself at a glance, Sir Clement Ermsby laughed, and said: "A rescue, sooth! A bunch of refuse,— rotten pieces of men. Come, back to your work!" And he renewed the attack on Ravenshaw; while Jerningham, calling out, "Ay, to him! these be helpless cripples," started again for the passage, his sword-point forward.

But with a wild whoop the beggars straightened out of their lame attitudes, swung their crutches and staves in the air, lost all regard of sores and patches, found arms for empty sleeves, showed keen eyes where white balls had plead for pity, threw off all the shams of their profession, and swept upon the captain's foes. A sturdy blow of a staff bore down Jerningham's rapier, a filching hook tore his dagger from his other hand. Iron-shod crutches and staves rained upon the heads of Sir Clement and the other men ; hooks caught their clothing, and dragged some to the floor. When at close quarters, the beggars drew their knives ; the women fought like men. Millicent, separated from Jerningham in the fray, ran shrieking in the one direction open to her ; this was toward the corner at the right of the front door. Ravenshaw, dashing through the confusion, placed himself triumphantly at her side. She essayed to run from him ; but he gently swept her with a powerful arm into the corner behind him.

" Oh, God, I am lost !" she cried, seeing Jerningham and his men brought to pause by the sturdy wielders of staff, crutch, and knife.

Across the captain's mind flashed a wild project of bearing her away in search of her uncle's house, which he knew was somewhere in the neighbourhood; but he heard a sudden fierce dash of the long-expected rain against the rear windows, saw how faint and exhausted she was, thought of the opposition she would offer, and considered the up-hill fight he would have to wage against an enemy desperate with the fear of losing his prey.   He had a better idea, — one in which prowess might be supplemented with craft.

Quite near him, in the wall at his right hand, was the open door to the porter's room which he had noticed upon arriving at the house; it had no other means of entrance or exit, its high-placed window being a mere slit. He purposely moved a little to the left. Millicent, seeing an opening, glided along the wall to escape him. He sprang forward, and confronted her just at the door of the porter's room. Recoiling from him, she instinctively darted through the door. "Good!" cried the captain, taking his place in the doorway, his face to the hall.

Millicent, in the little room, sank upon a pallet, which was its only furniture, and put out her hands to keep the captain from approaching her.   But she saw that he had stopped at the threshold, with his back to her.   It was, indeed, no part of his plan to follow her into the room.

Jerningham, startled at the maid's sudden disappearance, ran forward with a cry of rage; but Ravenshaw met sword and dagger with sword and dagger, and Jerningham was fain to draw back to save his body. Matters thereupon resumed a state of abeyance, during which men recovered breath, regained their feet, and took account of bleeding heads and flesh wounds.

"Hark you!" spoke the captain, in a tone meant for her as well as for Jerningham. "It is now for us to prove which of us means this lady no harm. Let her abide where she is, till the storm and the night are past ; then, together, we'll conduct her to her friends. And meanwhile, the man who attempts to enter this room declares himself her enemy."

Jerningham's face showed the rage of temporary defeat. "Then come from the door there," he said, sullenly, for want of a better speech.

"Nay, for this night I am the door here, — though she may close this wooden door an she please. These " — his sword and dagger — "she'll find true bolts and bars. She may e'en sleep, if she will, — there's a pallet to lie on."

Sitting weak and perplexed on the pallet in the dark little apartment, she wondered what purpose the captain might be about.

At the suggestion of sleep, Jerningham had an idea. Pretending to confer in whispers with Sir Clement, he secretly beckoned Gregory, who was still in his false beard. The servant approaching without appearance of intent, Jerningham, still under

cover of talking to Ermsby, asked in undertone for
the sleeping potion which Gregory was to have
obtained. The lackey transferred a phial in an un-
perceived manner to his master's hand. Pocketing
it in triumph, Jerningham turned to the captain :

"We shall see how honestly you mean, then.
And that the lady may rest freer of annoyance, send
these knaves of yours out of her hearing, back to
their ale."

"With all my heart — when you send away your
knaves also."

"I will do so ; but fear not, mistress," he called
out. "I will not leave this hall. 'Tis all for the
avoiding of bloodshed, and your better comfort in
the end."

"'Tis well, sir ; I am not afraid," she answered, in
a tired, trembling voice.

It was agreed that Jerningham's men should go
into the room on the left-hand side of the hall, diag-
onally opposite that in which the maid was ; that the
beggars should return to the kitchen ; that the sig-
nal for both parties to withdraw should be given by
Jerningham. He was about to speak the word forthwith, when the captain interposed :

"By your leave, I'll first have private speech with
my friends. You have already had with yours, and
may have again ere they depart."

Jerningham saw no way of refusing, or, indeed,

much reason therefor; doubtless the captain wished but to counsel his rascals to be vigilant for a possible second call. So Jerningham gave consent by silence. Ravenshaw had a conference with the beggars, in which chief parts were taken by the white-bearded rogue and the ancient cripple who had guided the maunderers to the Grange.

Presently Ravenshaw signified that he had done; whereupon Jerningham said "Begone," and the two parties filed out, each narrowly watching the other, Jerningham's men taking a torch with them, the beggars clumping with their iron-tipped wooden implements. Only Ravenshaw took note that one of the lanterns disappeared with the beggars. The captain, Jerningham, Mistress Meg, who had watched recent occurrences from the kitchen door, and Sir Clement Ermsby were left in the hall.

"How?" quoth the captain, staring at the knight. "Do you break faith? Why go you not with the other men?"

"Troth, sir, I am nobody's man," replied Sir Clement. "I am this gentleman's friend, and, when I choose, I fight for him; but my comings and goings are not to be stipulated for by any man."

Ravenshaw perceived that a minor point had been scored against him; but he was not much discomfited. He had merely to play for time, to guard the doorway of that room for an unknown number of

hours. As long as he could temporise, two antagonists were no worse than one ; if it came to
fighting, two were a little worse, but, as both must
attack in front, the odds were nothing out of his
experience.

"Have we not met before this, sir?" asked Ravenshaw, scrutinising Ermsby.

"My memory is but so-so," replied Sir Clement,
quizzically.

"Before God, I think we have," said the captain,
"and upon opposite sides, too, as we are now. Would
I could remember! I have had so many quarrels,
so many foes. I could swear you and I had clashed
once upon a time."

Sir Clement, who remembered the meeting well
enough, merely smiled as if amused at the captain's
puzzlement. Ravenshaw drew a stool to the doorway, and sat down, weapons still in hand. Sir Clement was leaning back against the table, at the
opposite side of the hall, with folded arms. He
made mirth for himself by suggesting various impossible places where the captain might have met him ;
while Jerningham, ever keeping the corner of his eye
on his enemy, went back and held a whispered conversation with Meg.

"Fear not," said Jerningham, heeding the peremptory question in her eyes. "The maid is in yonder
room. This captain, by a strange chance, knows her

as one he hath designs against. He would neither
have her go free, nor taken back to her father. He
thinks to find her at his mercy. But we shall outwit
him, and no more fighting. 'Tis for you to — "

"One would think he was her friend," said Meg,
glancing toward the captain.

"Poh! she fears him as he were the devil."

"Does he, then, desire her?" queried Meg, with
a curious feigned unconcernedness of tone and look.

Jerningham regarded her with the silence of sudden
discovery; then, restraining a smile, said, watchfully:
"He is another's instrument, I think. Such a man's
fancy would ne'er light upon a child; she is little
more. A woman of your figure were more to his
liking, I'll wager." He paused, to observe Meg's
blush, which was not resentful; then he added, sig-
nificantly: "If a woman were minded to make a
fresh trial of life, with a brave husband now — "

"Well, and what then?" said she, looking him
frankly in the eyes. "How if a woman were? The
man is not seeking a wife, ten to one."

"A few drops of this, mixed with a man's wine,"
said Jerningham, producing the phial in such manner
that his body concealed it from Ravenshaw's view,
"have been known to work a wonder."

"What is it?" she whispered, gazing at it.

"A love potion," he answered. "The surest in
the world, too. 'Tis the one with which — " But

he broke off, shook his head, and replaced the phial in his pocket.

"Let me have it," she whispered, excitedly.

"If you will swear to one thing."

"What?"

"That you will find means to use it this night."

"Why this night?"

He invented a reason. "So that, when it hath effect, you may use your power to draw him from that maid."

"I swear," she replied. He passed the phial to her, directed her in detail what to do, and returned to the front of the hall as if from a mere conference upon household matters. Meg went back to the kitchen. She failed to notice there that one of the beggars, a very old man, was missing; or that the window-seat was wet, as if the casement had been recently opened and closed again. Nor could old Jeremy have called her attention to these matters, for upon their return the other beggars had so crowded around him at the ale-cask that he had seen and heard only them and their clamours.

Ravenshaw and Sir Clement, having exhausted their topic of conversation, were regarding each other in silence. Jerningham, as his eyes fell upon the front door, suddenly exclaimed:

"The horse! Zounds, in this pelting rain—"
He seized one of the lanterns and ran to the porch.

"How now? The beast is not here!" He came back into the hall, looking puzzled.

"Perhaps the old man hath put him under roof," suggested Ermsby.

Jerningham went to the kitchen door and called Jeremy, who averred he had not been near the horse since he had tied it outside the porch.

"'Twas ill tied, no doubt," said Jerningham, "and hath got loose and sought shelter. Belike you left the stable door open. Go and see; and look in all the penthouses, too."

Jeremy went out. His return was awaited in silence, Jerningham pacing the hall, Sir Clement staying motionless at the table's edge, Ravenshaw sitting upon the stool before Millicent's room. She had not closed the door; she remained upon the pallet, able to see a little of the hall, but herself out of the light that came in through the doorway. Her thoughts were in confusion; at last they became so clouded that, obeying the impulse of fatigue, she lay down on the pallet, without heed of the act; soon she was in a state between anxious waking and a troubled dream.

Jeremy came back, dripping, and said the horse was not to be found.

Berating him for stupidity, his master sent him back to the kitchen. Jerningham presently sat down upon a chair near the table against which Sir Clement stood. Slowly the minutes passed, while the heavy beat of the rain against the casements was the only sound. Once Jerningham called out: "Is all well with you, mistress?"

Millicent, brought to a sense of her whereabouts after a moment's bewilderment, answered: "Yes, I thank you." The silence fell again.

At last Jerningham said to Sir Clement: "Those rascals yonder need not have all the good cheer to themselves. There's better drink than ale left in the house." He rose, and summoned Meg from the kitchen·

"Fetch wine," said he. Meg, returning to the kitchen, presently reappeared therefrom with a flagon and a pewter drinking cup.

"First fill a cup, I pray you," said Jerningham, "and carry it to the lady in yonder room."

She poured out a cupful, set the flagon on the table, and approached the door at which Ravenshaw sat.

"Nay, you shall not pass here," quoth the captain.

"What, will you deny the unhappy lady that small comfort?" said Jerningham, while Meg paused.

"No; I will convey it to her; but I'll first see you drink a cup of the same wine."

Jerningham shrugged his shoulders, took the cup from Meg, drained it, and turned it upside down. He then refilled it. Meg carried it to the captain,

and held it close to his nostrils in handing it. He
breathed its perfume, eyed it yearningly, then thrust
his left hand with it into the room.

"A cup of wine for you, mistress," called Jerningham.

Millicent, again roused from half-slumber, was
too gracious to refuse; she took the cup, sipped,
and passed it back to the captain's waiting hand.
He noticed that the cup was nearly full, but gave it
back to Meg, though a little reluctantly. Jerningham
emptied it down his own throat, and filled it for Sir
Clement, who made one long grateful draught of the
contents.

"Fill for yourself, mistress," said Jerningham,
affably. Meg shook her head, but, nevertheless,
proceeded to pour out another cupful. Her back
was toward Ravenshaw as she did so, but there was
nothing in that to strike attention. What Jerningham and Sir Clement saw, however, was this : she
held the cup with her thumb and little finger, against
her palm, so that her three other fingers lay across
the top. Along the inside of her middle finger was
placed the phial, a narrow tube, tied to the finger
with fine thread; the open end of the phial was
toward the palm, which she had hitherto kept tight
against it. But now, opening her fingers out above
the rim of the cup as she poured the wine, she released a part of the phial's contents into the cup

at the same time.   The sleight required but a
moment.

She put down the flagon, transferred the cup to
the other hand, and turned toward Ravenshaw.

"Eh? What?" exclaimed Jerningham, in feigned
disapproval, reaching out for the cup.

"Nay," said Meg, holding it away from him;
"hospitality ever, even to them you quarrel with!"

Whereupon she walked gravely over to the captain and offered him the cup.

Ravenshaw had thought he detected approbation
of himself in this woman's looks at the time of his
arrival; and now he thought he might flatter himself the approbation still existed.   Attributing all to
her good nature toward him, and not suspecting wine
in the same vessel, and from the same flagon, as had
supplied his enemies but a moment since, he grasped
the cup with a hearty smile of gratitude, and emptied
it swiftly down his throat.

Meg received back the cup, placed it on the table
beside the flagon, and passed silently to the kitchen,
followed by a faint smile of mirth on the part of
Jerningham.   The smile was supplanted by a look
of expectant curiosity as Jerningham turned his eyes
upon Ravenshaw.   The captain sat as before, rapier
in one hand, dagger in the other.   Jerningham himself had resumed his chair near the table, and Sir
Clement retained his old attitude.   In the little

room, Millicent relapsed into a dreamy half-consciousness, wherein she seemed borne by rough winds through black and red clouds; the room appeared a vast space wherein this occurred; and yet always she was vaguely aware of her actual surroundings.

Ravenshaw felt serenely comfortable; a delicious ease of mind and body came over him; the beat of the rain softened into a soothing lull; the hall grew dark before him. He opened his eyes with a start, amazed at himself for having let them close. A mist seemed to fill the place; through it appeared the faces of his two enemies, a curious smiling expression upon each.

"What is it?" cried the captain, sharply, and gave his head a shake to throw off the drowsiness that invaded him.

Jerningham's eyes shone with elation.

"God's death, the wine!" cried Ravenshaw, staggering madly to his feet. "Methought there was an aftertaste. Ye've played foul with me!"

He put his arms against the wall to keep himself from falling; his head swayed, and sank forward; the floor seemed to yield beneath him; darkness surged in upon him, and for an instant he knew not where he was or what he was about. But he flung himself back to life with a fierce effort, and began walking vigorously back and forth in front of his doorway. He knew that his sole hope of resisting the drug, if it was what he guessed, lay in constant action of body and mind.

Jerningham sat still; he had but to wait till the captain succumbed, delude Meg with the tale that the philtre sometimes began its operation by inducing a long sleep, find means to administer the rest of the potion to Millicent, and carry out his original design. The beggars were little to be feared without Ravenshaw; they would drink themselves stupid, and on the morrow, while they were snoring or bousing, the unconscious maid could be carried to the ship. As for Ravenshaw, once the drug overcame him he would be virtually out of the world for two days, at least. He could be locked in a chamber, and the beggars informed by Meg that he was gone. They would doubtless take themselves off when they had drunk the place dry. Meg would await with interest the termination of the captain's sleep. Thus all would pass without bloodshed and without any scandal reaching the bishop's ears too soon. Meanwhile, the slightest movement against Ravenshaw, or toward Millicent's room, was to be avoided; it would only stir the captain to action opposed to the effects of the drug. He was still striving against those effects, pacing with rapid steps the small stretch of floor he allowed himself, and thrusting in the air with his weapons.

He was continually losing his mental grasp and regaining it with effort. He wondered how they had contrived to drug his wine alone; doubtless the woman had the arts of a witch; a woman who talked so little was not natural.

How if, in spite of all his resolution, the drug should prove too potent for him? What of the maid then? He shuddered to think of her at the mercy of Jerningham, who had doubtless provided all means of dealing with her in safety from consequences. Should he, Ravenshaw, consign her to the protection of the beggars? Without his masterful and resourceful presence, they were like to prove fickle rogues. Should he remove Jerningham forthwith by killing him? If he did so, and then succumbed to the drug or to Jerningham's men, how might she fare at the hands of the survivors, rascals on both sides? This friend of Jerningham's was the only gentleman in the house, and he was without doubt a bird of Jerningham's feather. Where had the captain met him before? Ravenshaw, calling up anew his energies, stopped in his walk to stare at the man, and lurched toward him drunkenly. Suddenly the captain's face cleared, he stumbled back to the doorway, and cried:

"Mistress, look; look!"

So sudden and imperative a cry brought Millicent to the threshold, startled, white of face.

"Look!" went on Ravenshaw. "'Tis he — that night in the street — in February — they would not let you go — but I compelled them! And one gave me the slip — a man with a Spanish hat — a thick-bearded — Ah! 'twas you, you, you!" He had turned his gaze upon Jerningham. "That was the beginning, I trow! Ah, mistress, who were your enemies that night, and who was your friend?"

She stood bereft of speech, her hand against the door-post, recognising Sir Clement indeed, and dismayed at the frown — which to suddenly enlightened eyes was a betrayal of the truth — on Jerningham's face. And then she wondered at the wild, drunken movements of Ravenshaw, who had resumed his rapid pacing of the floor in a fresh struggle with the persistent opiate.

"The man will never sleep," said Ermsby, in a low tone, to Jerningham. "He will outwalk your medicine. You are not like to have him in a worse state than he is in now. Let me put an end to him while he is thus."

"But Meg — " objected Jerningham.

"If I give him a thrust in my own quarrel, she cannot blame you. Come; my weapons are itching."

"Why do you wish to slay him?"

"For the sport of it, i' faith." Sir Clement's face lighted up with cruelty. "'Tis your only sure way. He'll walk out of this cloud presently."

"As you will," said Jerningham, abruptly, after a moment's thought. "But 'tis between you and him."

Sir Clement, without moving, said aloud to the captain :

"I remember our meeting. You boasted you could be my teacher with the rapier. I knew not then you were Ravenshaw, the roaring captain ; else I had not put off the lesson."

"Lesson — put off lesson — what lesson ?" murmured the captain, dreamily, swaying and plunging as he strode.

"I said a time might come when I should see your skill," Ermsby went on. "I am bound on a far journey to-morrow, and may never meet you again." He drew his rapier and dagger, and stepped forward. "Come, knave! Remember your insolence that night ; for I shall make you swallow it !"

However vague an impression the previous words had made on the captain's mind, the sight of sword and dagger in threatening position roused and steadied him. Not fully sensible of how he had come to be opposed by these weapons at this stage, he met them with the promptitude of habit. The steel of his dagger clashed against the other's sword-point ; his own rapier shot forth to be narrowly diverted in like manner. There was exchange of thrust and parry till the place sang with the ring of steel. The jocund heat of battle woke in the captain's blood, its fierce thrill gladdened his soul and invigorated his body. And yet he went as one in a dream, with the lurches of a drunken man. But dazed as he appeared in countenance, wild and uncontrolled as his movements looked, his eye was never false as to the swift dartings of his enemy's weapons, his hand never failed to meet steel with steel. Some spirit within him, offspring of nature and practice conjoined, seemed to clear his eye and guide his arm, however his body plunged or his legs went awry.

Meg ran in from the kitchen at the first sound of steel. Jerningham hastened back and drew her out of the way of the fighters, saying :

"They fell a-quarrelling; I could not part them. See what effect the potion hath upon him; he should sleep now, but for this fighting. I hope 'twill end without blood."

The beggars, now drunk, were looking over one another's heads from the kitchen, not daring to enter without the order; and Jerningham's men, drawn from their dice by the noise, were crowded together beyond the left-hand doorway. Jerningham hoped that Ravenshaw would yet, in a moment of exhaustion, yield to the opiate ere Sir Clement found opportunity for a home thrust. So he stood with Meg at the fireplace, while Millicent, held by the interest and import of the scene, watched from her threshold. The fighters tramped up and down the hall.

"Never with that thrust, good teacher!" said Ermsby, blocking a peculiar deviation of his opponent's blade from its apparent mark — his right groin — toward his left breast.

"Nor you with that feint, boy!" retorted the captain, ignoring a half-thrust, and catching on his dagger the lightning-swift lunge that followed.

Furiously they gave and took, panting, dripping with sweat, their faces red and tense, their blazing eyes fixed. Now the captain threw himself forward when there seemed an opening in the other's guard; now he sprang back before a similar onslaught on his adversary's part. He swayed and staggered, and sometimes appeared to stop himself in the nick of time from falling headlong, but always his attack and guard were as true as those of Sir Clement, whose body and limbs moved as by springs of steel. It seemed as if neither's point could ever reach flesh, so sure and swift was the defence; the pair might have been clad in steel.

Ravenshaw had worked back to the front of the hall; suddenly he sprang forward, driving Sir Clement toward the fireplace. Ermsby made the usual feint, the usual swift-following lunge. Ravenshaw caught it, but with a sharp turn of the wrist that loosened his grip so that his dagger was struck from his hand by the deflected sword-point. Sir Clement uttered a shout of triumph, and thereby put himself back in the game by the hundredth part of a second; in that infinitesimal time the captain drove his old thrust home. Sir Clement dropped, limp and heavy, his cry of victory scarce having ceased to resound.

Ravenshaw turned fiercely about, his sword ready for new foes. Startled at the movement, Jerningham called his men to seize the slayer. The captain shouted to the beggars. These came staggering in from the kitchen, but he saw they were helpless with drink. The white-bearded fellow was feebly brandishing a pistol which he had made ready for firing, — the weapon he had pointed at Ravenshaw in the road. The captain seized it, turned toward Jerningham's advancing adherents, and fired into the band. A man fell with a groan, but his comrades passed over him, and Millicent recognised, as his false beard became displaced in his struggles, the fellow who had denounced Ravenshaw in her father's garden. The captain hurled himself upon the other men; brought down Cutting Tom with the sting of his rapier; felled Goodcole with a blow of the pistol; dashed through the opening he had thus made in their ranks; pitched forward as if at last all sense had left him; spun around, and grasped at the air like one drowning, and fell heavily against the front door, closing it with his weight. He stood leaning, his head hanging forward, his arms and jaw falling loose.

"No more, men!" cried Jerningham, though the half-dozen appalled survivors needed no command to refrain, any more than the beggars, who were stumbling over their staves. "The knave hath slain Sir Clement Ermsby, but he is done for, too. Now, mistress, for a better lodging!"

The captain, mistily, as if at a great distance, saw his enemy clasp the girl's waist. He tried to move, but could not even keep his feet save by bracing himself against the door. Suddenly, as the maid drew away from Jerningham's face of hot desire, Ravenshaw was thrown forward by a violent push of the door from without. Staggering to the table, he turned and looked. In stepped the old cripple, soaking wet; behind him was a portly, fat-faced gentleman, followed by several rustic varlets armed with pikes and broadswords. Lights flared in the porch, and with the sound of the rain came that of snorting, pawing horses.

"Well met, Master Etheridge," spoke Ravenshaw, thickly. "Look to your niece."

Jerningham stared in chagrin; Millicent ran with a cry of joy to her Uncle Bartlemy. Then the captain said, "Thank God, I may now go asleep!" and fell full length upon the floor.

CHAPTER XX.

"O, when will this same year of night have end?"
— *The Two Angry Women of Abington.*

MASTER HOLYDAY at first thought himself lucky
to be left alive, though naked to his shirt and bound
to a tree by hempen cords which were tied around
his wrists behind him, and around his ankles. But
he soon began to doubt the pleasures of existence,
and the possibility of its long continuance, in his
situation. There was a smarting pain between his
eyes, his face felt swollen all around those organs,
his arms ached from their enforced position, the chill
of the night assailed his naked skin.

He bemoaned the inconveniences of a stationary
condition, and for the first time in his life realised
what it was to be a tree, rooted to one spot all its
days. He no longer deemed it a happy fate that the
gods bestowed on the old couple as a reward for
their hospitality, in the Metamorphoses, — that of
being turned, at their death, into oaks. And he
became swiftly of opinion that the damsel who
escaped the pursuit of Apollo by transforming herself

338

into a laurel would have been wiser to endure the
god's embraces. And yet, as an accession of dampness — mist, if one could have seen it in the blackness of the forest — set his bare legs trembling and
shrinking, he envied the trees their bark ; and as
each arm felt its cramped state the more intolerably,
he coveted their freedom of waving their limbs about
in the wind. At this, he strained petulantly to move
his wrists apart, and, to his amazement, the cord
yielded a little. He exerted his muscles again, and
the hemp eased yet more. A few further efforts
enabled him to slip free his hands. In their haste
his two despoilers had made their knots carelessly.
They had been more thorough in fastening his
ankles. But, bending his knees, and lowering his
body, he set to work with his fingers, and after many
a scrape of his skin against the bark, many a protest
of discomfort on the part of his strained legs, he set
himself at liberty. Surprised at having been capable
of so much, he stepped forward with the joy of regained freedom, but struck his toe against a fallen
bough, and went headlong into a brake of brambles.

Cursing the darkness, and his fate, with every one
of the hundred scratches that gave him anguish of
limb and body, he backed out of the thicket, and
moved cautiously in the opposite direction, holding
his hands before him, and feeling the earth with his
toes before setting foot in a new place.

"This is what it is to be a blind man," quoth he. Often, despite his precautions, he hurt his feet with roots and sticks, and cut them upon sharp-edged stones. He began to think he was doomed to a perpetual labour of wandering through a pitch-dark forest; it seemed so long since he had known peace of body and mind that he fancied he should never again be restored to the knowledge. He knew not, in the darkness, which way he was going; he moved on mainly from a disinclination to remain in one place, lest he should experience again the feelings of a rooted plant.

He began to speculate upon his chances of falling in with dangerous beasts, and upon the probable outcome of such an enconnter. He had known of a man upon whom a threatened buck had once wrought the vengeance so vastly overdue from its race to mankind; in his poaching expeditions with Sir Nicholas the vicar he had often shuddered with a transient fear of a similar fate. In those expeditions he had always had company, had been armed and clad; the strange sense of helplessness that besets an undressed man was a new feeling to him.

At last, to his temporary relief, he came out of the wood, as he knew by the less degree of darkness, the change of air, and the smooth turf which was delicious to his torn feet. But presently the turf became spongy; water oozed out as it gave

beneath his feet. He turned to the left, thinking to avoid the marsh without entering the wood
again ; but the ground became still softer ; a few
more steps brought him into sedgy pools several
inches deep.

"This is worse than the wood," he groaned, and
put his face in what he took to be the direction of
the trees. But the farther he went, the deeper he
sank in water. He now knew not which way to
go in order to find the wood, or even the comparatively solid turf on which he had formerly been. So
he stood, railing inwardly against the spiteful destiny
that had selected him for the butt of its mirth.
He had a sensation of being drawn downward ; he
remembered, with horror, the stories of people sucked
under by the marshes, and he lifted first one foot
and then the other. He kept up this alternate
motion, trying each time to set his foot in a fresh
place, and yet fearing to move backward or forward
lest he find himself worse off. The dread of becoming a fixture in the earth came over him again, as a
greater probability than before, and impelled him to
move his legs faster.

"Would I were a morris-dancer now, with practice
of this motion," he thought, as the muscles of his
legs became more and more weary ; and he marvelled
understandingly at Will Kempe's famous dance to
pipe and tabor from London to Norwich. "Better,

after all, to be a tree," he sighed, "and not have to toil thus all night lest the earth swallow me."

His legs finally rebelling against this monotonous exercise, he resolved to go forward whatever befall; and just at that moment he saw, at what distance he could not determine, a faint light. He uttered a cry of satisfaction, supposing it to be a cottage window, or a lantern borne by some night-walking countryman. As it moved not at his cry, he decided it was a cottage window, and he hastened toward it, through the tall grass, careless how far he sank into the marsh. But, as he drew near, it started away from him; then he told himself it was a lantern, and he called out to its bearer not to be afraid, as he was but a poor scholar lost in the fen. The light fled all the faster. As he increased his pace, so did it. At last, out of breath, he stopped in despair. The lantern stopped, also. He started again; it started, too.

"Oh, churl, boor, clodpate, whatever thou art!" he shouted. "To treat a poor benighted traveller thus, that means thee no harm! These are country manners, sure enough. Go to the devil, an thou wilt. I'll no more follow thee."

But as the light now came to a stand, he ran toward it, thinking the rustic had taken heart. He was almost upon it, when suddenly it separated into three lights, which leaped in three different directions. Knowing not which to follow, he stood bewildered. After a moment, he made for the nearest light ; it disappeared entirely. He turned to watch the others ; they had vanished.

"Oh, this is ridiculous !" he said. "This cannot be real. I perceive what it is. It is a dream I am having ; a foolish, bad dream. It has been a dream ever since — since when ? I was writing a puppet play, and I must have fallen asleep ; I wrought my mind into a poetic fever, and therefore my dream is so troubled and wild. My courtship of that maid, — but no, that was in bright day, 'tis certain, and 'tis never bright day in dreams. Well, when I wake, I shall see where I am, and learn where the dream began ; perchance I am still at that horrible tree. No ; alas ! these aches and scratches, this wretched marsh, are too palpable. 'Tis no dream. Would it were. Perhaps those rascals killed me in the wood, and I am in hell. Well, I will on, then, till I meet the devil ; he may condescend to discourse with a poor scholar ; he should have much to tell worth a man's hearing ; no doubt, if he cannot talk in English, he can in Latin. Ah, what ? I am again on *terra firma :* but *terra incognita* still. I'll go on till something stops me. Oh !" he ejaculated, as he bumped against a tree. "Here is another wood. Or is it the same wood ? I know not ; but I will on."

A brief uncovering of the moon — the same which revealed to Millicent the huddled roofs of Marshleigh

Grange — gave Holyday a view of his surroundings. Looking back across the fen, he saw what must be the wood from which he had come. He stood, therefore, on the border of a second wood. He knew the wind was from the west; hence, noting the direction in which the clouds were flying, he perceived that his course had been southward and from the river. He ought to be on familiar ground now, which he had often scoured with the parson and their fellow poachers; but ere he could assure himself, moon and earth were blotted out, and he was again in a world of the black unknown.

Turning his back to the marsh, he traversed the second wood. A swift, loud wind raced over the tree-tops, bringing greater dampness. He came into what might be a glade, or a space of heath, which he proceeded to cross. As he had been gradually ascending in the past few minutes, he had no fear of another bog at this place. He was by this time ready to drop with fatigue. Stumbling over a little mound, he fell upon soft grass. He lay there for some minutes, resting, till his body seemed to stiffen with cold. Then he rose, and plunged wearily on in despair. Suddenly, to the joy of his heart, he heard voices ahead.

"I'll take oath 'tis no deer," said one. "Come on; the keeper is abroad in this walk; I tell you I spied the candle in's window to light him home."

" I'll have a shot at it, for all that," said another.

Poachers, thought Holyday; and they were speaking of him. He flung himself down, just in time to hear the twang of a crossbow where the voices were, and the whizz of a bolt through the air where his body had been.

" 'Fore God, thou hast laid the thing low," said a third voice. Recognising it, Holyday leaped up with a cry, and ran forward, calling out:

" Sir Nicholas! oh, Sir Nick, thou poaching rascal, 'tis I!"

"God save us, 'tis a ghost; a human ghost!" cried the first speaker.

" 'Tis a white thing on two legs, sure," answered the vicar, with trepidation.

" 'Tis the devil come for you; he spoke your name," said their companion, affrightedly; and instantly came the sound of feet running away like mad.

Holyday pursued, shouting, " 'Tis I, Ralph Holyday!" But the poachers, hearing the name, and thinking it to be the spirit of Holyday come to announce his own death, were soon quite out of hearing.

Losing their direction, and knowing his wornout legs were no match for their fresher ones, Holyday sank to the earth, ready to weep with vexation.

"I see," he wailed. " 'Tis a mockery devised to torment me. To lift me out of the mire of despair into the very arms of my friend, and then to fling me back deeper! A fine joke, no doubt, on the part of Heaven; but why one poor scholar should provide all the mirth, I do not clearly perceive. Was it indeed Sir Nick, or was it but an illusion of mine ears? 'Tis all the same. Well, I will sit shivering here till daylight; what else can I do?"

But suddenly came the rain, a wind-driven deluge, showing its full fury at the outset. In a trice the scholar was drenched; the drops seemed to beat him down; there was no surcease of them. He ran for cover, and presently gained that of another part of the wood. But even the trees could not keep out this downpour. Water streamed from the branches upon his head and body. He was flung upon, buffeted, half-drowned. Never had he received such a castigation from man or nature. He thought the elements were arrayed against him, earth to trip and bruise him, air to chill him, fire to delude him, water to flog him to death. But on he went, moved always by a feeling that any spot must be better than that whereon he was. At last he saw another light.

"Nay, nay," said he; "I am not to be fooled so again. Go to, Jack-with-the-lantern! I chase no more will-o'-the-wisps."

But he bethought him that such a rain would put out

any false fire; moreover, he was in a wood, on high ground. And then, as he approached, the light took the form of a candle in a window. He remembered what the poacher had said. This must be the keeper's lodge; if the candle was still in the window, the keeper had not yet come home, — the rain had caught him too. The keeper being still abroad, his door might not be fastened. With a sense of having reached the limit of endurance of the rain's pelting, — for his thin shirt was no protection, — he dashed blindly for the window, which was on the leeward side of the lodge. He felt his way along the front of the house to the entrance, pushed the door open, and stepped into a low, comfortable apartment, like the kitchen and living room of a yeoman's cottage. Out of the rain and wind at last, his grateful legs bore him across the room to a bench. He sat down, nestling back to a great deer-skin that hung against the bare wall of wood and plaster.

At one side of the room was a door to another apartment; at the back was a ladder-like set of wooden steps leading to a trap-way in the ceiling. Holyday had scarce observed these details by the candle in the window, when a coarse female voice, as of one suddenly roused from sleep, called out from the other room : " Is't thou, Jack ? Time thou wert home ! — hear the rain."

Holyday kept silence. Then he heard a bed

creak as under the movements of a heavy body. The woman was coming out to see what had made the noise. And he, clad only in the briefest of shirts! A double terror shook him; he sprang across the room and blew out the candle. The door opened, and a heavy, unshod tread sounded upon the floor.

"Ecod, the light's out!" said the woman. "And the door open." She found her way in the dark to the door which Holyday had neglected to close upon entering. "'Twas the wind, I wis. Fool Jack, to leave the door ill-fastened! Well, he is served right, for the wind hath blown out his candle. I must make another light, forsooth."

Holyday, standing perfectly still near the window, heard the woman grumbling about the task of striking a light. He felt himself blushing terribly in the dark; he was surely undone. But with a timely inspiration, and glad for once that his feet were bare, he went tiptoe back to where he had sat, stepped over the bench, and slipped behind the deer-skin, flattening himself as much as possible against the wall as he stood.

The woman got the candle aflame, looked around the room, replaced the light in the window, and went back to the other chamber. Hearing the bed creak again as it received her weight, Holyday came out from his hiding-place. What should he do in order to profit for the rest of the night by the comforts of this abode without discovery? He knew who this woman was, and who Jack, her husband, was. He had fallen foul of this keeper before he had left for London, and the keeper was a fellow who would take revenge when occasion offered. Pondering on the situation, Holyday was almost of a mind to face the stormy night again rather than risk capture by the man in such circumstances. Before he could make up his mind, he heard a gruff voice outside ordering a dog to its kennel. It was Jack's voice. Master Holyday fled panic-stricken up the narrow stairs, through the open trap-door.

He was in a place of darkness. He forgot that the height of the cottage — which served but to house an under-keeper and his wife, and was not the principal lodge pertaining to this chase — forbade that the upper story should be more than a mere loft; but of this he was speedily reminded by a bump of his head against a rafter. The loft was warm and probably unoccupied, for Jack rarely had a guest. The rain upon the roof made a din in Holyday's ears. He felt his way to one end of the place, and lay down, near a small window. He heard Jack entering below, swearing at the storm, fastening the door, and finally joining his spouse in the sleeping-chamber. There was some conversation in low tones, and then the house was still.

Holyday's foot struck against the end of a wooden chest. Crawling to it, he opened the top, and found what he had hoped for, — soft garments in which to lie. He tore off his wet shirt, rolled himself up in what seemed to be a woman's gown, — Jack's wife required dresses of ample capacity, — and sank away in sweetest comfort to oblivion.

He woke from a dream of delicious warmth and wondrous light, and found the sunshine in his face. His window was toward the south. The sun had passed the line of noon. Holyday gathered himself up; surveyed the garment of russet wool he had slept in; and finally dressed himself in it in proper manner. It hung loose upon him, but it covered his nakedness.

A creak of the stairway drew his eyes toward the trap. There rose into view the frowsy head and fat face of Jack's wife.

"Ecod, I knew I heard somebody!" she cried, staring at Holyday fiercely. "And dressed in my clothes, too! Oh, thou thief, I'll tear thy skin from thee!"

She came up the steps as fast as her bulk allowed. But Master Holyday, with one glance at her great clenched fists, kicked open the casement behind him, fell upon all fours, and backed out of the window, from which he dropped as the woman reached it. He alighted on a bank of flowers, scrambled to his feet, and, holding his skirt above his knees, trusted all to his bare legs. He heard the woman's furious threats from the window, but tarried not to answer. Plunging through the forest with the new strength derived from his long sleep, he was soon far from the cottage. Easing into a walk, he crossed heath and fields till he came in sight of a pleasant mansion on a green hill. Between him and the hill lay a road, which he must needs cross to reach Sir Nicholas's house. He gained this road, and, seeing nobody about, walked along it some distance so as to skirt the base of the hill. Unexpectedly, from a lane he was passing, came a resonant voice :

"Well, God-'a'-mercy ! what transformation have we here ? "

Holyday turned, and beheld Captain Ravenshaw.

CHAPTER XXI.

THE CAPTAIN FORSWEARS SWAGGERING.

" My follies and my fancies have an end here." — *Wit without Money.*

WHEN Ravenshaw came to his senses, after losing them on the floor of the hall, he gazed around in wonder. He was in a soft bed, in a handsome room which he had never seen before. Bright sunlight streamed through an open casement which let in also the music of birds. Beside his bed lay his clothes, neatly arranged; his sword and dagger; and Master Holyday's puppet-play, which he had carried in his doublet. At sight of the manuscript, full remembrance rushed upon his mind. Though his bodily craving was to sink back on his pillow, and a fierce ache was in his head, he leaped out of bed. There was too much to be learned and done.

He pounced upon the ewer and basin he saw at hand, and speedily soused himself into a more live and less fevered state. While putting on his clothes, wondering where on earth he was, he looked out of the window upon a sweet prospect of green hills, fields, a few distant sun-touched roofs, and a far-off steeple among trees. It was plain that he looked from a house on a low hill, and that noontime had arrived.

A door opened, and in was thrust the head of a man whose blue coat betokened a servant, and whose manner declared a rustic.

" Dod, then your worship be up ! " said this fellow, awkwardly entering. " Young mistress did vow she heard somewhat stirring. I ask your worship's pardon. If your worship had called — " He set about trussing the points of the captain's doublet and hose.

" Who art thou ? " asked Ravenshaw.

" Your servant, sir. To tell truth, sir, Master Etheridge's servant, sir ; but yours while you be here, your worship."

" Master Etheridge ? Master Bartlemy Etheridge, meanest thou ? "

" Yes, sir, by your leave, sir. He bade me attend in the gallery here, sir, to serve your worship an you called."

" This is his house, then ? "

" Yes, sir ; his country-seat, your worship, — not that he hath any town house, begging your pardon."

" How came I here ? "

" Dod, upon a stable door we found loose at Marshleigh Grange last night. I'fecks, I'll never forget such rain ; and to be roused out of bed in the black o' the night, too ! But as to fetching your worship hither, the young mistress wouldn't come if you were left; so master must needs bid us seek somewhat to bear you hither upon. And never once you woke, e'en when me and Dick took off your clothes and put you to bed."

A strange warmth glowed in the captain's soul. Lost in his thoughts, he passed out to the gallery as soon as he was dressed. It was a wide, airy gallery, with doors along the sides, and a window at each end. In one of the windows sat a figure, which rose the instant he appeared. It was Millicent. For a second he paused, fearing she would meet him with her old scorn, or flee down the stairs. But she stood motionless, returning his look with some timidity, blushing and pensive.

"So," said he, quietly, "you would not come if I were left."

"I was much your debtor," she faltered.

"And you, watching here, heard me stirring, and sent the manservant?"

"Why, I was watching here," she replied, confusedly, "lest my father should come unawares. We were seen and followed, Master Holyday and I, and my uncle thinks my father would go first to Master Holyday's house, and then come hither. But let him come what way he will, I can see him afar from this window."

"And how if you see him?"

"There is an old chest in my aunt's chamber that my uncle hath made ready, with holes bored in it for air. They will lock me in, and feign that the key is lost, and that the chest hath not been opened this year."

"Your uncle hath stood your friend indeed in this."

"Yes, he and — others, — more than I deserve. My uncle is no coward, in truth, — save to his wife, and when he is in London against her will and knowledge." She smiled faintly.

"He must have shown courage enough to Master Jerningham to fetch you off safe — and me, too, when I was o'erthrown at last by their drug."

"Why, of a truth, my uncle came to that place with so many men — every Jack on the estate, and all that could be roused quickly in the village — that Master Jerningham would have done ill to contest. The heart was taken out of him, I think ; four of his men were killed, and of the rest, those that had come with me fled when they saw their leader slain."

"Four men killed, troth !" said Ravenshaw, "of whom I shall be asked to give account."

"But you will not be asked," she replied, quickly. "'Twas in self-defence — and in defence of me. But there will be no question made of the affair. Master Jerningham seemed as much to desire that as — as my uncle. He hath his own reasons ; he said he and his men would keep silence. So my uncle agreed to say nothing; those drunken beggars and the rascals that betrayed me will hold their tongues for their own sake; and Master Jerningham said he would dispose of the slain."

"But the slain have friends, — that gentleman will surely be inquired after."

"Master Jerningham said he could explain his disappearance, and the other men's. I know not how, but I would warrant he spoke in good faith."

"More false dealing, belike. I'll go and see."

"Nay! whither would you go?" Her face showed alarm.

"Back to that house. I must see how matters stand there. I must seek out the knaves that betrayed you, and learn what hath befallen Master Holyday. Where did they leave him?"

"Alas! I know not where 'twas. They beat him down in the wood, and left him, — tied to a tree, one said; and they robbed him of his clothes. I should not know where to look for the place."

"Be of good cheer. I'll find him, though I search the forest through; and, if he be alive, I'll not eat or sleep till you are wed."

"Then 'twas indeed your planning?" she queried, looking not too well pleased. "I had begun to think as much, after last night."

"Why, troth, I — ah — did give the plan my

countenance," admitted the captain. " But we durst
not let you know I was privy to it ; you thought so
ill of me — and rightly. But the bringing you to
Marshleigh Grange was pure treason against us.
I was too trustful; but I will undo my error if
Holyday be alive."

" I marvel why you should have plotted so for
me."

" To save you from wedding Sir Peregrine Medway; and to put you out of Master Jerningham's
ken, as well. You said any husband was better — "

" But why chose you Master Holyday ? "

" Faith, is he not young, and a gentleman, and
comely ? And he will be well provided for upon his
marriage, e'en though he bring a wife without dowry.
And then I was pleased at the chance of benefiting
him, too. I could think of no better remedy than a
husband, and no better husband than he."

Millicent was silent a moment, her brows a little
bent as if she would say something she knew not
how to say; then seeing him move, as if to depart,
she resumed :

" You spoke of Master Jerningham as well as Sir
Peregrine."

" Yes ; I knew of his intent toward you. What
I said last night was true. He employed me to —
what will you think of me ? "

" But you did not," she said, holding his glance.

"No," he answered, in a low voice.

"Why did you not?"

"Faith, I cannot tell — I was formerly a gentleman — and you were — troth, when I talked with you in the garden, I could not. And when I came again, though I kept my false name, knowing how people held my true one, 'twas indeed to plan your escape from that old knight."

"I know not how I can ever prove my gratitude, — and for last night." She paused, and dropped her eyes; her heart beat fast while she awaited his answer.

"You have put the debt on my side," he said. "You would not come from that place if I were left. And but now you were attentive to my waking."

Evidently the answer fell short of her hopes.

"Oh," she said, a little pettishly, "I am on the watch here lest my father come, as I told you. As for your waking, yonder clodpate is a stupid fool. My uncle thought, being drugged, you might sleep all day and longer; but I said you were no ordinary man."

"Troth," said Ravenshaw, smiling, "I somewhat broke the drug's power by resisting till your uncle came. And now that I am so soon awake, the sooner may I seek your husband that shall be." He turned toward the stair-head.

"But hear me, I pray ! If you go back there, you hazard your life again."

He touched his sword and dagger, which he had girded on in the bedchamber. "I still carry these," quoth he ; "and I must thank you for recovering them."

"Nay," said she, blushing again ; "the sword never left your hand. There was but your dagger to seek. But go not back there, I beg of you !" She could scarce conceal the depth of her solicitude.

"Why, why, mistress, fear not for me. There is no danger."

"I entreat you not to go."

"Nay, the more you concern yourself for my safety, the more am I bound to go and serve you."

"Take men with you, then."

"Nay, your uncle must keep his men here to protect you. But one to show me the way, — the old beggar that summoned your uncle last night, — perchance he came hither with us."

"No, he stayed with his comrades ; my uncle paid him for his service."

"I must e'en thank your uncle for that ; and for his care of me."

"I will take you to him, and my aunt," she replied, eagerly, seeing a chance of delaying his departure and gaining time for dissuasions.

But he seemed to read her thought ; he took a

sudden resolution, and said: "Nay, I'll thank him when I return. Farewell, and — "

"You will return — soon?" she said, with quivering lip.

"Ay, with Master Holyday — or news of him," he answered, and turned to the servant: "Show me the way to Marshleigh Grange, and make haste."

Avoiding her glance, he hurried down the stairs ere she could frame a further objection. The servant, wonder-eyed, followed him. When he was out of the house, he shook his head, and said within himself: "Another minute in her presence, and 'twould have been she that bade me go, I that begged to stay."

He dared not look back; had he done so, as he hastened down the hillside, he might have seen that she had changed her window for one which looked toward his road. When he disappeared in the lane to which his man conducted him, she dropped her face upon her arms.

The lonely plain whereon the Grange stood was nearer than he had supposed. When he reached the house, there was no sign of life about it. He called and knocked; and finally was admitted to the hall by Jeremy. The old man was its only occupant, living or dead. He was engaged in washing out sundry stains that reddened the floor.

"Hath your master taken them away?" asked

Ravenshaw, bluntly, nodding toward the stained places.

"Ay, but a short while since," said the old man, unconcernedly. "I trow they are to have sea burial. He came and had them carried aboard a ship. He and they are e'en now bound seaward."

"That is strange. Where is the woman, Mistress Meg?"

"He hath ta'en her along on the ship. Troth, she swore she would not stay another night under this roof. There was much talk atwixt 'em. She is to be a queen on an island where 'tis always summer."

Wondering if the old man had lost his wits, the captain asked, "And you are alone here?"

"Ay, and well enough, too. I have no mind to go a-voyaging. I shall have all the milk, now, and all the eggs; and no foolish woman prating ever of ghosts and witches. I'll have some peace and quiet now."

"The beggars have gone, then?"

"Ay; when they came sober, and saw slain men upon the floor, they fled as if the hangman were after 'em. Ha! I knew enough to hide the chickens over night." The old man chuckled triumphantly.

From what further information he could draw, the captain made out that Jerningham's own men had embarked with him, and that Cutting Tom's followers had gone their way unheeded. Not till days afterward was he assured that Jerningham had indeed set sail for some far country. To the bishop and others, the voyager had accounted for the absence of Ermsby and Gregory by a tale of their having preceded the vessel to Gravesend, where they were to come aboard. He and his ship were never heard of again.

The captain left the Grange, thinking next to inquire of Sir Nicholas the vicar. If Holyday had not contrived to find his way to his old friend's abode, the parson would doubtless help search the woods for him. Ravenshaw's attendant knew where Sir Nicholas lived. The way passed near his master's house. The captain made him lead at a rapid pace. It was when they were emerging from a lane into the road that Ravenshaw came upon Master Holyday, attired in the loose-hanging garb of the keeper's wife.

The captain, after the briefest salutations, grasped the scholar's arm, and ran with him up the hill toward Master Etheridge's house. Millicent, seeing them coming, and recognising only Ravenshaw, made haste to join her aunt and uncle, who had gone to discuss her situation out of her presence. She found them in the orchard at the rear of the house.

To that place, having inquired of the first servant he met, the captain dragged the breathless and

protesting scholar. Millicent's wonder, at sight of
Holyday's distressed face, was almost equal to that
of her portly uncle and his stately, angular spouse.

"Good-morrow, madam," said Ravenshaw, with a
bow which at once surprised the dame's severity into
fluttering graciousness. "And to you, sir." He
then turned to Millicent. "Know you not Master
Holyday, mistress? I met him by chance; he was
hastening hither for news of you."

But Millicent's astonishment at the poor scholar's
appearance had given place to a look of decided
disapproval. Holyday himself stood red-faced and
sullen.

"You are welcome, sir," said Master Bartlemy
Etheridge, in an uneasy voice. His countenance
was worked into a painful attempt to convey something to the captain's mind privately; in his concern
upon that score, he paid no heed to Master Holyday,
whom his wife greeted with a curtsey.

"I am much bounden to you, sir," said Ravenshaw. "For your care of me, and your hospitality,
my gratitude shall balance my want of desert. At
our last meeting — "

"Meeting, sir?" broke in Uncle Bartlemy, in
despair at the evident failure of his facial exertions.
"I'll take oath I never met you before; it must have
been some other gentleman of my appearance."

"Our meeting last night, sir, I meant," said Ravenshaw, with a smile ; "though, indeed, 'twas a brief matter on my part."

"Oh, last night, forsooth ; oh, yes, yes, yes," said the old gentleman, with a look of infinite relief. "Troth, yes, certainly, indeed.   And you, Master Holyday, God save you.   'Tis long since I have seen you ; you have changed much."

As Uncle Bartlemy's gaze was upon the scholar's dress, Holyday's assumption was that the remark was concerned therewith.

"Faith, sir," said he, resentfully, " 'tis fine manners in you to jeer ; my wearing this gown comes of my willingness to marry your niece."

"Oh, indeed !" quoth Millicent.

"Troth," went on the poet, miserably, "it hath been ill upon ill, e'er since I ran away with her.   If such a night be the beginning of our marriage, what shall be the end of it, in God's name ? "

"There shall be no end of it," retorted Millicent ; "and no beginning, either.   Last night, say you? Ay, you showed bravely then.   You are well suited in a woman's gown, I think.   A fine husband you would be, to protect a wife ! "

The scholar's face cleared somewhat ; turning to Ravenshaw, he said :

"Give me my puppet-play.   I'll go back to London.   You see she will not have me."

"Softly, softly !" cried the captain.   "Would you

mar all at the last, mistress? Reflect, I pray; your only true safety lies in marriage ere your father finds you. You will not bring all my plans to nothing? I do entreat you —"

He stopped at a sudden parting of her lips; he looked around to see what alarmed her. There, coming from the house to the orchard, were Master Etheridge the goldsmith, Sir Peregrine Medway, and a ruddy, irascible-looking country gentleman.

"Plague take it!" muttered Uncle Bartlemy to Millicent; "this comes of not watching."

As Sir Peregrine was the embodiment of lagging weariness, and the goldsmith was himself well fagged, their companion was first within speaking distance. With scant greeting for the elderly couple, he turned fierce eyes on the scholar.

"How now?" he burst out. "Thou unthrift! thou ne'er-do-well! thou good-for-naught! Wouldst run away with my old friend's daughter? I'll teach thee, knave!"

But the captain stepped between the elder Holyday and the son, for he felt the quarrel to be his own, and saw his painfully reared structure of events ready to fall about him.

"Sir," he said, "he did it for your behoof; he marries to perpetuate your stock."

"Sir," replied Holyday the father, "I can attend to that myself. I am taking a wife next Thursday;

my rascal son would not seek one when I bade him ;
so I sent him packing ; but now he shall come home
and be kept out of mischief."

The goldsmith, coming up, ignored his brother,
bowed stiffly to the latter's wife, and stood before
Millicent, his hands open as if he would fain clutch
her.

"Thou baggage, thou'rt caught in time! Thou
shalt not sleep till thou'rt tied in marriage to Sir
Peregrine." He made to grasp her by the arm.

"Touch me not!" she cried, with a sudden
thought. "You have no power over me; I am
married!"

Her father stared. Master Holyday, taken by
surprise, said, emphatically :

"Not to me, that I'll take oath ; so I am a free
man, of a surety!"

Ravenshaw could have struck him down. But
Millicent, after one crestfallen moment, said, quietly :

"Not to Master Holyday, certainly ; but to this
gentleman." And she went to the captain's side.

There was a moment's general silence, during
which Sir Peregrine, overcome by his long exertion,
leaned limply against a tree.

"To this villain?" cried the goldsmith ; "this
cozener, this notable rascal, this tavern-cheat. 'Tis
not possible ; there hath not been time ; not even
for a license."

Millicent looked up at Ravenshaw's face, whereby he knew she desired him to take up the ruse.

"Sir," quoth he, "there hath been more time than you wot of; we have all been in the plot together for three days now."

"A pack of knaves!" shouted the goldsmith. "An there hath been a marriage, 'twill not hold. She was bound by pre-contract."

"'Tis not true," cried Millicent. "Sir Peregrine knows I would not receive his tokens."

"Oh, good lack!" quoth the old knight, faint of voice; "'tis all as well. I am glad your daughter hath released me, Master Etheridge. She is much inclined to jealousy, I see that; belike I should give her cause, too. I thank her for my liberty."

The goldsmith cast on the old knight a look of wrathful disgust, and walked precipitately from the place, breathing out plagues, murrains, and poxes. Sir Peregrine laboriously followed him. But Holyday's father dragged the scholar aside to talk with him privily.

Ravenshaw turned to Millicent. "The device served well. But the truth must out in time. Your father will have his revenge then."

"Alas, I have told a great falsehood," said she, braving her blushes. "I know not how to clear my soul of it — unless you — " She hesitated.

"I, mistress? What can I do?"

"Make it the truth," she faltered, dropping her eyes.

For a time he could not speak.

"Oh, mistress!" he said, at last, with unsteady voice; "would to God I might — But think you of my reputation."

"You will amend that; 'tis no great matter."

"I am no worthy mate for you."

"You have fought for me."

"You will learn to hate me again; you hated me but yesterday."

"'Twas because I had loved you the day before; else I should not have heeded."

"You are a world too good for me."

"Troth, I am not good in all eyes. Sir Peregrine is glad to be rid of me, and Master Holyday will not have me."

"I am penniless."

"My uncle hath said he would provide for me."

Ravenshaw looked at Uncle Bartlemy, who had been calming his wife's wonder. The old gentleman, with a fine attempt at hidden meaning, thus delivered himself:

"Sir, I owe you much upon the score of our first meeting — whereof you spoke awhile ago. If you can be content here in the country, with a wing of our poor house, while we live — 'twill all be Millicent's when we are buried —"

Ravenshaw felt her hand steal into his; he turned and took her gently in his arms.

Master Holyday, having come to an adjustment with his father, callously interrupted this embrace with the words, " Give me back my puppet-play now, and I'll wish you joy, and pardon all my calamities, even this dress."

Ravenshaw drew forth the manuscript from his doublet, saying: " If you return to your father's house, we are like to be your neighbours. And your friend Sir Nicholas shall earn a fee in spite of you."

" Troth, then, I'll write your nuptial hymn," said the poet, tenderly handling his puppet-play. " 'Twill have a rare sound, — ' Epithalamium to the Beauteous Maid of Cheapside and the Roaring Captain.' "

" Nay, the roaring captain is no more," said Ravenshaw. " I am a gentleman again. Believe it, sweet."

" I care not what you are only that you are mine," quoth Millicent.

THE END.